LONG TRIP HOME

DUTCH JONES

LONG TRIP **HOME**

TATE PUBLISHING
AND ENTERPRISES, LLC

This novel is a work of fiction. Names, descriptions, entities, and incidents included in the story are products of the author's imagination. Any resemblance to actual persons, events, and entities is entirely coincidental.

The opinions expressed by the author are not necessarily those of Tate Publishing, LLC.

Published by Tate Publishing & Enterprises, LLC
127 E. Trade Center Terrace | Mustang, Oklahoma 73064 USA
1.888.361.9473 | www.tatepublishing.com

Tate Publishing is committed to excellence in the publishing industry. The company reflects the philosophy established by the founders, based on Psalm 68:11,
"The Lord gave the word and great was the company of those who published it."

Cover design by Anne Gatillo
Interior design by Jake Muelle

Published in the United States of America

ISBN: 978-1-62994-354-1
Fiction / General
13.12.20

DEDICATION

To the only people who motivate me,
Ori, Jesse, and Jake.
Thank you for your support and for believing in me.

MUSICAL CHAIRS

Troy has been on the road for over three weeks, covered five countries, had countless meetings, lunches, and dinners; and he's exhausted. He has eaten more meals where he was unsure of exactly what he was putting into his mouth or that had names that he could not pronounce than all of his other trips combined. Troy has calculated that on this one business trip alone, he has traveled over thirty thousand miles! His internal clock is wound so tight you could tell him it is three o'clock in the afternoon when it's really three in the morning, and he'd believe you. To make things worse, this last stop is absolutely the furthest it could possibly be from his home—Chicago. Troy is done, and he doesn't care about anything else right now; all he wants to do is get on board the plane and start the long trip home.

Troy arrives by taxi at the Djibouti International Airport where he works his way through the crowd and gets in line to check in. After many minutes of dealing with the clerk at the counter and her almost nonexistent English, he is checked in all the way through to home. Troy is about to embark on the final leg of his trip; it will take him around thirty-six hours to get home. He knows he will have several stops with plane changes and layovers, but he is so tired he just doesn't care; he just wants to get going. He needs to get home. The one thing he does care about right now is the very real possibilities of any delays or missed connections. That would be a nightmare. The mere thought of missing a connection makes him sick, so he tries not to think about it. The trip home is already unbelievably long; the last thing Troy wants is for it to be any longer because of something stupid like a late or delayed flight. Troy is certain this is the hardest trip he's ever been on, and he knows with 100 percent certainty that this is the most exhausted he's ever been in his life!

The terminal area is very, very crowded. *People move about looking like they are in a rush, with nowhere to go.* Troy figures this may be the only flight from this small, in the middle of nowhere "international airport." Troy thinks to himself, *I suppose it has to be "international," the only places any of the flights go from here are out of the country!* Troy takes up a position in the terminal area well away from the crowd, hoping to make one more attempt to call or Skype his kids before he has to board the plane.

Troy, thirty-four, is married to April, the boss's daughter, who is one year younger than him. Together, Troy and April have two children, Maggie, twelve, and Justin, nine. Good kids. Troy is in international sales for a large-parts distribution company where his father-in-law is president. Troy has been working for the company for thirteen years, exactly two weeks longer than he has been married. He's been promoted once, which came with virtually no pay increase but somehow managed to increase his travel by thirty percent. It did come with a cool title, though: Vice President of International Sales. Troy likes his job and he does it well; he travels too much, but that's just part of the job, and he accepts it. While he doesn't like the travel, he really enjoys meeting new people from all parts of the world, many who he has become friends with.

All of the travel hasn't been easy for Troy and his family. For some time, Troy has felt that he and April have been losing their grip on their marriage. He isn't completely sure why, but he is confident the travel has something to do with it. It is Troy's father-in-law who put him in this position. Troy has never liked his father-in-law and has always felt he has had it out for Troy. For years, Troy has felt that April's father has been trying to undermine their marriage.

Troy hates it; he can't believe that his marriage has reached this place. But it's come to a point that, even after a long trip like this one, when he gets home, April acts as if she's really not all that happy to see him. Together, he and April have done everything they can to protect the kids from any of their 'outbursts,' but even that has gotten out of control. Troy is looking forward so much to going home to see his kids, but he can't help but reflect on when he left for this trip. At the last possible minute, April changed her mind about driving him to the airport and told Troy she had already called him a cab. The second before he got into the cab, April announced to Troy that she thought they should consider getting a separation! Troy was not shocked at the proclamation but still stunned at the timing. *Wow! That was seriously a chicken way to handle that*! The whole way to the airport he was pissed but only thought about his kids and how much it might affect them if he and April got divorced. Troy had hoped it wouldn't come to that, thinking that some day they would be able to work through their problems.

Troy is above average height, being just over six feet tall. He has short dark hair; he is thin but has an athletic quality, although no one would consider him an athlete. He's never been able to throw, catch, hit, or run; so sports were never a part of Troy's life. Although for some strange reason, he's always liked professional hockey. He goes to games every chance he can. April hates the sport, so Troy is usually on his own with a buddy or business associate. It's the nonstop action, and the gladiator sense he gets that draws Troy to the sport, at least that's what he's told a few friends.

Troy is a handsome man. He has had to wear glasses from the time he was a kid and has only accepted that fact since being in college, when wearing glasses became, in a word, 'cool'. Troy got his degree in business, and he minored in history; his whole life he has been a great student. Most people would refer to Troy as a nice guy who is quiet, kind of nerdy, not much of a *conversationalist*, and isn't home very much. Troy never managed to have any *real* long-term friends; he gets along with almost everyone he meets, but he never seemed to connect with a guy or two that he could just be himself with. At least not until he started working for April's Dad. There he has several friends, and one "best friend" named Eddie, to some Crazy Eddie. Troy has often thought it must be the common ground the job creates, a common bond that opens up the opportunities to have friends at work. Crazy Eddie says it's the scared masses bonding together for security.

While Troy is waiting for his flight to be called, he tries again to get ahold of his kids. He's unsuccessful by Skype or by phone. *It figures,* he thinks to himself. *I haven't gotten a decent signal in days.* So he starts to do some work on his computer. While working, Troy decides to put on some music and plugs his headphones into his phone. Minutes later, Troy is asleep. It must have been a pretty deep sleep because he never heard a single one of the calls to board the flight. Troy was literally the last passenger left in the terminal when he was spotted by the woman who checked him in. She walked over to Troy and nudged him awake. As he sat up, he took a look around, and instantly, he felt he was living his nightmare. "Oh my God!" he yelled very loudly. In one frantic swoop, he grabbed up all his stuff and ran for the gate.

Standing alone at the gate was a woman airline employee who saw Troy running toward her; she smiled at him as he approached. "Do not worry, sir, you made it."

"Thank God," Troy said as he fumbled around for his ticket. He checked his coat pocket then his pants pocket then his back pocket—no ticket! Troy really started to get visibly upset. *Maybe in my case*, he thought as he put his case on the counter to open it. The woman waiting to take his ticket said to Troy very calmly and politely, "Sir, if I may," as she reached out toward Troy and removed his boarding pass from his front shirt pocket. The woman smiled as she handed Troy his boarding pass back to him.

Embarrassed, Troy simply said, "Thank you" and started for the gangway. *Holy smoke! I can't believe I almost missed my flight!* he was thinking as he walked toward the plane. Had Troy missed his flight, he might have had to wait two or three days to catch the next one!

Troy was definitely last to board. As he entered the plane, Troy looked down the aisle; all he saw was a mass of people. "Ah, coach again." The company Troy works for, even with all of the miles he has traveled, has never upgraded Troy, ever. His boss, the father-in-law, feels the miles belong to the company and are then distributed as the company sees fit—usually as a bonus, which Troy has never received. Troy recognized the type of plane from his youth when he used to collect plane models. The plane was an older Boeing 747 jumbo jet made in America. A big plane first developed in the late sixty's for longer coast to coast and international flights. *This was definitely one of the early models!* Troy thought. Each row in the plane consisted of two seats on each side of the plane with a middle row of five seats. *I wonder*

if this was the first one ever made! He was thinking as he entered deeper into the plane. You could easily tell the plane was a bit beat up—some missing arm rests here and there, a few missing tray tables, and tape in place of stitching to cover up tears in the upholstery. He proceeded toward his seat, which of course was in the back of the plane. Troy actually prefers to sit in the back, especially on longer flights; this way, he is closer to the bathrooms, and he can stand up and stretch out a little easier. As he maneuvered his way toward the back of the plane, he kept thinking how close he was to missing the flight. *At least I'm on*, he thought.

Troy got to his row, three aisles from the back of the plane, but he realized as he approached there were no empty seats. He looked at his ticket. "Yup, right row," he said to himself, then he looked at the middle seat that was supposed to be his. The only thing worse than sitting in the middle is not being able to fly at all, especially when you are so ready to go home, at least that's what Troy was thinking when he booked the flight. There in his seat sat a young woman, maybe in her early twenties with an infant in her arms. Worse, it appeared she was nursing. There were no stewardesses around so even though he felt like an idiot asking, he said to the woman, "Is this your seat?" She looked up at him with a puzzled look and said something very quietly in something other than English. *Arabic*, Troy thought. Troy knew immediately he was in trouble! As he began to try again to communicate with this young mother, he could tell he was upsetting her. Just then, a stewardess walked up behind him. "Can I help you, sir?" she asked in very good English.

Troy turned to the stewardess and handed her his ticket. "I think this woman might be in the wrong seat," he said calmly. The stewardess looked at his ticket then looked at the row and seat number. Troy was right. The stewardess spoke to the woman in what Troy assumed was Arabic. It appeared the stewardess was asking the woman in his seat to see her ticket. The woman was now visibly upset and started to cry. She was trying to explain something to the stewardess, all the while pointing at the older woman sitting next to her by the window. Troy had no idea what the stewardess was saying to the woman, but the woman reached over her baby to try to grab her bag. The baby started to cry.

What a mess! Troy was thinking. He did not want to make any trouble, especially for a young mother, but he had to be on this flight. Then the older woman reached to help the younger woman retrieve her bag. The young woman combed through her bag and produced a boarding pass. Her boarding pass indicated she was in an aisle seat seven rows back toward the front of the plane. The stewardess turned to Troy. "This woman wanted to sit next to her mother; that is why she sat here. She didn't think anyone else was going to board, so she thought it would be okay."

Troy, relieved, responded, "Sure, I understand, I don't care where I sit". The stewardess nodded to the young mother as if to say it was all right and pointed Troy back toward the front of the plane.

As Troy and the stewardess started moving back toward the front, the stewardess told Troy, "This is no problem, we will just put you in her seat." Troy smiled. He was good with that. He didn't want to sit in a middle seat anyway, and he definitely did not want to be anywhere near a baby! The stewardess walked Troy to row twenty-six and stopped. She looked at the ticket and looked at the people sitting in the row. Troy was a little panicked again—all the seats were full! The aisle seat that was supposed to be that of the young woman who was in Troy's seat was taken up by a man who appeared to be in his early fifties or so—a very, very large man, hard-looking but dressed nicely. The stewardess, Troy was assuming, asked the man for his boarding pass. He unbuckled his seat belt and stood up in the aisle. He was so big his sides were touching both sides of the aisle! His head had to be inches away from the ceiling of the plane. The man smiled, reached into his pocket, and produced a boarding pass. The stewardess looked at it, handed it back to the man, and in the one word Troy knew, said thank-you to the man.

Now Troy was moving past panic to a complete meltdown, way out of the range of normal for Troy. He knew part of it was because he was so tired; part of it was the thought that this was it, the stewardess was going to kick Troy off the plane and part of it was the plane felt like it was ninety degrees inside. He started to sweat. The stewardess turned to Troy and said, "There seems to be two tickets for the same seat," she told him. "Of course!" Troy said with a great deal of sarcasm. "Now what do I do?" he asked.

She could see the sweat starting to come down Troy's face. "Come with me." She directed him toward the front of the plane.

Troy assumed she was walking him off the plane. A ton of different thoughts were running through his head. *The next flight is in a couple of days, but even then, there's no guarantee I'll be able to get a ticket. Man, this sucks! Maybe I could rent a car and drive to the next airport?* he was thinking. *No, that border is too dangerous, especially for Americans.* Troy also knew the chances of getting on a plane there were even more remote. Just as Troy was weighing all his limited options, the stewardess stopped in the galley area, near the plane's door. She started to speak to a steward who was there. Troy had no clue what they were saying to each other, but it was definitely about him. Every few seconds, one or both of them would look at Troy and then continue talking. The steward kept nodding his head.

As the steward and stewardess continued talking to each other, Troy turned back toward the main body of the plane to see if he could see any open seats. Not only were there no open seats, but he could tell the people on board knew that Troy was the reason for the extended holdup, and they were not looking too happy. Troy quickly turned back to the stewardess. The steward looked at Troy and said, "Come with me." Troy followed. He was immediately excited that they walked past the door of the plane. It looked like he wasn't getting off. He took a deep breath and breathed a sigh of relief. Together, they walked through what Troy thought must be like a business class section. When they got to the end of the section, they reached a closed curtain. The steward asked Troy to wait as the steward pulled aside the curtain and walked through.

It was a very uncomfortable feeling standing there looking at a closed curtain knowing that everyone behind him was staring at him. He felt like he should say something, but what would he say? Even if he tried, most of the people would not understand him. Just as Troy was beginning to panic again, the steward appeared from behind the curtain. He held back the curtain and told Troy to follow him. They passed out of the business class section and entered the first-class section. They walked to the very front of the section to the first row. Each row only had four seats, two large seats on each side of the isle. There was one seat open in the very first row. It was an aisle seat. As they got to the first row, the steward indicated to Troy that he should sit there! Troy was very excited and anxious at the same time. He leaned into the steward, "Thank you" Troy said very politely.

"Yes." He nodded. "Just for now." Troy stood in front of the seat and started to take off his jacket. He was thrilled, relived beyond words. *Even if this is only until the next flight, I'm on board and I'm in first class, this will do!*

The person in the seat next to him was a young woman, at least as best he could tell. She was almost completely covered with her legs folded up on the seat. She had on a sweatshirt with a hood over her head, and she was wearing big, oversized, very dark sunglasses. She had a blanket that was covering the rest of her. *Strange*, Troy thought but could care less. As he sat down, he was approached by a different steward who asked Troy if he would like a drink before they took off. Troy looked around, and except for the woman next to him, pretty much everyone else had a drink. "Yes!" he answered and ordered a beer. "I think I deserve it!" he told himself.

As he settled into his large, comfortable first-class seat enjoying his beer, Troy was thinking how he almost missed his flight. "Finally something worked out for me! And worked out really well!" He quickly brushed off the thought of what *could have been*, smiled, and took another drink of his beer. He turned to the woman next to him to share his good fortune. *Wow, she must really be out!* he thought. *She hasn't moved once. Oh well, this flight will be much more peaceful than I thought it was going to be.* The steward picked up everyone's empty glasses and handed each of them a hot towel. As Troy was wiping his hands with the little hand towel, a stewardess was making some type of announcement over the loudspeaker. She never made the announcement in English, but Troy knew by the standard show that flight crews have to do on every flight; the flight crew was going over the safety features of the plane. The steward in the first class was very enthusiastic about each of the steps when putting on your mask. Troy thought this was the first time he's actually seen a flight crewmember put the mask all of the way on. They finished the safety instructions, and the plane started to push back. Troy looked over at his row mate and the woman still had not moved, even through all of the very loud announcements!

Wow! he thought to himself.

The plane started to pick up speed; it started to shake and get loud as the jet motors hummed at a fever pitch. As the plane was lifting off the ground, Troy couldn't help himself as he stared at the woman next to him, pretending to be looking through her window. He was waiting to see when the woman was going to move. Twenty minutes later, already at cruising altitude, she didn't move one time. Troy was actually a little concerned. *I wonder if she is okay*, he was thinking. It will be a four-hour flight and already twenty minutes in, *This is going to be a breeze*, he thought. Troy was so tired. He was finally coming down off his stress; he was fighting to keep his eyes open. Within minutes, he was out.

Sometime later Troy woke to some turbulence. At first it startled him but then he realized where he was. As he tried to get oriented, Troy immediately realized the woman who did not move the entire time so far was now resting her head on his shoulder! For the first time, he could see a little of her face. *She is young*, he thought—a white woman. *Wonder what she's doing here? Especially by herself? Kinda strange*, he thought. Troy's shoulder was getting numb, but the woman was still out. He didn't want to wake her. He was weighing his options, which is something Troy always likes to do, when the steward came up to him.

"Oh, I see you are awake," he said in very broken English. "You missed the meal, would you like me to get you one?" he asked. Troy looked at him then looked at the woman then looked back at the steward.

"I don't think I would wake her," the steward suggested to Troy.

"Why?" he asked.

"Just my opinion, sir."

"Well, that's just odd," Troy said to the steward. The steward nodded and smiled. Troy told the steward he would pass on the meal but would love some water. The steward headed off to the galley. Before the steward could come back with Troy's water, suddenly the plane hit some strong turbulence again. This time, the woman woke up. She didn't just sit up like you would think; her head was still on Troy's shoulder, but she murmured something and reached for her sunglasses. She took off her sunglasses and looked up at Troy without lifting her head. Troy was a little surprised now that he could see her whole face. Troy's guess was pretty close; she looked like she might be in her late twenties. She had very dark, almost black hair, hard to tell if it was short or long because it was tucked into the hooded sweatshirt she was wearing.

Her eyes are huge! Troy observed, big and dark. Troy is hardly an expert, but to him, it appeared the woman didn't have any makeup on. Even so, she was very attractive in a hard and dark kind of way. *She has beautiful skin and full, red lips*, he admired. Even in the plane's low lighting, he could tell. *Whoa, what am I thinking?* Troy was not the type to dwell on something like this, but he found himself curiously interested.

"Who are you?" she said with a quiet but direct voice.

"I'm Troy," he told her. She started to lift her head off Troy's shoulder; as she did, a thin trail of drool followed her. Now Troy knew she spoke English, which was a huge relief.

"Who said you could sit here?" she asked sharply. She wiped the drool from her mouth and smiled at Troy. "Oops!"

Troy told her the steward moved him there because his seat was taken. As Troy started to explain the details, the woman held up her hand, indicating she didn't want to hear it.

"That's my seat." she said matter of factly. Troy was puzzled. "I'm sorry, do you want to switch?" he asked as politely as possible. "No! These are *both* my seats," she sternly stated with a heavy dose of attitude. "Both of these seats are yours? I'm sorry, I didn't know. This is where they sat me, and there are no more seats on the plane," Troy quickly tried to explain. She reached for Troy's shoulder and tried to wipe her drool off his shirt with her hand. "That's a little embarrassing!" she said and started to put her sunglasses back on. "Well then, I guess I have no choice," she said as she turned away from Troy toward the window. She covered herself back up and seemed as if she went back to sleep. "Now I know why the steward didn't want me to wake her!"

EXPERIENCE COUNTS!

They were about halfway into the four-hour flight; Troy was reading some articles he had downloaded earlier onto his laptop computer. The mystery woman sitting next to him really never moved again, except for a slight repositioning of one foot. Troy only knew this because she kicked him as she moved it. Troy was thinking, *Either this woman is really sick, or she must have taken a sleeping pill. No one can sleep like that!* Troy returned to the article he was reading. He was feeling a little guilty like he should get some work done, but he was still so tired he couldn't muster up the motivation. *I'll try to do some work on the next flight*, he thought, knowing he had plenty of time to get his paperwork done while he sat in planes and airports over the next thirty-two hours. Then, there was a strange sound coming from behind him, like a metal rubbing on metal sound. Troy wasn't sure if the sound was coming from inside or outside the plane. The noise got louder and louder, then suddenly only a few seconds after it started, the noise went away. But before Troy could take a breath, there was a loud explosion, "Oh God! What was that?"

Troy let out as the plane made a sudden hard right turn and rapid decent. It felt as if the plane was falling out of the sky! Alarms started going off, the oxygen masks fell from the ceiling; people started screaming. Troy's laptop and water fell to the floor, but he didn't notice. Even the mystery woman couldn't sleep through this; she sat straight up with her eyes wide open. The plane started to shake violently; it felt and sounded like it was coming apart. The pilot straightened out the sharp turn but the plane continued to fall; people were in a total panic! As far as Troy could see, all the crew made it to their seats except for one stewardess who was draped across a row of passengers, who were trying to hold onto her. Troy was scared, but with as much flying as he has done, he wasn't yet convinced they were going down. Still, the only thing in Troy's mind was the faces of his children. It helped keep him calm. After what seemed like several minutes, the plane started to level off. The captain came over the loudspeaker to make an announcement. People were crying, some still screaming, and all sitting in their seats with the oxygen masks over their faces. Troy's leg started to hurt him. He looked at his leg as he started to move his hand toward the pain. The woman sitting next to him was literally driving her nails into Troy's leg. He looked at the woman who hadn't put on her mask; she looked completely terrified, although Troy does not remember her screaming. Her sunglasses were now off, hood down, blanket on the floor, as she stared straight ahead. He touched her hand gently, she looked at her hand and realized she was hurting Troy, and quickly released it. *Wow, that really hurt*, without saying it out loud. She even managed to draw a little blood!

As the plane seemed to stabilize, it was obvious there was something very wrong. The captain continued to make announcements over the loudspeakers, as did one or more of the crew. Unfortunately, Troy could only understand one or two words, none of which made any sense to him. The first-class steward was now out of his seat and moving about the front of the plane. Troy waved him over. "What happened?" Troy asked with a little concern in his voice. The woman sitting next to Troy was now focused and listening intently to the steward as he talked with Troy.

"One of our engines went out," he said with a strange smile on his face; maybe he was trying to soften the blow. "No cause for alarm, sir, the captain has everything under control," he offered.

"Okay," Troy said. "Are we going to be able to make it to the airport?" he asked very concerned.

"The captain has indicated that to be safe, we are going to have to land at the closest airport to make repairs" the steward explained.

"Okaaay," Troy said again, this time with some outward concern on his face. "Where is that?" he asked. "The Captain said the closest airport is a small airport in Asmara, Eritrea. We are going to land there. We should be on the ground in less than twenty minutes," he explained further.

"Eritea?" he asked. "I've never heard of it!" he said to the steward.

"Yes, not many have, it's a very small country," he replied. "It will be fine," he told Troy as he went back to his duties and the other passengers.

Amazing how people change when the circumstances change. Within minutes, Troy now knew the mystery woman sitting next to him—the same woman who barely said three words to him in the first two hours of the flight. Troy now knew her name, Isabelle; he knew she was divorced, and she lived in Los Angeles. And she had a remarkable grip as she squeezed his hand tighter and tighter with each new shake or shimmy of the plane. Troy didn't mind; he was kind of happy she was there. He thought about what it would have been like for him if he were in the middle seat in the back of the plane during this whole thing. *Well, if I'm going down, at least I'm going down first-class!* he joked with himself, trying to calm his nerves.

The plane started descending; only this time, it felt like it was under control, at least at first. It started to shake again, and the passengers who had finally calmed down were once again starting to cry and scream. Troy was sure much of what he heard were prayers being said as loud as they could; Troy himself was quietly praying in his mind. Isabelle was now speaking with Troy as if they were friends, and they knew each other for years.

"Do you think we are going to be okay?" she asked Troy very softly. Troy looked at her, this was the first time Troy could actually see his row partner. Isabelle had long silky black hair and big dark eyes. She was very pretty, even without makeup, Troy observed. She seemed softer now, maybe not as hard as he originally thought. The woman who seemed to care about nothing but herself was a new person, a scared young woman. She had tears flowing down both of her cheeks.

"Without a doubt!" he responded with confidence. "One thing I know about these planes is they are very strong. I bet the pilot could fly this plane with only two engines!" he said, trying to comfort her. He realized as he was saying it, it probably wasn't what she wanted to hear. Troy quickly added, "We will be on the ground soon, it will be fine. We'll be fine."

As they descended lower and lower, the plane's shaking calmed a bit. Troy could see lights off in the distance. *Must be the airport*, he thought. He knew they were getting close to landing. Everyone was seated including the crew. One of the stewardesses came over the loudspeaker to make an announcement; everyone started to lean forward, putting their heads in their laps.

Isabelle grabbed Troy's hand again. "We are supposed to get into a crash position!" she told Troy. "Hmmm," Troy knew something else about her; Isabelle understood the language. As Troy began to ponder that thought, he could see the airport lights coming up fast. The plane was very close. He heard the landing gears coming down. *That's a good sign*, he thought. The plane was slowing, the closer to the ground they got, the harder Isabelle squeezed Troy's hand. Troy was looking out the window next to Isabelle; there were no visible buildings around, not many lights that he could see either. *Strange*, he thought. Now the runway lights were racing by the window as they were seconds away from landing. The screech sound from the first touch of the wheels!

Troy felt the nose of the plane touch; as it did, they went past a small fire truck with its one emergency light flashing. "That's it!" Troy said out loud. Everyone on board, including the crew started to clap.

"What?" Isabelle asks.

"We must be waaaay out! They only have one emergency fire truck!"

The plane came to a safe stop. Troy lifted his hand, the hand that Isabelle was still holding onto so tight. She let his hand go and smiled warmly at him. "We made it!" she said with a cute little in-her-seat celebration. The rest of the passengers and crew were clapping, laughing, and some still praying. The captain spoke over the loudspeaker. People got very quite and listened. Troy turned to Isabelle, expecting she could understand. Isabelle told Troy the captain wanted everyone to disembark the plane and wait in the terminal for further instructions. Troy thought for sure they were going to have to slide down one of those emergency slides when they got to the door. Kind of strange, but he was looking forward to it. As he and Isabelle approached the door of the plane, Troy could see the ground crew had put stairs up against the plane. He asked the steward that was with him in first class why there was no emergency slide, especially since no one really knew at that point if the plane was safe yet. The steward explained to Troy that the plane was perfectly safe and they didn't want to deploy the slide if they didn't have to because it would be impossible to get a replacement and they couldn't take off without one. Troy looked at Isabelle; she smiled like it was no big deal and started down the stairs.

ADVENTURE WITHIN AN ADVENTURE

It was cold, rainy and the wind was whipping hard, mixing water with sand, making it nearly impossible to see. As the passengers approached the terminal at this remote little airport, Troy noticed it was pretty much the only building around, except for a couple of out-buildings that looked more like shacks than actual buildings. They waked into this very small one-room terminal. It was about as simple as it could possible be. It had a one-person counter, a couple of dozen chairs, not nearly enough to accommodate all the passengers from this flight, and it had a couple of vending machines. Oh, and it looked like there may have been three employees present in the terminal—a counter person, a security guard, and a baggage guy, who Troy is sure he saw driving the fire truck! They definitely were not prepared to handle this group!

Most of the passengers seemed very disoriented when they first walked in. Partly due to surviving what they were sure was going to be a crash, partly because of the unusual surroundings. The terminal area quickly filled to capacity. As were many others, Troy was looking around for a restroom. It was quickly learned that the only restroom they had was outside, and the line was already forming around the building. Troy decided he was going to hold it for a while. When he went back inside the terminal, someone was standing on the only counter speaking to the group of passengers. Troy tried to understand what was being said, but the only thing he picked up was the word for plane and time. Whatever was being announced, the other passengers were not happy. Troy needed to know what the announcement was, so he started looking around for Isabelle. There were so many people jammed into one small area it was impossible to find her. Troy started asking those around him if they spoke English and if they could tell him what was said. After going through a dozen passengers, the fire truck guy was suddenly standing in front of him and he said he could help. *This was unexpected*, Troy thought. The fire truck guy, who's name was Mohammad, Troy gathered from his name badge, told him they announced that the planes engine cannot be fixed and they were going to try to bring in a different plane. "That completely sucks!" was Troy's first reaction. "How long did they say until the new plane gets here?" Troy asked Mohammad.

"They are saying it should be here by six or seven AM tomorrow morning," he answered.

"That's over eights hours"! Troy yells out louder than he expected to.

Eight hours! Troy was thinking to himself. *Now I'm going to miss every connection and may not be home for days!* He grabbed his cell phone out of his pocket—zero bars. *Of course!* There was no way for him to start making flight changes or even contact his family. Troy was about to ask Mohammad if there was a phone around he could use when someone put their hand on his shoulder.

"Lost stranger?" Isabelle asked. Mohammad smiled.

Troy turned to see it was Isabelle "I guess so, and apparently I'm going to stay lost for at least eight hours!" he said, very frustrated.

"Well…we can stay here in this lovely private club with the other four hundred members, or we can get out of here and go find something decent to eat? I'm starving!" Isabelle strongly suggested. "I'm pretty sure I owe you at least that much!" she told him.

"Uh, that's sounds great, but I haven't seen any taxis around, actually I haven't even seen any camels around!" Troy said, more as a matter of fact than trying to be smart. "Man, oh, man, you're not one of those the glass is half-empty guys, are you? That would be a major bummer!" she joked.

"No, not normally, but I am a bit of a planner, and I'm not really seeing too many options here," Troy replied.

"That's because you're not looking in the right places or talking to the right people, right Mohammad?" Mohammad smiled and nodded. The mystery woman still had her mysteries, but hiding or being reclusive was no longer one of them.

Next thing Troy knows, they are back outside in the rain and wind getting into the fire truck! "The fire truck!" Troy laughs. Isabelle climbed into the middle, and Troy got in behind her. Troy wanted to say something but thought it might be better to keep his mouth shut. Isabelle says something to Mohammad in apparently a language he understood. He smiled and started to drive away from the terminal.

Troy had to speak up. "Do you know where we are going?" he asked a little skeptical.

"Not exactly, but Mohammad says there is a village that is not too far, and it's supposed to have the best food and entertainment for a hundred miles! It should be fun," Isabelle said, showing an adventurous side Troy hadn't seen till now. This time, Troy just smiled and said nothing.

They drove on dirt roads the entire time—not an easy or comfortable ride, especially in a nearly antique fire truck! The moon was not out at all. Some parts of the drive were so dark the only thing you could see that were not in the headlights was the faint outline of the mountains and stars—lots and lots of stars. Every once in a while, they would pass through what looked like a small village with a couple of buildings and what Troy assumed were houses. There were only a couple of lights visible in each of the villages; no one was outside. Troy started to wonder how safe they might be. They were in a country were there was an active civil war, but the conflict was mostly tribe against tribe and was usually not going on in remote areas like they were in. Still, it was hard not to worry about it. There have been many, many stories about Americans being kidnapped or killed in situations just like this one. Just as he was starting to freak out a little bit and was about to suggest they turn around, Mohammad excitedly exclaimed, "We're here!"

As they drove into the village, Troy could see it was much larger than any of the others they passed on the way. It was more like a small town than a village, Troy thought. According to Mohammad it was called Dekemhare. It had only one street, still a dirt road, with several buildings along it.

"Here we are!" Mohammad said as he pulled in front of a single-story building that was dimly lit from the outside; you could see that lights were on on the inside through the only window. "This looks great!" Isabelle said excitedly. There were people inside, and Troy could hear music and singing.

"You hear that?" asked Isabelle. "This looks fun!" she said very anxiously. They jumped out of the fire truck; Mohammad waved and started to drive off.

"Wait!" Troy yelled out. "Why is he leaving?" he asked as he turned back to Isabelle, who was almost to the establishment's door.

She stopped and turned to Troy. "I thought you said you weren't one of *those guys*?" she joked.

"Well, I'm not, but—" Troy was interrupted.

"Don't worry about it. Mohammad had to go back, and when the new plane arrives, he will come and get us," Isabelle said reassuringly.

"Oh" was the only response Troy could come with.

"So let's go! I'm starving!" Isabelle said as she waived for Troy to hurry up.

Troy and Isabelle walked through the front entrance, which was an arch with some drapes where you would expect to see doors. There was a small step up and then you were inside. "They have floors!" Troy said a little too excitedly to Isabelle. Inside they saw they had six tables, all of them full with men. Most were eating and drinking. Many were smoking those Turkish pipes, which were placed at the center of each table. Music was playing in the corner; three men each playing a different instrument, none of which Troy recognized. Troy immediately liked the music, it was light and fun. Isabelle obviously liked it; she was already dancing where she stood. Within seconds of them walking in, everyone in the place stopped what they were doing, including the musicians, and were staring at Troy and Isabelle. Troy felt very uncomfortable, but Isabelle was completely oblivious. Just then, a small middle-aged man with a full beard and mustache came up to them. "Welcome, welcome to our little oasis in the desert," he said with his arms open wide, a big smile on his face, and in a very delightful tone. Troy assumed he must be the owner.

"We would like to eat?" Isabelle asked.

"Of course, of course," the man said as he gestured them to come further inside. All the tables were full, but with a wave of his hand and a quiet whistle, one of the tables immediately cleared. "Wow!" Troy exclaimed. Isabelle turned to Troy and smiled.

As they sat at their table, the music started again. The men at the other tables began to go back to their conversations. Troy was a little more comfortable. A young boy showed up at the table with bread and water. He bowed before he placed the items on the table and then bowed again as he backed away from the table then turned and walked away.

Impressive, Isabelle thought. "What do you think?" Isabelle asked Troy with a big smile on her face.

Much prettier than I thought, Troy was thinking as he turned his attention to Isabelle. "This is great!" he said with more enthusiasm than he thought he would. "I hope the food is good!"

After a minute or two, the owner was back. In pretty good English, he introduced himself as Basil and explained he was, in fact, the owner. "I am delighted to have you here at my restaurant. It is my honor to serve you," he said very excitedly. Isabelle could not stop smiling. Basil was explaining the food choices to them, and as he did, the young boy was back. The young boy placed a glass in front of each of them with a beverage already in it. Troy looked at the glass, picked it up, and smelled it.

"Whew!" It gave off a very strong liquor smell. "What is this?" he asked Basil.

"That is our house wine. You'll like it very much, the drinks are from me," he said. "Please try."

Isabelle and Troy each picked up their glasses. Troy was not a big drinker, so he was sure this was not going to go down easily. But he did not want to insult the owner so he decided he had better at least take a sip. He raised his glass up toward Isabelle and said, "Cheers!" Isabelle responded by clinking Troy's glass, and they both took a drink. Well, Isabelle took a drink; Troy took a sip. "Umm, that's really good," Isabelle told Basil. Troy had to agree. "Wow, I really like it!" he told Basil. *An unexpected surprise*, Troy thought to himself.

As Troy and Isabelle listened to Basil continue to explain the menu, Isabelle politely interrupted him. "I think *you* should choose for us," she suggested as she glanced over at Troy.

"Please do," Troy agreed.

Basil was delighted. "This will be a feast like none other," and he quickly walked away. Then things became a little awkward for Troy. Even with the music in the background and the sound of men laughing and talking, it became uncomfortably quite at his table. Troy was looking at Isabelle smiling and enjoying the music, quietly clapping along. "Who was this unusual woman, why is she here, why am I here?" He couldn't help but ask himself. He could not believe this was the same woman on the plane who was so rude to him. As Troy continued to stare at her, he felt like he knew her. Or maybe he just wanted to know her. Before he could care less, now she seemed so interesting to him. Hours ago they were perfect strangers sitting next to each other on a plane, and now it's just the two of them stuck in the middle of nowhere in a strange country, eating at a place where normally only local men eat, an hour away from their plane. *How strange*, Troy thought to himself, "I'm not sure I can tell anyone about this, I don't think they would believe me anyway!"

Troy could see that Isabelle is a very attractive woman, more than he realized. She was tiny and slim. When she smiled, her whole face lit up. She has a positive energy about her that is very seductive. *Boy, the opposite of when I first saw her*, he thought. Troy figured she had to be in her late twenties, but then he's never been any good at guessing peoples ages. He thought maybe she was a model or an actress or something like that, but he couldn't place her. Which is not saying much. Troy rarely goes to the movies and knows nothing about the fashion world. Isabelle was dressed in all black. She had on some kind of black tights, a tight black top with a black hooded sweatshirt over, and a black leather jacket over that. The only reason Troy knew any of this was because Isabelle took off the jacket and the sweatshirt when they went to sit down at their table. She wore no jewelry at all. Every once in a while, Isabelle would pull her hair back behind her ear and Troy could see a small tattoo behind her left ear, but he couldn't tell what it was. *She must be successful*, Troy was thinking. *How could she afford to be in first class, especially on such a major trip? Why would she be traveling alone?* he asked himself again. This troubled Troy more than anything else.

"Isabelle," Troy called out over the music.

She turned to him. "Call me Izy." She paused. "All my friends call me Izy." That sounded strangely familiar.

"Okay, Izy. I wanted to say thank you for bringing me here with you."

Isabelle turned her full attention to Troy. "You may have very well saved my life, the least I can do is buy you dinner! Besides, I would never come to a place like this by myself!" Troy smiled, and they toasted their glasses again. "Troy, I know nothing about you, except I can tell by looking at you, you're a good person. What do you do for a living . . . and why were you on this dreadful flight?" she began to ask. Just then, the young server brought out some plates, and behind him was Basil with another round of drinks.

Troy said, "No, no. I cannot drink anymore, but thank you" in an attempt to refuse the drink. Isabelle accepted hers. "These are not from me," Basil said. "The gentlemen over at the far table bought these for you. They are very excited you are here, we don't get Americans here—ever!" he explained.

"Oh," Troy said. "Well, please tell them thank you very much" and accepted the drink.

Troy was already feeling a little light-headed from the first drink. Maybe the fact that he hasn't eaten in ten or so hours might have something to do with it too. With her chin in her hand, Isabelle coyly smiled at Troy. Troy smiled back.

"Well, it's kind of boring." Troy suggested as he started to answer Isabelle's question. "I'm in international sales for a parts distributor based out of Chicago. My job is to find out what parts our clients need, usually big manufactures, and then I find a manufacture that can make them at the best price, no matter where they are. For my job I have to travel all over the world. I'm sure I spend more time on a plane than I do on my own couch. Anyway, on this trip alone, I've been to five different countries, well . . . six now!" He laughs. "And I've been away from home for over three weeks. I ended up on our flight, which I nearly didn't make, because there is one small manufacture in Djibouti that makes a very unique part that we need, and it was important for me to go visit them." From there, Troy went on to tell Isabelle the crazy details of how he almost missed the flight and how he ended up in first class sitting next to her.

Isabelle was listening intently and would laugh at some of the crazier moments of Troy's plane mishaps. "That *is* a crazy story," Isabelle admitted. "But not boring! I am very glad that you ended up sitting next to me…see, it all worked out" She took a long pause, "So tell me about home," she requested. "Are you married? Do you have any kids?" The young server just arrived with several dishes of food. The plates were piled high with food, some chicken, some rice, one plate looked like it might be vegetables, and a fourth plate with something Troy did not recognize. It all smelled fantastic. Troy, not usually the talkative type, and rarely about himself, continued, "Yes, I'm married and have two children—Maggie, twelve, and Justin, nine. I'm lucky, they are great kids. I just wish I could see them more," he complained. "I've been married for about thirteen years and my wife is a busy homemaker, more busy with her own life than actually being a homemaker, but that's okay." Troy felt kind of bad after saying that, and Isabelle could tell.

"I know what you mean…it's okay," Isabelle said supportively.

Troy added, "It also just so happens I'm married to the boss's daughter!" He laughed. "Stupid, right?" he asked.

Isabelle only smiled bigger. "I know this is going to sound *really, really* stupid, but I'm pretty sure that's why I have to travel so much," he told her.

"What does that mean?" Isabelle inquired. She was very curious about such a remark.

"I know you'll think I'm nuts, but I think my father-in-law sends me on these trips just to get me out of my own house. He and I don't get along very well, and sometimes I think as my boss he takes advantage of that," he told her.

"Wow," Isabelle remarked. "That's terrible if it's true! Why would he want to do such a thing?" she asked. "Especially to his own daughter's husband?"

"Right? It's not too hard to figure this out, when I'm home he never comes over to the house to visit the kids or my wife, but when I'm away he's there almost every day. He takes the kids places and takes them all out to dinner almost every night. I know he loves them and loves being with them, but he avoids any involvement when I'm around, except when he has to, like birthdays and things like that." Troy continued talking for some time, telling Isabelle many things about his life—his dreams and his goals. He spoke a great deal about his children, how he misses them all of the time, and how much he loves them. When he spoke about his wife, their marriage, and his job, which to Troy were all tied together, it seemed he was releasing many of his pent-up issues in this very rare and unique opportunity. He even fessed up to the remark April laid on him as he got into the cab when he was leaving for the airport. He admitted, "Well, that didn't exactly work out as planned." For whatever reason, Troy felt comfortable talking with Isabelle, maybe it was the drinks doing the talking or maybe it was being able to open up to a perfect stranger. He didn't know, but for Troy this was a first, and it felt tremendously liberating.

PARTY OF TWENTY

Troy felt like he's never eaten this much food in his life! Every bite was excellent, a new and exciting taste. Both he and Isabelle remarked throughout the meal how great it was. "This is so fantastic, it's like every bite is fun!" said Isabelle.

"Who knew!" said Troy.

They nearly finished every plate. They were both sitting back in their chairs sipping on their drinks, which they long ago lost count of, when one of the men from the back table was suddenly standing in front of Troy and Isabelle. Not a big man, long beard, full Middle Eastern dress. He said nothing, it was a little intimidating to both of them. The man smiled. Troy thanked him for the drink. The man nodded his head in response. "I don't think he understands us," Troy said. The man stood there a few more seconds, smiling, when he put out his hand with his palm up toward Isabelle. Troy had no clue what that meant, but Isabelle did. Troy was about to say something when Isabelle stood up and set her hand in the palm of this man's hand; together they stepped a few feet away from the table. The man dropped Isabelle's hand and sort of did half a bow toward her. Isabelle returned the gesture.

The music restarted—lively and fun tune, very Middle Eastern. The man reacquired Isabelle's hand, and he started to turn them both to the sound of the music. Every once in a while, he would make a big clapping gesture above his head to the music. Within a minute or so, the other men in the restaurant would all clap at the same moments. Isabelle was having a blast; she was laughing and dancing, even though she had no idea what she was doing. She was definitely going with the flow! Soon, other men were dancing, and within minutes, they were all dancing! It was quite a sight. Troy started taking pictures with his phone when Basil approached Troy. "Come, come, you must dance!" he told Troy. Troy started to say no, but between the drinks and the strength of his host, Troy was on his feet. One of the men pulled Troy into the middle of everyone dancing, then they nudged Isabelle into the middle with Troy. Everyone was dancing and clapping, having a great time. The music was so energizing. Isabelle reached out for Troy's hand; Troy took it, and they began to slowly turn in a circle. They were quickly joined by some of the other men who took a hand, and they all danced in two big circles. First, one way, then the other. This was truly a first for Troy. He's only danced one other time in his life, and that was at his wedding; even then, he did so because he had to, plus he wasn't going to be the first groom in history to not dance the "first dance" with his new bride.

After the dance was over, nearly all the men gave both Isabelle and Troy a hug. Many of them wanted to shake Troy's hand. It was amazing. Smiles and pleasantness all around. Isabelle was able to thank them; all the men seemed impressed at her attempts to speak their language. Troy and Isabelle were having so much fun. It was like they forgot where they were and the circumstances they were in. They had a chance to be free, to really be themselves, just themselves. When Troy and Isabelle returned to their table, there were fresh drinks waiting for them and a new plate of food, but not just any food. It was a "desert for lovers" is what Basil called it.

"Uh-oh," Troy murmured. "Isabelle busted out with this huge laugh and started clapping.

"Really, it's funny, but is it that funny?" Troy suggested to Isabelle.

"Are you kidding? It's not funny, it's perfect!" she exclaimed.

"Oh"—he finds himself saying that a lot. Basil stood by their table and raised his own glass. Everyone in the place raised theirs glasses, as did Troy and Isabelle. Basil made a toast that started in English and ended in Arabic. He ended the toast by saying, "Much happiness, health, and many, many babies" was the part Troy got out of it.

Holy crap! he thought to himself. Then everyone drank and cheered. It was very cool. Troy, a little embarrassed, looked at Isabelle; she was literally beaming as she smiled and cheered with all of the men. Troy decided not to say anything and just go with it.

"Are you going to cut the cake, honey?" Isabelle laughed very loudly as she handed Troy a knife. Troy laughed with her and cut them each a slice of the desert.

"Okaaay," Troy says, breaking the moment for a second. "We've spent the last—I don't know how many hours—talking about me, I think it's your turn! I mean, after all, *we are married*! I should know something about you!" Troy laughingly suggested.

Isabelle broke out laughing. "I suppose so? What is it you'd like to know, kind sir?" She was really having a good time.

"Well, I guess the basics to start, like are you married, and do you have any children?" He started off.

Isabelle calmed down a bit. "Really . . . do we have to talk about me? I'd much rather talk about you some more!" she pleaded.

"No," Troy said. "It's only fair."

Isabelle shook her head in agreement and started, "Well, okay, since it's only fair. Ah-umm." She cleared her throat. "I am not married. I was once, but it didn't last long," she started.

"That sucks! I'm sorry," Troy injected with sincerity.

"No, it was never meant to be, we were both very young and I wasn't exactly focused on the right things back then," she said.

"Are you focused on the right things now?" Troy asked.

"You know, I'm getting better. Every day, yes, I think my life is coming more into focus. My priorities are changing, and I'm becoming a better person," she stated.

"Wow, that's very cool!" Troy remarked. "How about kids?" Troy asked again.

"No, no kids either. Don't get me wrong, I'd *love* to have kids, but I haven't found the right guy, or anything remotely close actually, and really my career makes it nearly impossible," she explained.

"Your career?" Troy asks.

"Yes, like you, I have to travel often. Only when I travel sometimes I can be gone for months at a time," she went on.

"Really! Months? I promise not to complain about my travels anymore!" he laughed. "Why do you have to be gone for so long at a time?" Troy asked her. Now he thought he might be right about the acting or modeling thing. *Those guys are always on the road for long periods*, he thought to himself.

Isabelle went on to answer. "I'm in the music industry, and I have to be wherever, whenever I'm needed," she said.

"Music industry, that's sounds exciting. What do you do in the music business?" Troy is more and more intrigued.

"It's no big deal, and no, the excitement went away a long time ago," she said with a great deal of heaviness in her voice. "I guess you could say that basically I'm a producer ... this is boring, ask me something else," she said rather sternly but still smiling.

Troy could tell she was getting a little upset with the subject, so he asked her a different question. "So when you find your Mr. Right and you find time for the guy, what does Mr. Right look like? What does he do?" he asked.

"Great questions!" was Isabelle's response. "You know, I haven't thought about Mr. Right in a really long time. I guess I just gave up on him, I think."

"That's sad," Troy said. "Let's talk about him now, who knows . . . he may just be right here in the building!"

Isabelle laughed so hard she thought she was going to pee!

Isabelle talked and laughed like she has never done before, telling Troy things she has never shared with anyone—ever. For hours, they talked, laughed, and even cried once while sitting in this remote little restaurant in this remote little village in this remote little country. They were lost, completely engrossed in each other's experiences and life stories. They shared and talked and shared and talked. It came so easy for both of them. Isabelle, at one point, interrupted herself and said to Troy, "You know, you're my best friend!" She said with excitement and a big smile on her face. Troy wasn't sure how to respond and looked at her, puzzled. "I mean it, I've told you things that I have never told anyone else. Doesn't that automatically make you my best friend? I don't have a best friend, and I'd be honored if you would be it!" Again Troy was not sure what to say. They'd both drank a lot, more than either could remember, but this didn't sound like it was anything but real.

"Sure, I'd be happy to be your best friend," he said as he smiled. *Nothing wrong with that*, he thought. *It's not like I have a best friend either!* As soon as Troy said yes, Isabelle asked Troy for his phone.

"My Phone? Why?"

"Please just give it to me."

Troy handed Isabelle his phone. "It's not like your going to get a signal out here!" A minute later, she handed Troy his phone back. "Look!" she said excitedly. Troy looked at his phone and saw that Isabelle had added a new contact: Best Friend, with what he was assuming was her phone number and her e-mail address. "I've added you to mine too, see?" as she pointed out "Best Friend" on her phone to Troy. And yup, she had his number and e-mail too.

"Isabelle," Troy said in a low but meaningful voice. Isabelle was already ahead of him,

"Troy, don't you worry. We are friends, right? Best friends! That only means when you need someone to talk to, or if you just want to catch up, you can call your best friend…me too! That's okay, isn't it?" she asked in a concerned voice.

"Yes, that would be great. Izy is my new best friend."

Isabelle smiled, and they continued to talk.

Apparently they talked through the night. The sun was sneaking in from under the curtains. Troy and Isabelle lost all track of time. No one bothered them all night. The music had stopped hours ago. Even the owner, Basil, was nowhere around. They were the only ones there, until Troy noticed the young server sleeping on a chair in the corner. "Oh my God!" Troy let out. "What time is it?" The young server fell to the floor, startled from Troy's outburst. "How come Mohammad didn't come back for us?"

The young server ran to their table to see if they needed anything, they both politely waived him off. Isabelle tried to stand, but she started feeling the alcohol right away. "Whoa, that drink is hitting me now, and not in a nice way!" Troy had no idea how much their bill was, so he asked the young server. He told Troy it would be two hundred thousand munies (the country's currency). Troy, also feeling the pain of drinking all night, asked him again, "How much?"

"Sorry, sir, my boss says that is forty dollars, US," the young server replied. Troy was dumbfounded.

How could that be? he thought to himself, with all of the food and all of the drinks. Troy handed the boy a fifty-dollar bill and asked, "Please give this to your boss and thank him very much from both of us."

"Yes, sir" was his reply.

"And this is for you," Troy said as he took the young server's hand and put a twenty-dollar bill in it. The young server stood there with his mouth open, staring at the bill. He wanted to say something but didn't know what to say. A voice comes from behind Troy. "Hello!" In walks Mohammad. "Are you guys ready?" he said loudly in an excited voice with his arms raised over his head.

"Ouch!" Isabelle said, feeling a headache coming on strong. "A new plane will be here in an hour or two, so we need to get going." They waived to the young server as they walked out of the restaurant. Isabelle asked, "Wasn't I supposed to buy *you* dinner!"

THE NEW BEST FRIENDS

On the way back to airport, Troy and Isabelle, although exhausted, continued to laugh and talk. Mohammad enjoyed the fun conversation and tried to get involved every now and then. As they passed through one very small village, the mood became somber quickly. Several structures, maybe homes, were burnt to the ground, several still smoldering. Villagers were walking around aimlessly, children were crying. At first glance, no one appeared to be hurt. Isabelle asked Mohammad to stop the truck. They all got out and walked up to one elderly man who was visibly shaken but did not seem hurt. Mohammad asked the man what happened. As the man explained, Isabelle was trying her best to interpret for Troy. The village was attacked at dawn by a band of rebels. They took all the young boys and left only the elderly men and all of the women and children. The rebels burnt down several homes to remind the villagers who was in charge.

"There must be something we can do?" Isabelle said to Troy and Mohammad in a very distressed voice.

Mohammad spoke up, "Unfortunately this is not uncommon. It has become the way for many small villages like this one. The rebels come and take the young men to fight for them, most never come back." The old villager spoke to Mohammad again; Isabelle was having trouble following. Mohammad responded back to the old villager, then Mohammad turned to Isabelle and Troy. "You have already helped them," he said with a big smile on his face.

"How's that possible?" asked Isabelle.

"How did we do that?" Troy curiously asked Mohammad. "The young server who helped you at the restaurant last night, he is from this village. Because he stayed with you all night at the restaurant, he did not get picked up! You may have saved his life!" The older villager was shaking Troy's hand vigorously and petting his head. Repeatedly he was thanking Troy and Isabelle for saving the young server's life, which they now knew as Abraham. Troy and Isabelle looked at each other and smiled, but underneath, they felt they did nothing and wished they could do more.

In the terminal, people were sitting or lying all over the floor. The few seats that were there were being used by some elderly women. Children were playing, people were talking to each other; some were perfect strangers before they were forced into this situation.

Mohammad came up to Troy. "We have a plane now," he stated. Troy looked out the window and saw a jetliner just touching down on the runway. He could hear the screech of the plane's tires. Everyone in the terminal started to clap and yell. All the passengers started to get up and get their things together. The plane was coming to a stop directly in front of the terminal building; you could hear the engines winding down. An airport official, someone Troy had not seen before, was making an announcement. Isabelle explained he wanted everyone to line up for a count, and he told them when they boarded the plane they were to go back to their same seats. Calmly, every passenger in the terminal moved in an orderly fashion to be counted and then went to the stairs to board the plane.

Once on board, it was a little chaotic but people were generally calm and tried to get to their former seats. Troy and Isabelle were in the middle of the group. Once on board, they turned left toward first class. When they got to the first row—their row—people were in both of their seats.

"Not again!" was Troy's immediate response. Isabelle tried to talk to the two people, a young man and woman, who appeared to be together. Just then, the first class steward approached. "Is they're a problem here?" he asked Isabelle. The steward noticed right away before Isabelle could say anything the two passengers sitting in Troy and Isabelle's seats. He stepped in front of the two passengers and told them they were in the wrong seats and that they'd need to move back to their original seats. The woman spoke to the steward like she was trying to explain something. The steward got very stern with them, and they got up.

As they worked their way around Isabelle and Troy, Isabelle whispered into Troy's ear, "They are on their honeymoon! Apparently they are not able to sit together in their assigned seats. That's very sad, don't you think? It's their honeymoon, how cute is that?" Troy knew where this was going. As the two newlyweds started to walk away, Troy asked them to stop. Troy looked at the steward.

"We'd like them to have our seats," he said with much reluctance.

"Really?" asked the steward who was very surprised by the generous action. The steward told the two honeymooners to come back and explained that Troy and Isabelle gave up their seats for them. The response was not what Troy or Isabelle expected. They were showered with hugs, kisses, and blessings. Much more of a big deal than Troy needed, but it was nice to see them so excited and happy.

After some seat shuffling in the back of the plane, the stewardesses were able to arrange it so Troy and Isabelle could sit together. The crew thought that was the least they could do after Troy and Isabelle gave up their first-class seats. Troy was a little upset while Isabelle was totally enjoying it. They ended up in two of the middle seats in the middle of the main section of the plane. It was a tight fit, but once Troy relaxed, it was fine.

"See, this will be great!" Isabelle said enthusiastically. "I'm pretty sure we made those kids' day!" she told Troy.

"You're amazing!" Troy said as he turned to look at Isabelle. "Those weren't my seats to give, that was very generous of you."

Isabelle's response? She stuck out her tongue at Troy and simply said, "It felt good!" Troy laughed. The plane was in the air, and they were on their way.

Troy and Isabelle, new best friends, continued to talk as if they had never left the restaurant back in Dekemhare. They shared many stories and personal things about each other for the remaining two hours of the flight. Some of what they talked about was good fun, other things much more personal and heavy. At one point, Isabelle started to cry as she shared something very personal with Troy. Troy comforted her by giving her a hug. The time went by too fast for both of them. The pilot made an announcement over the loudspeaker. They are approaching for landing. Twelve hours late, but they were landing where they were supposed to. Troy's first thought was he wasn't ready to have his time with Isabelle end. But he knew the monumental task in front of him to try to reroute and rebook all of his flights to get home. Even though he finally made it to Cairo, he still might be stuck for sometime.

Isabelle asked Troy, "I never asked you, where do you go from here?" Isabelle wasn't ready to be separated from her new "best friend" either.

Troy responded with a depressed look on his face. "I'm not sure. Originally I was supposed to go from here to London, then from London to New York, then New York to Chicago. I have no idea what I'm going to be doing now. I guess I'll be on the phone for awhile when we land."

Isabelle explained she was also supposed to go to London, onto New York, then New York to Los Angeles.

"Really? I guess that makes sense," Troy responded.

"I'll tell you what," Isabelle started, "let me make some calls, I may be able to get us on the same flights at least through to New

York. Why don't you call your family and your office while I see what I can do?" she said enthusiastically.

Troy was surprised, but not like you would think; he was surprised at himself because he thought it was a great idea, and he wanted it to work out. "That would be great!" he answered. "That would be really great! Thank you."

Once they were off the plane and in the terminal, they knew they were in an international airport, it was huge! The place was bustling with people. Isabelle and Troy agreed to meet at a restaurant they spotted when they first got into the main terminal area. Troy stopped at the men's room, as Isabelle continued walking on. "See you in a bit," she said as she waived her hand high in the air without looking back at Troy. Troy couldn't help but smile; he turned and went into the men's room. Troy was very happy to finally be able to call home. He sat down at a table in the restaurant that he and Isabelle were to meet at. Troy called home; his wife answered the phone.

"Troy! Oh my God! I've been worried sick, are you all right?"

But before Troy could respond, April continued on, "Why didn't you try to call me? I called the airlines, and all they would tell me is your plane had to make an emergency landing and that everyone was all right. They wouldn't even tell me where you landed! I called Daddy, and he tried everything, but no one would help him either. I thought maybe you were kidnapped or something!" Troy accidentally laughed out loud as he thought that someone might think of his little trip with Isabelle as a kidnapping. "What's funny? Why are you laughing?" April asked with her familiar stern and forceful voice.

Oops, Troy thought. "I'm sorry, April, I was perfectly safe . . . really. I couldn't call you because where I was had no signal at all, and there were no landlines around anywhere. Trust me, I tried. I was stuck until they could get us a new plane, which took ten or twelve hours!" he tried to explain. There was no way Troy was going to tell April about his new friend. He didn't want to lie to her, and even though Troy didn't feel as if he had done anything wrong, he knew no matter how he explained it, his wife was not going to process it well. He continued, "I'm trying to arrange for new flights right now, as soon as I have a new itinerary, I will forward you all the details. I'm really hoping to be home by tomorrow," he told her.

"That's good news," April said. "The kids and I really miss you!" she said, shifting into a much lighter and sweeter tone.

Troy responded in kind. "I miss you guys *too*. Are the kids around? I'd love to talk to them," he asked.

"Yes, yes, but it's the middle of the night here, they're asleep," April said.

"Oh, right," Troy responded. "I guess you wouldn't want to wake them?" he asked sheepishly.

"Are you kidding?" April was now back to her "other" voice. "But Daddy's right here, he wants to talk to you." Dread came over Troy—physical dread. The father-in-law was on the phone.

"Troy? Are you there? Listen, I'm glad you're okay. April and the children were very worried about you, but I kept them busy so they wouldn't have to worry too much. It's not good for the kids, you know what I mean?" Troy wanted to respond differently, but he didn't and only said, "Yes ... thank you."

The father-in-law continued, "I know you're tired, and you want to get home to see your family, I understand that. So take a day and relax, but I'll need you and your reports in the office right away after that! Are you good with that?" Now Troy's boss was talking to him.

"Yes, sir" was the only thing Troy could muster up to say.

"Good, I'll see you then. Have a safe flight." And the phone went dead. "Well, at least I don't have to try to call the office now," Troy said to himself as he tried to shake off the call. He was really saddened that he didn't get to talk to his kids; those were the two people that he actually *wanted* to talk to.

NO PROOF NECESSARY

Troy was deep into his computer when Isabelle walked up. "May I sit down?" she asked with a little excitement in her voice.

Troy looked up and smiled. "It would be my honor" he replied.

"It's all set," Isabelle said excitedly.

"What's all set? The flights?"

"Yup. I've got you covered to Chicago, and I'm ticketed through to Los Angeles. We are on the same fights and sitting next to each other all the way to New York!" Isabelle said even a little more excitedly. Then it suddenly struck Isabelle; she didn't even think about asking Troy if this was okay; she just went off and did it.

"Troy?" she said quietly and almost in a teasing voice. "I just realized I really didn't ask you. Maybe you don't want to sit next to me all those hours? I feel like an idiot now. I'm soooo stupid. I didn't think to ask you. I'm sorry, if you like, I can—" Troy interrupts her by touching her hand as she sat down to the table.

"Are you kidding?" he said. "Not only have you made this trip bearable, especially when we were stranded, but you have made this the best road trip I've ever had to go on . . . ever!" he told her. "It has been my honor to meet you and to be your new 'best friend'!" Troy said with a big smile on his face. Isabelle had hoped that would be his response.

"How did it go with your family? Did you get ahold of them?" Isabelle asked with genuine concern.

"Yes," Troy answered. "I spoke to my wife and somehow my father-in-law, but unfortunately, I didn't get to talk to my kids, they were in bed," he said.

"Oh, I'm sorry," Isabelle offered. "Did you say *your* father-in-law?" she inquired.

"Yea, I know, strange, right? Apparently he has been staying at the house with them since I've been gone."

Isabelle smiled. "I'm not so sure I'd say strange, after some of the things you've told me! How'd it go?" she asked.

"Fine," Troy answered directly and with no emotion in his voice. Isabelle knew to let it go; she could see that Troy was upset.

"Okay! Let's eat!" Isabelle's attempt to change the subject. "And this time, it's on me, no exceptions!" She added with a stern voice but sweet smile.

Two hours later, they were in the air headed to London. When they boarded the plane initially, Troy was a little concerned as they again sat in the first row in first class! *Oh man!* he thought. "I don't know why I didn't think about it," he started to explain to Isabelle. "I never thought about the fact that you will want to fly first class! My company will never approve the difference in fares, and it would be hard for me to cover it," he said, feeling embarrassed and stupid. Isabelle smiled and said reassuringly, "Don't worry, my company will!" Not used to hand outs, Troy didn't respond and sat down in his seat.

Troy sat back and was enjoying the thought that he was going to be flying first class all the way to New York. "This is great!" he said to Isabelle, who smiled in response. Troy noticed Isabelle had started acting a little differently when they went to the gate to begin boarding. She put back on the sunglasses she had on from the first flight when he first saw her and she put on the hooded sweatshirt with the hood on over her head. Troy didn't try to read too much into it, he figured maybe Isabelle is more comfortable traveling this way or maybe his model theory still had some wheels. Even after they sat down, Isabelle left on her sunglasses, and she kept the hood over her head, nearly covering her whole face. *This looks strangely familiar!* he thought to himself.

Troy reached out to Isabelle. "Are you okay?" he asked.

"Yes, thank you, I'm fine," she replied, smiling. "I'm just cold," she told him.

Well, okay, that might explain the sweatshirt, Troy thought. *But not exactly the need for sunglasses!* They continued to talk for some time. Isabelle was not as fun or outgoing as she had been for so many hours before, in what Troy figured out had to be well over twenty-four hours. *Maybe that's what it is*, Troy was thinking to himself. *She's tired.*

"Isabelle?" Troy began to ask. "Izy," she politely corrected him. "Sorry, right, Izy. Would you like to stop talking for a bit, maybe try to get some sleep?" he suggested.

"No, no" she replied. "Let's keep talking . . . please."

Troy nodded. "Okay." Troy was exhausted, but like Isabelle, he didn't really want to stop talking with her either. So he had a question, "Izy, I don't think we talked about it. How did you end up in Djibouti anyway? Was there some kind of artist around there you were looking at or something like that?" Troy tried to offer up an answer for her.

"No, actually I ended up in the always lovely Djibouti because it was the only flight out of Saudi Arabia where I was working," she explained. "Bad luck on that choice," he said jokingly.

"No, not really." She lowered her sunglasses and looked directly at Troy as she answered the question while smiling the same little koi smile she had done a few times before. Troy smiled back, a little embarrassed. Isabelle continued her explanation, "I was working in Saudi Arabia when I got in a huge fight with some of the people I work with. I guess you could call it creative differences. I quit, and like a spoiled little brat, I walked out!" she told him.

"*Really*?" Troy asked somewhat surprised at the admission.

Isabelle said, "At that point all I wanted to do was go home and I didn't care which flight I got on as long as it pointed toward home."

"Wow, that's a bit of a surprise! I mean I only just met you, but somehow that doesn't sound like you." Troy said. "Yeah, sorry to disappoint, but sometimes that is me. I don't like it either . . . I am trying to work on it." She confessed.

"Well, if you quit, what are you going to do now?" he inquired. "I have to imagine positions in your field can't be easy to come by?"

Just as Isabelle began to answer Troy couldn't help but think, *I can't believe this didn't come up before.*

Isabelle went on to explain, "You know . . . I'm going to piss off a lot of people, a lot, but I think I'm going to take a little break and rest. Maybe just sit around home, read a few books I've been wanting to read, and watch a lot of movies," she said with some of the enthusiasm coming back into her voice.

"That sounds good," Troy said, not actually sure if it did sound good to him. "It's great that you can do that. I could really use some time off, I can't even remember the last time I took more than three or four days off. I'd love to spend that kind of time with my kids. But . . . not really my call, if you know what I mean!" he explained.

"I do," Isabelle said, showing support. "I'm not sure I really can either, it's just a thought . . . but I'd love to."

The pilot came over the speaker system. "We should be landing in about thirty minutes. Right now, it's raining in London and about forty-two degrees. Please fasten your seat belts and prepare for landing. Thank you for flying with us today."

Isabelle turned to Troy. "Look at that! Only eight hours or so before your home! You're nearly there!" They both laughed as Isabelle stood up to grab her bag from the overhead compartment. As she did, someone from behind her in first class yelled, "Izy!" Izy turned toward the person and a flash went off.

"What was that?" Troy asked, very puzzled as Isabelle quickly sat back down.

"I'm not sure" was Isabelle's reply. "Strange, don't you think?" she added.

"Yea, very strange," Troy agreed. Isabelle could see Troy's mind was racing. "Troy...listen, there is something else I've been wanting to tell you. At first I wasn't going to, but now I feel like we are *really* becoming good friends, and I don't want that to change, I think we could be such good friends, don't you?" Isabelle offered with a little desperation in her voice.

"Yes...yes, I do, I think we can be friends. Aren't we already friends?" Troy jokingly replied, trying to be supportive, but now very curious. With a serious look on her face, Isabelle leaned in toward Troy took his hand and said, "Look...I have to make a little admission to you." Troy was kind of glad he was already sitting down; this sounded serious.

"You might want to get off the plane before me when we land in London," she started her "admission."

"Uh, okay. Why?" *Strange thing to say*, Troy thought. Isabelle started to explain to Troy something she thought she would not have to, but then she thought she and Troy would only be temporary travel buddies, until Isabelle realized just how much she liked Troy and maybe just how much she needed him...as a friend. For the first time in as long as she could remember, someone wasn't treating her differently. Troy wasn't pretending to like her or care about what she thought or cared about. Isabelle was sick of being surrounded by "yes" people; this was so refreshing to her. Troy allowed Isabelle to be herself and not be judged. Troy could be a real friend to her, and she didn't want to lose that. London was under their feet, and Isabelle realized she was running out of time. She didn't want to "blow it" with Troy, but she had no choice now...she had to tell him the truth.

She turned her body as much as she could to be facing Troy. She sat up straight and smiled. Then she said to him in a very lighthearted way, "Hi, my name is Izy, and I'm a rock star." As she rocked her head back and forth, throwing her hair around and flashed Troy the devil horns with her fingers, a popular way of expressing your passion for rock and roll. Troy laughed as Isabelle moved the hair from in front of her face.

"Okay, that's cool. That's a slight promotion from producer, isn't it?" he suggested.

Isabelle laughed too. "No really!" Still being lighthearted about it, she said, "I mean *I am* a producer," she tried to explain, "and a writer, and a musician, and a singer. I didn't want to tell you because you seemed so real, and you didn't seem to know me, so I felt I could be myself around you. Trust me, I never…ever get to be just me," she told him.

Troy was puzzled again. He knew the name Izy, everyone knew the name Izy. "Why am I always a little puzzled around you?" he asked. "So…your telling me your Izy the rock star?" Isabelle said to Troy with a great deal of emotion behind her eyes, "From the minute we left the airport in Cairo I have been nothing but truthful with you, and that's a whole lot of truths coming from *me*! Okay, maybe I didn't tell you *everything*, but I told you the truth." Troy was trying to think if there was a difference, when Isabelle spoke up again, "Look, put these on." She handed Troy the headphones to her phone. He listened. "Okay, sure I've heard of 'Izy', I mean who hasn't? My kids are nuts about her…or you, against my better judgment really. So you have 'Izy' on your phone, doesn't half the world have her on their phone?" he asked with a fair amount of sarcasm in his voice.

"Right!" Isabelle said, shaking her head. "You're right! Here! How about this? Take a look at these!" She said as she handed Troy her phone and opened her photo gallery. Isabelle was amazed that Troy did not believe her. "I know I look different without my makeup or costumes, but this is crazy," she was thinking to herself. She was having fun with the challenge and Troy was being very cool about it. She started scrolling through some of her photos from a recent concert. "It is definitely an 'Izy' concert," Troy said to her. The photos appeared to be from backstage at a concert and 'Izy' was in most of them. As Isabelle continued to scroll through the photos with Troy, Troy made her stop on one particular photo. It was a close up of Izy and a famous musician that Troy recognized, but that's not why he stopped on the picture. In the photo, he could clearly see a tattoo of an angel behind Izy's left ear. Troy expanded the photograph with his fingers to look closer. He looked at Isabelle, Isabelle pulled her hair back, and behind her left ear was the same tattoo of an angel. Troy handed Isabelle back her phone. The stewardess yelled at them both, "Hey! Put that away!" Isabelle quickly jammed the phone in her bag.

Within a matter of minutes, the wheels of the plane touched down. As they taxied their way to the gate, Troy asked, "So you didn't tell me before because you were afraid I'd act differently toward you?" he asked.

"Basically, yes," Isabelle answered. "And why is it you're telling me now?" he inquired. "Because," she started to explain, "someone just took my picture, so now it is very likely people on the ground know I'm here. I was trying to get home without being noticed. I'm concerned I'll be mobbed when I get off the plane, and I didn't want you to freak out!" she said, again with a little desperation in her voice. Troy shrugged his shoulders and opened his hands in a questioning gesture and replied, "Okay, I guess that makes sense, sort of. Of course, you're assuming I'm not freaking out right now!" Isabelle looked at him with a face of concern, then they both started laughing; Isabelle hugged him. "Now that I've gotten to know you, I really don't want to screw this up. Will you wait for me on the next flight?" she asked. "Sure. I'll even save you a seat!" he said jokingly. "But this last flight together, I'm going to have some serious questions!" he told her.

"That's fair," Isabelle's replied. "Be nice to me!" she said as she laughed. The plane stopped at the gate.

Troy was one of the first passengers off the plane. There was a small crowd around the gate area, which wouldn't normally seem unusual except some people had their phones held up as if they were preparing to take a picture. There was more than the usual amount of airline employees hanging around too, trying to look as if they had a reason to be there. Troy was too curious so he stepped back behind the group as the other passengers continued to get off the flight. Not long after, the last passenger must have gotten off the plane because then the crew came out of the gangway and the airline employee at the gate started to close the door. "Hmm, what happened to Izy?" Troy wondered but wasn't bothered by it. Troy could hear some of the people standing around talking as they began to turn away from the gate. "I guess it was just a hoax," one young teen said to another. Troy continued on to his new gate and on to the next to last leg of this very long but totally unique adventure, which just twenty minutes ago became even more unique. *Huh! I've been with* ***the*** *Izy all this time, how crazy is that?* he laughed to himself.

THE LAST LEG

Troy was on board the flight to New York; so was everyone else. The stewardess in first class had already served drinks and gave out towels and was now collecting them back, but no Isabelle. *Izy!* Troy said to himself, shaking his head. *I guess I'm going to have to get used to that*, he thought. A stewardess was announcing the usual preflight instructions when all of a sudden Izy was crossing in front of him and sat down. "You cut that a little close, didn't you?" Troy asked Izy.

"Hi, my new best friend Troy!" Izy said excitedly. "I wasn't 100 percent sure you would be here?" She said with a smile.

Troy laughed. "Miss out on flying first class to New York with Izy, are you kidding!?" Together, they laughed as the plane began to taxi out. Izy sat looking at Troy. She was so happy he was there and even happier that he really didn't seem to care about who she was. She felt like she might have found a real friend, someone she could trust and confide in, and in the strangest place under the strangest circumstances. *How cool is that!* she thought.

The plane had hardly lifted off when Troy turned to Izy and said, "Okay, now about those questions!"

Izy laughed. "Well, if you really want to," she replied. "But I'm not totally sure you're going to want to be my friend after you hear some of the answers," she said.

"I'll be the judge of that," Troy replied. "Besides, you're still *my* friend after finding out about my boring and pathetic life!" he told her. Izy laughed. Troy pauses and takes a deep breath. "I guess my first question is . . . what was that 'I quit my job' thing all about?" he started.

"I *knew* that was going to be your first question! I knew that bothered you!" She was laughing as she said it. "But . . ." she slows down her voice and tone. "I guess it's a bigger question now that you really know me," Izy goes on to explain.

"I feel like an idiot, and telling you this now only makes me feel more like one. The truth is I walked off stage in the middle of my last concert. It wasn't even a concert really, more like a show," she said.

"I had a feeling it was going to be something like that," Troy replied.

"Ya, stupid and selfish, I know. I guess I have a little of that diva thing in me. It is so hard to explain. It was literally the last performance of an eighteen-city tour. It was such a strange gig to begin with—against my wishes my management booked this concert, if that's what you want to call it. Turns out this concert was for about five hundred people. It was 'requested' by one of the princes of the country. It was for him, his family, and his friends," she explained.

"Really?" was Troy's first remark. "That actually sounds kind of cool, unusual but cool. But it doesn't sound like it went so well?" he asked.

"The whole thing was very unusual, and not something I'd normally do. I only did it as a favor for my manager; something to do with the prince and the fact that he is major investor in the label. It started out okay, or at least I thought so. We were scheduled to perform for two hours, basically my normal concert time. I sang two or three songs, two I think, we were rocking this small venue really hard. That part was actually pretty cool, we were totally getting into it because of the acoustics in the building. It's been a long time since I've played somewhere so small. All of a sudden, just as I started to get into the third song, my manager walks on stage with some other man dressed up in some expensive-looking robes and a headdress. Of course we stopped playing. I looked at my manager, like 'what the hell is going on?' This other guy just bows at me and smiles. My manager told me the music was a little too loud for the prince, and he would like it if we could turn it down a little! Can you believe that!" Izy asked Troy, "They wanted me to turn down rock and roll!" she was still feeling it as her face was turning red; she was still very upset about it.

"Wow, that's a little crazy!" Troy responded. "What did you do?" he asked.

"My manager looked so upset, I know he would never ask me something like this if the pressure on him wasn't so intense, so what else could we do? We turned it down," she told him.

"So did that work out?" Troy asked. "It did for about another two songs, then my manager and this guy were back on stage again! I was getting pretty pissed off!" she said.

"What did they want now?" Troy asked, very interested, and completely fascinated with the whole story. "They wanted me to sing something else, something softer," Izy said while gritting her teeth.

"I don't understand, what does that mean?" Troy asked.

"Exactly!" Izy responded. "Apparently it meant they didn't want me to sing any more of *my* songs, can you believe that! Then this other guy, the guy in the fancy robes, hands me a list of songs provided by the prince, songs the prince thought I should sing for him!"

"Holy crap!" Troy let out. "What did you do then?" he asked excitedly.

"I screamed some pretty nasty things and walked off stage. That was it, I'm not someone's puppet. I don't care who you are or how much money you spend, if you ask for me, guess what, you get me!" Just retelling the story was getting Izy pretty pumped up.

"I jumped in a taxi that was out back, went straight to the airport, and got on the first flight that looked like it was headed west," she further explained.

"That is an amazing story, Izy. I'm not so sure, though, you should be so upset with yourself for walking out," Troy offered.

Calming down a bit, Izy said, "No, it was all me, me, and my ego. I found out later this prince was actually one of the tours investors, would have been nice to know that earlier! We're talking about a lot of money here, and my selfishness may have hurt the label. After I thought about it for a while I realized should have just done my job and sang those songs. It wasn't like I didn't know the songs, but they weren't *my songs*. Man, oh, man, there are going to be a lot of very pissed off people when I get home, starting with my manager and my label," she said, thinking about the consequences of her recent actions.

Izy is an international rock star. She is known all over the world for her hard-hitting rock and roll and her personal and intoxicating lyrics, but she is almost equally known for her oversexed costumes and wild performances both on and off the stage. Some of her fans are fanatics—all love her—but to the media and the paparazzi, she is a field day, always giving them something; most of the time not on purpose, just Izy being Izy. Every hour of every day, she is stalked by the paparazzi. She is rarely ever able to be outside her home and almost always has armed security with her. There is never a day when the paparazzi aren't waiting just outside her gates, looking to get that one shot. Not a part of the deal that she likes, actually hates, but she puts up with it. Izy is smart enough to know that good or bad, her fans like it, and she sells more music because of it.

Izy has been on stage since being about sixteen when she sang and played guitar in a local garage band. Her band played a few local gigs, mostly bars and some high school parties. Her music was a cross of some lightweight punk and traditional hard rock and roll. An unusual mix, but it worked for them. Loud was a requirement and always part of the equation. Eventually Izy got away from the punk music that she felt was holding them back and focused on her own version of rock and roll. She wrote most of the music and all the lyrics; she wouldn't have had it any other way. She was quickly discovered by her manager who got her signed with a big record label. She was put together with a new band, and they were sent out on tour within months of being signed. Thankfully her manager, who Izy always felt cared about her, pushed the label to use several of Izy's own songs, both on tour and in her first album. The label wasn't happy about it until each single became an immediate hit, then they were all on board.

It was like "being on a roller coaster," Izy was often heard saying. Now ten years later, she has won three Grammys, has thirteen number one singles, and too many gold and platinum albums to name. Every single concert, every year, all over the world, sold out to capacity. She was rich and famous—very famous. Sometimes famous for the wrong things, like getting arrested for almost causing a riot in Germany when some fans got too carried away and Izy started spitting on them. But to Izy, it was all about being a true rocker—that and she didn't care. She has several homes, many cars, more clothes and jewelry than anyone could wear in a lifetime; what she didn't have was love or someone she could call a true friend. Even before Izy became Izy, she didn't really have any friends, except for her early bandmates who she was closest to at the time. She always thought that because she was so much of a rebel, none of the other girls in school liked her, most of the boys were scared of her and because she started touring so young, she never had the time to develop any real friendships. The only friends she has are her managers and handlers, who these days are less about just being there for her and are more about giving advice and working hard to keep her pacified. Izy doesn't treat them badly but gave up a long time ago trying to be "herself" around them. It was easier to play the role of the spoiled star and be "on" for everyone, including them.

Troy never had to ask another question the rest of the way to New York. He opened the floodgates, and Izy was pouring her heart out. Troy was fascinated. Many of Izy's stories were very funny, and they would both have a good laugh; many of her stories were not. Troy tried not to judge and tried to only be supportive. When Izy got to the parts about her family, none of which she has seen or talked to in many years, she got very emotional. She grew up in a broken home and lived most of her young life with her dad, who was never around, and when he was, it wasn't exactly a healthy environment. Izy talked and talked; it was a newfound freedom she has never experienced. She told Troy about some of her most outlandish escapades, like the time she and a couple of members from her band swam naked in the Triton fountain in Rome. They were arrested but let out later when they mayor of Rome found out who they were; all she needed to do was sign a T-shirt for the mayor's daughter. Izy admitted to Troy that it was actually kind of sad the things she could get away with just because she was Izy. "Not!" she said, laughing very loud. "It's a total blast!"

Troy felt like he learned more about this person on this six-hour flight than he did in the first forty-eight hours they spent together. And he felt really good about it. Izy to him was not a superstar; she was a young, beautiful, exciting, and talented woman whom he could now call his friend. *Pretty cool*, he thought. This was more important to Troy than her fame. Although sometimes while Izy continued to talk, Troy would daydream about the reality of this new relationship.

How could we ever really be friends? he'd asked himself. *I mean she lives in Los Angeles, I'm in Chicago, she's a superstar, I'm ... well, a dad.* But he decided that whatever it is, it is, even if their friendship never went any further, this has been completely amazing and something he will never forget. He may not be able to tell anyone about it, but for Troy, that's okay.

They were about twenty to thirty minutes from New York, you could see the ocean below getting closer and closer as the plane started to descend, Izy stopped herself mid-sentence. "Troy," she started. "I have been absolutely yacking the whole time, I am sooo sorry. You *must* think I'm just nuts!"

"Well, yes" was Troys calm response with a smile. Izy hit him in the arm as he laughed. "Izy … really?" Troy said. "We've been friends now for what, three days? Learning about you and your life has been awesome. Now I know you better, and I'm glad I do!" he stated with confidence.

"Really?" Izy asked. "I'm afraid you know more about me than my managers, doctors, and family combined!" she laughed.

"That doesn't bother you, does it?" Troy asked. "No, just the opposite," she said. "That's how much I trust you! Some of the things I told you could really hurt me, you know, if it ever got out in public, I mean," she admitted to him.

"I know!" Troy said. "This is good black mail stuff!" he laughed.

Izy continued as if she felt she had to get something out. "We're going to be landing soon, and this is where we part ways," she said.

"I know," Troy answered. "It feels sort of strange after being together for so long." There was a long pause.

"Listen … Troy. I don't want to make you feel uncomfortable or think this is just too weird, and if you do that's fine, I'll stop. I know I keep saying this, but I really mean it, I want for us, you and me, to be friends. Is that crazy? Is that okay with you?" she asked with genuine concern. Troy wanted to answer right away with yes, but as he had in his previous daydream wondered how that would be possible?

"It's not likely my wife would be okay with it," he said.

"I know, I know," Izy responded in a sad tone with her head dropping down.

Another long pause. "Wow, Izy, this is way out there for me, I mean...way out there! I don't want to lie to anyone, especially my family," He paused again. Izy lifted her head back up in anticipation. "But I'd really like to stay friends with you too. I think I might be nuts, but I'm willing to try. I just don't know how," he told her.

Izy released an audible sound of relief and hugged Troy hard. "That's perfect!" Izy said so excitedly. "I don't know either, but maybe we can just talk once in a while over the phone, or text, or e-mail—really whatever you are comfortable with. And if you don't want to tell anyone, that's okay with me. Just so you know though, I'm telling everyone about my new best friend!"

Troy looked completely startled. "Well, I don't have to give them your name, right?" Izy said. Troy laughed.

After they landed in New York, they both stood in front of their seats. Izy spoke first. "I'm not going to go out with you," she explained.

"No, I get it, I understand now," Troy answered.

"My people are here to pick me up, so I'm going to go with them. They'll be waiting to take me to a different plane," she said. Little did Troy know at the time that she meant *her* plane.

"Okay, have a safe flight home." Troy started for the door of the plane.

"Troy," Izy called out. Troy came back to her. "Thanks for being my friend," she said in his ear as she gave him another hug. Troy wasn't sure what to say, so the only thing he could offer was "I really enjoyed meeting Isabelle *and* Izy, to me your both you know." he said with a smile. Izy held onto this hand as long as she could as Troy walked away.

What a surreal feeling! Troy was thinking to himself as he sat down in the oversized seat in first class. *Not a bad thing to have friends in the right places*, he thought as he enjoyed a cold beer. No sooner did he finish thinking about whether or not he would ever hear from Izy again, his phone vibrated with a text:

> Troy, we are just about to take off, I already miss my friend! It feels funny to sit on a plane without you here! Have a safe flight; I hope you get to spend as much time as possible with your beautiful children. I'll talk to you soon?
>
> Izy

Attached to the text was a photo Izy took of the two of them when they were at the restaurant in the village of Dek'Emhare. Troy smiled. Before the plane door was closed, he was asleep. He did not wake up until the plane came to a full stop at the gate in Chicago.

HOME AGAIN, HOME AGAIN

As Troy was getting off the plane, he wasn't sure what to expect. He called his wife from London and then again from New York, but they hadn't really established how he was getting home from the airport. He walked through the airport, anxious to get home to see his family…and sleep in his bed. When he got outside of security on his way to baggage claim, he heard his kids yell out, "Daddy!" He looked over and saw his kids running toward him with his wife coming quickly behind.

"My babies!" he yelled out. He picked them both up at the same time and squeezed them tight. He must have kissed them twenty times! Troy was so happy to see them, feel them, and smell them again. April came up as Troy put the kids down. Completely out of character, she gave him a kiss and a hug.

"We missed you," she said, looking straight into his eyes. "You don't know how scared I was that something happened to you!" she told him.

"I know, I'm really sorry," Troy started to explain again. April stopped him. "Troy, you're home, safe and sound, that's all that matters! Why don't we catch up at home, let's go get your bags."

April is around five foot four inches tall; she has shoulder-length, dirty blond hair, and is very "cute" many would say. She has a very outgoing personality and a voice to back it up. Troy and April first met in college. It wasn't exactly love at first sight, although Troy thought this energetic and somewhat outspoken petite, blond was very cute, he could never seem to catch her eye. He could easily see why she seemed to have so many friends; her personality was her most attractive feature. They finally met by accident one day in the hall at school during Troy's senior year. She mistook Troy for the senior class president. It was awkward, but it lead to a conversation, which led to a date. They dated for a while and not long after came marriage. Within the first year of marriage, their first child, Maggie, was born. It's all kind of a blur to Troy now. April is considered a full-time homemaker who got her degree in animal physiology. Troy never understood the thought behind getting a degree in animal physiology.

Useless, he often thought to himself. He assumed his wife never actually intended to use it. Troy always felt school was more about the social life to his wife, and going to college was something expected by her family, especially her father.

Troy loves his wife, he's just not sure he *likes* her anymore. Their relationship has been unraveling for several years. Troy has tried many times, in many different ways to find out why, what has changed, but has never gotten any kind of real answer. April has always been a devoted mother, very involved with the kids, their school, and in all the kids' "other" activities. Almost anyone who meets April thinks of her as being very nice, outgoing, and strong-willed. But in recent years, April has become bitter, almost angry, and not just to Troy. At first it was just once in a while, but it has become more the "norm" lately. Troy keeps hoping it's a "phase" even though it's already been a couple of years. For no real reason, April will take a small incident, like one of the kids spilling milk, literally, and scream at them as if they just burnt the house down. She never answers a question directly; she will often only answer with sarcasm, snapping at you in a hurtful way. At one point, it got so bad, the kids were afraid to talk to her, unsure of why their mom would be so angry at them all of the time. Troy finally talked to April about it one day, but the talk wasn't very productive. She dealt with it by being defensive. For a while after the talk, she did seem to back off, almost to what the family considered "back to herself." April has always been tough—tough on her husband and tough on her children. It's just who she has always been. She tends to scream a lot, usually because she doesn't feel she is getting her way or not being taken seriously. The only person April is not tough on and never screams at is her dad—a true Daddy's girl.

For the longest time, Troy brushed off April's attitude change as stress, but he was never able to decide what she has to be so stressed about. One possibility is April's weight. From nearly the beginning of their relationship, she has been on a perpetual diet. It hasn't been very fun for anyone. April will go on a diet, make everyone around her miserable, and then within a couple of days, be right back to eating her favorite ice cream. Since being married, April has put on an extra twenty to twenty-five pounds that she does not carry very well, that's Troy's best guess since she won't admit to gaining anything but a few pounds. She used to blame her extra weight on having the kids, but she pretty much started putting the weight on right after getting married, and it only got worse with each pregnancy. It's been nine years since the last pregnancy, so Troy is convinced, *that* excuse is played out. Troy and April have for the most part always gotten along and when they don't they have an unwritten pact that they never argue in front of their kids. One rule they have never broken. Troy travels a great deal for work, and April has become more and more involved with her charity work, keeping her out days, nights, and many weekends, between them, being home at the same time has become somewhat rare.

After picking up his luggage and getting many more hugs from his kids, they headed out of the airport. Troy was pleasantly surprised about April, not so much by his wife's level of affection, which was great, but more surprised they were there without his father-in law. *That's a nice change*, Troy thought. "Maybe this trip was good for all of us?" "Daddy, I'm so glad your home!" Maggie said as she hugged her dad on the way to the car.

"When are you going to tell us about your plane crash?" Justin asked, pulling on his dad's arm. "I'll tell you the whole story soon. Let's get home first," he replied.

"Where's the car?" Troy asked April. "It's just over there." She pointed toward the outside curb where taxis and limos park. Troy immediately spotted the company limo, "The limo ... that's a nice surprise," he said as they walked out to the car. Just as they got to the car, out of the back steps his father-in-law, Frank. "Hello Troy, welcome back," Frank said. "Crap!"was Troy's immediate thought. "Thank you, sir, good to be back." The driver grabbed the bags, and they all got into the back of the limo. Troy sat in back with Maggie and Justin on either side of him. April and her Dad sat on the bench seat.

"So, Troy, tell us about your trip, sounds like it may have gotten a little scary there for a while?" Frank asked in about as genuine a tone as he can manage. April actually spoke up for Troy. "Daddy, Troy is exhausted. Let's get him home first and feed him. Then he can tell us all about his trip, okay?" she asked a little sternly.

"Okay, that's fine," he replied. "I was just trying to be polite!" he added. The rest of the way home, Troy mostly talked to his kids. He wanted to know everything they were doing and what things he missed. His daughter, Maggie, kept saying to her dad, "Daddy, I really missed you. I'm so glad you're home. I hated how long you were gone!" Troy looked up to see if his father-in-law was listening. If he was, it didn't show.

After a hot shower and a much-needed good meal, Troy and his family sat down in their family room to catch up. Thankfully after dinner, Frank excused himself and went home. Not much fanfare, he just told Troy, "Welcome back. I guess I'll see you on Thursday." It was Tuesday. Troy was really hoping to get the rest of the week off, but then, this would have been the nice thing to do. Troy kissed his wife as he went to sit down on the couch. His kids climbed onto the couch next to their dad, squirming with excitement. "I think I may have brought back a couple of things for you guys from this trip!" Troy said jokingly with a big smile on his face. They clapped with excitement. The kids always looked forward to this part. Every time Troy comes home from a long trip to some far-off place, he always brings something back for the kids. This time was no exception.

As he opened the piece of luggage that had the gifts in it, he started to explain. Every gift had an explanation. About what it was, if it wasn't obvious, where it was from, and what it meant, if necessary. His kids always soaked it up. First was something for Justin, a book on Middle Eastern kings. It was a big, thick book with many pictures and sketches. Justin loves this kind of stuff. "Oh, thank you, Daddy, this looks great! I can't wait to read it!" Next, he pulled out an opal and turquoise necklace, and he handed it to Maggie. "Wow, Daddy, this is so beautiful!" Maggie attacked her dad with a bear hug and a kiss. "I'll wear it every day!" she replied as she put it on. April nodded at Troy with approval. Troy gave the kids several other smaller but unique gifts, each one having its own story. "That's it!" Troy said. Everyone applauded with approval. "Oh, wait! I think I have one more," he said coyly.

Then Troy pulled out one more present from his luggage, only this one was wrapped. This was something new; Troy had never done this before. The kids kept asking, "Who's that for, Daddy? Who's that for?" He got up off the couch walked over to April and handed her the nicely wrapped gift. She looked up at Troy with a look of astonishment. "It's for you," he told her.

"Really? Wow, thank you, Troy, this is a surprise." Because Troy takes so many trips, he rarely buys his wife anything unless it's for a special occasion. April began to unwrap the gift. It was a beautiful handcrafted scarf. April loves scarves and can never have too many. She loved it. "Troy, it is absolutely beautiful! Thank you so much!" She said as she put the scarf on. "I will be wearing this one a lot!" She went to Troy and gave him a kiss on the cheek and a hug. The kids started to clap and cheer.

The next morning, Troy woke to the sounds of his kids playing outside and the smell of freshly brewed coffee. *Now it feels like I'm home!* Troy was thinking. He got up from the bed and pulled back the curtains to the bedroom window. Out back, his kids were playing. Maggie was kicking the soccer ball around, and Justin was sitting at the patio table, reading. Troy could hear Maggie asking Justin to play with her. "Come on, Justin! I promise I'll let you score some goals!" She said with no response from Justin except a hand held up that indicated Justin had no interest. "Awe!" Maggie was disappointed but not surprised.

Maggie is outspoken like her mom but was always respectful. She is tall for her age and very lean. Maggie has long, blond hair that she almost always wears in a ponytail. Usually, the only time she ever takes her hair down is when her dad asks her to. Maggie loves her dad, and she loves being with him. She will go to hockey games with her dad as often as he will let her. She is a very good student with many good friends. Maggie is often referred to as the hip one in the house. She always knows what's going on in pop culture, loves to listen to music, loves to dance, and is actually a pretty good soccer player.

The opposite can be said about Justin. He's not a very good student; he's an exceptional student. He has already skipped one grade and is getting A's in every one of his classes, which are all honors classes. He's not athletic in any way. Justin is quiet and shy. He rarely speaks unless called upon. He has one friend that he does everything with; they seem to have an intellectual connection. About the only thing that he and his sister have in common is Justin likes music too, and when Maggie will let him, he loves to dance. Never when anyone but Maggie is around—never. And unlike Maggie, Justin never seems to want to "hang out" with his dad. Troy has invited him many times to hockey games and other guy types of things, but Justin never wants to go. He would rather read or play his one buddy in a video game. Troy knows Justin loves him; he just shows it differently.

Troy quickly dresses and goes out to the kitchen where his wife greets him. "Good morning! I thought you might not wake up till tonight! How are you feeling?" she asks.

Troy laughed. "I'm actually feeling pretty good, thank you. But some of that coffee might just make the difference!" With his coffee in hand, Troy walked out to the backyard. "Daddy!" Maggie shouts as she runs to him. Justin looked up and ran to him as well. They both gave him a huge hug. Maggie immediately asked if he would kick the soccer ball around with her. "Sure," he said to her, as Maggie's face began to light up. "But let me finish my coffee first and just sit here with Justin for a minute," he told her. "Awe!" was Maggie's reply.

"So, Justin, how are you doing? I feel like I haven't talked to you in so long," Troy asked his son.

"I'm good, Dad, I really missed you. It was a little scary around here when Mom couldn't find you for a while," Justin said to his dad in a sincere and concerned voice. "I know, it must have been scary. I'm sorry I worried you, but I was never in any danger," he explained. "When we have some time, I'll tell you all about it, it turned out to be quite an adventure," Troy told him.

"That'd be great, Dad. By the way, thank you again for the cool things you brought me. I especially love this book!" Justin said as he smiled at his dad. Troy didn't even notice that the book Justin was reading was the one he just brought him.

"You're welcome, I'm glad you like it. You'll have to tell me all about it when you're done."

"Come on, Daddy!" Maggie pleaded with him. "Oops, duty calls!" he told his son. Justin just smiled and went back to his book. "Okay, I'm ready now, let's go!" He said to his daughter as she kicked him the ball. They kicked the soccer ball around, trying to steal the ball from each other. Troy tried to score in their little backyard goal, but the only times he did was when Maggie let him. But he was having fun. Maggie pretty much ruled the day, and no matter how much Troy tried, really tried, he could not stop Maggie from stealing the ball when she wanted and making a goal. "You're really good, Maggie. I can't wait to see one of your games," he said as he was breathing really, really hard. Troy just does not have the skills, but he tries, and Maggie loves the fact that he tries. Troy loves just being able to be with his kids and enjoy what they enjoy. This is what Troy missed the most.

Soon, April was calling Troy in for breakfast, the kids had already eaten hours before, but they came into the house with their dad anyway. Troy enjoyed the breakfast so much he felt as if this was the first breakfast he's ever had. He ate everything on his plate and then some. April and the kids joked with him about how much he was eating. Troy laughed while he was finishing his third round of pancakes. After the plate was clear and April was out of food, Maggie asked her dad, "Daddy, can you tell us about your trip now?" "Especially the part about your plane that crashed!" said Justin, who was beaming with excitement. "Sure. Okay," Troy started. April sat down at the kitchen table next to Maggie; Justin was sitting right next to his dad. They were all ears.

"Well, to start with, the plane did not actually crash!" Troy started. Justin almost looked disappointed. "But it was very close to crashing!" Justin's face lit back up. "We were about halfway into the four-hour flight when I heard an explosion from the back of the plane," Troy continued to explain.

"Was the explosion close to you, daddy?" asked Maggie. "No, not really, it turned out it was one of the engines, and I was in first class so I wasn't very close, but—" he was cut off.

"First class!" April belted out, interrupting the story. "*You were in first class*?" she questioned with a great deal of cynicism. "Actually yes," he stated, "but I only ended up there by accident. Trust me, that's an even longer story that I'll tell you about later," he said, clearly a little upset with his wife's tone. "Anyway…" Troy went on telling the story about his scary but exciting adventure. He told them in great detail about how the plane had to make an emergency landing at a small remote airport in a different country that was at war with itself. He told them how they were going to have to wait for ten hours for a new plane and instead of waiting at the overcrowded airport, he went to a small village where he ate and met many of the locals. He told them how he may have saved a young boy's life because he kept him from going back to his village that had earlier been burnt down by rebels and all the young males from the village were taken. He told a great story that was all true. The only thing he didn't include in his story was one word about Izy.

THE NEXT DAY

Troy may have been at his desk for five, maybe ten, minutes when Frank, his boss and father-in-law, walked in unannounced. "Morning, Troy" he started. "I read your reports, nice work. Looks like we may have picked up two new major suppliers." That was more kudos than is normally handed out by the boss.

I wonder what's going on? Troy was thinking. *Must be something bad coming*, he thought.

"Listen, you continue what you were doing here, we have a phone conference at eleven with Zeito, which is a major account, and then you and I need to go to lunch. You good with that?" he sort of asked or demanded, pointing his finger at Troy.

"Good," Troy responded. Frank walked out of his office. *Hmm, lunch? He never takes me to lunch. Yup, something's wrong. One day off, first day back and the pressure is already on!*

Just as Troy began to feel a little sorry for himself, in walks Crazy Eddie, his "other" best friend. Loud and obnoxious, nothing's changed with Eddie, which is why Troy likes him. Always guaranteed to make you feel better. "So, traveling man, how are you?" Eddie started. "I heard all the rumors, so which ones are true?" he asked laughingly.

"Rumors?" Troy responded. "What rumors?"

"Oh, you know ... your plane crashed in the middle of nowhere, stranded for days with all of these exotic women ... you know the back-of-the-penthouse types of stories! It's okay, you can tell me!" he said with a big goofy grin.

"Yeah that was it! No more no less." Troy smiled back. Eddie knows Troy better than most. He knows he can joke with him, and Eddie tries to help Troy not take things too seriously, especially when it comes to his father-in-law.

Eddie always refers to Troy as his best friend, so Troy's goes along with it. It's not like Troy has many options, and he does enjoy being around Eddie, who is generally totally the opposite of Troy. Eddie is loud and fun, athletic, outgoing and a bit of a troublemaker. That's attractive to Troy because he's none of those things. Troy really likes it when Eddie goes to hockey games with him; Eddie is the guy who is always too loud and screaming at both the players and the referees about every play. Eddie makes almost everything more fun for Troy. The only real problem with Eddie is Troy's wife. April doesn't like him, but thankfully, he is married to *her* best friend, Barb. So she has no choice and has to put up with him but does her best to minimize her involvement.

"So ... we going to lunch so I can hear all the details?" asked Eddie.

"That would be my first choice, but unfortunately, I can't. I'm going to lunch with Frank," Troy said.

"Frank!" Eddie belted out a little too loud. "Eddie!" Troy snapped at him. "Close the door," he demanded. After Eddie closed the door, he turned back to Troy. "Lunch with Frank? Frank never goes to lunch with anyone. What's up with that?" Eddie asked, a little concerned. "I'm not sure actually. He came into my office earlier, it seemed like everything was fine, actually he told me I did a good job," Troy was explaining.

"Really?" Eddie was just as surprised. "That's a biggie! Maybe he missed you!" Eddie joked, knowing there is not a lot of love between the two. Eddie and Troy started laughing. "What do you think the lunch thing is all about?" he asked Troy.

"I've been thinking about it, I have zip. Maybe he just wants to go over my trip," Troy was saying.

"Yea, maybe that's it," Eddie offered, not very reassuringly. "Well, listen, we have to catch up, so how about a barbecue at my house this Saturday?" Eddie asked.

"You know, Eddie, that would be great! Let's do that," Troy responded. "Let me clear it with the other boss, and I'll let you know tomorrow," Troy told him.

"Great!" Eddie said as he walked out of Troy's office.

After the conference call, which Troy thought went well, Troy was waiting in the reception area making small talk with the main receptionist when Frank walked up. He looked sternly at the receptionist as he said to Troy, "You ready?"

"Yes," Troy answered, and they walked for the elevator. Troy turned his head back and smiled at the receptionist in an "I'm sorry" face; she shrugged her shoulders and smiled back. No conversation in the elevator or in the lobby of the building, so Troy tried to start up some kind of conversation while they walked. He asked Frank, "Where are we going for lunch?"

"There's a little place around the corner that I like, we're going there," he responded.

"Oh, okay. That's sounds good," he said, rolling his eyes in his head. *Wow, this guy amazes me. Hard to believe he's my father-in-law!* Troy was thinking to himself. They walked about a block and a half in downtown Chicago, where it was clear out, but with the wind, it was especially cold. Frank stopped. They arrived in front of a subway sandwich shop!

"Subway?" Troy questioned. "This is the place you want to take me to lunch?" he questioned.

"Sure, they have great food, and I always get my drink for free here!" he explained.

"Wow!" was the only thing Troy could come up with.

"Why…you don't like subway?" Frank asked sarcastically.

"No, I'm okay with subway. Just a little surprised, that's all," Troy answered.

"You were expecting some little fancy Italian bistro or something?" Frank asked a little smartly again.

"No, this is fine. Let's go eat," he suggested. The truth is, Troy was relieved they were eating here. It won't be one of those long drawn-out lunches where he will have to sit and listen to Frank for hours and only maybe be able to offer up one or two points of topic. Generally Frank owns the conversations.

After ordering their food and sitting down at a small table in the corner, Frank spoke up first. "That must have been a hard trip for you?" he started, referring to Troy's most recent trip. "But you were successful and some good things are going to come out of it."

Troy was a little surprised and a little worried where the conversation was going. *He's not going to ask me to go again, is he?* he was thinking. *Or maybe he wants me to expand even more? Oh my God, please don't be that!* Troy was praying to himself.

"I've decided we need to change some of your responsibilities, mix up some of your territories." Troy was holding his forehead with one hand, looking down at his sandwich as Frank continued. "So I think I'm going to scale it back some, I was thinking of letting you handle some of our domestic accounts. But…I will still need you from time to time to handle some of our more important Asia and the Middle East accounts. I think that would be good, and besides, it would keep you closer to home." Troy looked up at Frank as Frank took a bite of his sandwich.

In shock, he responded, "Sure, Frank, that sounds great. Whatever you need." Inside, Troy was losing his mind with excitement. He could spend more time with his family and be there for many more of their important events. "This is great!" he added as the thought of the change starting to take hold. He started in on his sandwich, trying not to smile while he ate.

Barely back at the office, Eddie was on him in minutes; this time, he closed the door to Troy's office. "So? That was a short lunch, what happened?" Eddie asked excitedly.

"Well," Troy started, "definitely one of the more unusual lunches I've been to, especially with Frank."

Eddie was about to burst, "Did you get a raise? A new office? What?" Eddie was losing it.

"No, nothing like that, he changed my areas of responsibility," Troy said.

"What he heck does that mean?" Eddie asked with a puzzled face.

"It means no more international trips, for the most part anyway. I'm going to be taking over primarily domestic accounts," Troy explained with a big smile on his face.

"Really? That's fantastic, dude, I'm so happy for you!" Eddie told him. "Although this means you'll be in the office more, and you know what that means!" Eddie suggested.

"Yea, I do. But still worth it. Being able to be with my kids and be at all their important events, it's a no-brainer!" Troy said somberly. "I totally understand. I bet the wife will be happy!" Eddie added. Troy paused for a second, thinking, "The wife?" he asked.

"Well, yea, she'll be happy to hear the news, won't she?" Eddie asked like it should be common sense.

"Yes, of course your right, she will." He paused again. "Actually, I have a feeling she already knows the news!" Troy didn't say any more and Eddie didn't say anything, but he knew what Troy was talking about. This new change in Troy's "areas of responsibility" likely came from April. She has always had a pretty stronghold on her dad; it was almost obvious it was her influence. "Great news, bud! Don't forget...barbecue on Saturday!" Eddie left Troy's office.

Troy got home a little early, still feeling the effects of his trip. Both kids were out front when he pulled up.

"Daddy!" They both ran over to greet him.

That's a nice sound, Troy was thinking as he knelt down for hugs and kisses. April came out the front door and walked over to hug Troy. "Come on in, I hear you have some good news!" she said.

Just as I thought, Troy said to himself as he walked to the front door with his kids in tow. But after Eddie left his office earlier today, Troy had time to think about it. He was wishing Frank had offered the change himself because Troy had earned it, or because Frank needed him to be involved with some important domestic accounts. But that's not the important thing. Troy was happy no matter how or why it happened because he got what he really wanted, and that was to be home with his family more often. Besides, if April made this happen, really, that only makes it better because she was looking out for him and their kids.

Izy at home in Los Angeles was still coming down off the trip, too. But no breaks for her, not even one day. Almost immediately, she was thrown into one meeting after another with her managers, the record label, and the press. She was exhausted and really needed a break. All any of them could talk about was the need for the next new album. "You've got to get something started, Izy!" her manager told her. Even after such a hugely successful tour, the label wanted her to get to work on the next album. Izy, on the other hand, was more interested in what Troy was doing. She was constantly thinking about him. She tried several times to call him but couldn't muster up the courage. She was concerned that she would interrupt his life, and she was convinced the last thing Troy needed was someone like her in his life. So, she didn't.

ALMOST FORGOT!

Weeks had passed since Troy's last road trip. He's never been home for this long at one time. He was defiantly liking the new position and the reduced travel. Troy has had the opportunity to watch Maggie play in several soccer matches, he really enjoyed it, and he was really impressed with how good she really is. He also got to hang out with Justin more; he even talked him into going to a hockey game with him. Justin said he had fun, but Troy is pretty sure he was just being polite. Troy was putting in a great deal of hours in the office, something Troy was not used to and didn't like at all—but a necessary part of the job. His first business trip was scheduled for a west coast sweep. First Seattle, then San Francisco onto Los Angeles, ending in Las Vegas. He's scheduled to be gone for two weeks, but that was a walk in the park for him.

Troy was also enjoying the time he got to be with his friends, especially Eddie. They went to lunch often and a hockey game now and then; they even managed to get the families together for a family barbecue that was always at Eddie's house. Eddie was definitely the master of the barbecue! Troy's relationship deepened with Eddie, and they talked often. Unfortunately Troy's relationship with April didn't. The more Troy was home, the less they seemed to get along. Although since being home April has not brought up the 'separation' bomb she dropped on him before leaving on his last trip. *Maybe she's finally interested in trying to work something out*? Troy wondered. Troy tried several times to take his wife out, just the two of them, but most of the time, she turned him down because of "other obligations." The couple of times they did end up out together was not much fun for either one. They found little in common to talk about, except for the kids, and often found themselves just sitting at dinner in silence, or worse-arguing. No matter how often Troy asked, April would not go to a hockey game with him. Troy even tried volunteering to go to a play with his wife, which is something she loves and something he hates, but that didn't work out either. Between April's social activities, her father, and her volunteer work, Troy was home more than she was.

Troy was in the office early on Monday, hoping to get some work done before most of the others came in. He was scheduled to head out of town on Wednesday for Seattle and needed to be ready. He was making a pretty good dent in his work when Frank came into his office. "*You're here early*?" posed more as a question than a remark.

"Good morning, Frank," Troy said. "Yes," he continued, "I'm trying to make sure I have everything ready for the trip," he told his boss.

"Oh, that's good, I'm sure you'll be ready," Frank said. Troy couldn't help but think, *Whaaaat was that! Some kind of an attempt to be supportive? Okay, that was just strange*, he thought.

Frank asked, "Are you looking forward to the trip and meeting some of these clients? You haven't been on the road in a while," Frank inquired.

"I am," Troy replied. Just as he was about to go into more detail about one of the clients he wanted to talk to Frank about, his phone that was sitting on his desk began to vibrate. He continued to talk with Frank as he glanced at his phone. It was a text message from "BFF!"

"Holy crap!" Troy said out loud, startling Frank.

"Everything okay?" Frank asked in an unusually high pitch.

"Um," Troy cleared his voice. "Yes," he said. "A friend of mine's dog just had puppies" was the only thing Troy could come up with. *Oh my God, what an idiot!* he was saying to himself as he half smiled at Frank.

"Oh," Frank responded. "That's nice . . . I guess," he was looking at Troy as if Troy had no clothes on. "Okay, well, I have to go, let's meet up later so we can go over your trip."

"Sure, that would be fine," Troy said as he was thinking his father-in-law must truly think he's nuts.

Frank barely walked out when Eddie walked in. "Hey, adventure dude!" Eddie's new nickname for Troy. "Your headed on your next adventure soon, right?" he asked.

"I am . . . Wednesday," Troy answered. "Two- to three-week West Coast sweep," he added. "Well, that should be a nice change for you," Eddie said. "Nice weather, same language, same money, and no one's at war on the West Coast! At least I don't think they are!" Eddie and Troy both laughed.

"So lunch today?" Eddie asked.

"Sure that'd be great!" Troy said.

"Cool, I'll come and get you around twelve thirty?" Eddie suggested.

"Perfect" was Troy's response.

After Eddie walked out of his office, Troy got up and walked over and closed his office door. *Finally!* he was thinking. He went back and sat at his desk. He was a little nervous about reading the text. It's been several weeks, and while Troy thought about Izy often, and he was tempted to call her or text her so many times, he didn't want to be the first one to call. Truthfully he never really thought they would talk again.

He picked up the phone and opened the text:

> Hey, BFF! How are you?! I hope you are well. I am so sorry I haven't bugged you sooner, it's been nuts since I got back. I think about you and our crazy trip together often. I really

need to talk to you... can you possibly call me sometime today? If that's okay? Let me know! Yours@Izy!

"Whoa!" was Troy's immediate reaction. He sat there staring at his phone where he pondered the text for some time. His office phone rang, startling Troy so badly he nearly fell out of his chair. After he finished the call, he picked his cell phone back up. He was really struggling with whether or not he should respond to the text. *It's no big deal, right?* He was thinking. *We're friends, and that's just cool*, he thought, trying to talk himself into it. *Ahhh, but if anyone, especially April, found out I was communicating with this woman, especially a rock star of all things, I'm pretty sure that would not go over well! No, I shouldn't respond!* he decided and put his phone back down on his desk. Thirty seconds later, he picked his phone back up and replied to Izy's text: "Hey, back at you." *No! That's just stupid*," he thought and started over: "Hi, Izy! Great to hear from you! Everything here is good, family's good. It's been awhile! I've been thinking about our adventure quite a bit too! Is everything okay? I can call you later around five thirty or so, will that work for you? Troy."

And he hit send. *A friend in need—it's the right thing to do*, he said to himself convincingly. Troy was in truth very excited Izy contacted him and was now very excited to talk to her, no matter what the reason. He loved talking to Izy; he felt she was the only person he could ever really open up to—well, maybe besides Eddie. Within seconds, Izy texted him back: "Perfect, talk to you then!" Troy couldn't help but smile.

At lunch with Eddie, Troy was acting a little unusual—excited.

"Are you all right, Troy?" Eddie asked, smiling at Troy. Troy was acting like a kid before his birthday, all this nervous energy. He couldn't sit still. Troy felt he was going to bust wide open if he didn't tell someone. He's been holding it all in for too long. Who else would he tell but his best friend Eddie?

"Ya, I'm good. Thanks for asking, how are you doing?" Troy responded.

Eddie bursts out laughing. "Did you take something you weren't supposed to?" he said still laughing at Troy's actions. "You know you could share!" Eddie said jokingly.

"Na, na. It's nothing like that,"Troy said, laughing with Eddie.

"Okay then, fess up, what's going on? I don't think I've ever seen you like this before!" Eddie asked.

"Okay, okay ... but listen,"Troy said with a serious face and in a serious tone, "you cannot tell anyone. You cannot discuss this with anyone, even your wife! You understand?"Troy asked sternly of his friend.

"Sure, Troy. I can do that, I think you know that," Eddie responded. Eddie has always been a man of his word. Eddie was thinking this must be a pretty big deal; he's never seen Troy act this way, and his excitement was becoming contagious. "I am so glad I am finally talking about this. It's like a huge relief for me!" Troy was explaining.

"Uh, okay. That's a little out of the norm for you. What'd you do, rob a bank, have an affair?" Eddie probed. Troy's face lit up. "Oops, I hit a soft spot!" Eddie said with a big guilt-ridden smile. "What did you do!?" he asked.

"No! No! It's nothing like that!" Troy exclaimed. "This is a long story that I have to make really short, so just sit there and listen, and I will try to explain."

Troy went on to tell Eddie in great detail the whole crazy story about his trip home from Djibouti and how he met his new friend Izy. Actually, he only referred to Izy as Isabelle until he got to the end of his story. "That is an amazing story," Eddie said enthusiastically. "Why were you keeping this from me? I mean it wasn't like you were having an affair or anything like that, right? What's the big deal?" he asked. "That's not quite the end of the story, Eddie. There are a couple more ... important details to add," Troy told him. "Let me ask you, do you know anyone who goes by the name Izy?"Troy asked Eddie.

Eddie thought about it for a few seconds, "No, not really, why?" he asked.

"Really, no one?" Troy asked again. "Well, except for the rock star!" he joked.

"Rock star, that's right!" Troy said. "Do you like her music?" Troy asked.

"Sure, who doesn't, she's blasting around my house all of the time, why?" Eddie returned the question.

"Well, Isabelle ..." Troy paused.

"Yeah?" asked Eddie.

"Isabelle is Izy!" he explained excitedly. Now it was out; he actually told someone. *What a relief!* he thought.

"Okaaaay, your story just took a bizarre turn!" Eddie laughed. Troy said nothing. He pulled out his phone and showed Eddie the photo of him and Izy in the restaurant in Dekemhare.

"Holy Crap!" Eddie yelled loud enough that most of the other patrons in the restaurant turned their heads to look.

"Eddie! Keep it down, man! Are you nuts!" Troy said in a scolding way.

"You're calling me nuts!?" Eddie laughed. "So *this* is your new friend?" he asked as he held his hand over his mouth to prevent another outburst.

Troy went on filling in some of the blanks. Eddie was all smiles and all ears, laughing loudly the whole time.

"Okay! Okay!" Eddie started. "So you're telling me you spent, like, three or four days hanging out, just you and Izy, out doing the Indiana Jones thing? Wow! I mean wow! And you're telling me I can't tell anyone about this?" Eddie asked sheepishly.

"Oh my God, *no*!" Troy said, scared that he may have screwed up by telling Eddie. "I'm just messing with you, dude! Don't worry, but really, don't you think this should be on something like *Entertainment Tonight* or something?" Troy would have gotten more upset, except Eddie was laughing too hard for Troy to take seriously.

"Wait!" Troy said. "There's more."

"More!" Eddie said a little too loud again. "How could there be more?" he questioned.

Troy went on, "The whole reason I had to tell you and especially today." Troy took a long pause. "Is because she contacted me today." Eddies mouth was literally hanging open.

"She contacted you…today?" Eddie asked. "Why? How?" he asked.

Troy told Eddie how she thought of Troy as her new "best friend" and how they exchanged numbers, planning on talking when either wanted or needed. He explained to Eddie that he never thought in a million years she would actually ever contact him, but she did. He also told him that he and Izy have a strange connection that he cannot explain, and that other than Eddie, Izy was the first person in his life he felt he could tell anything to and how quickly they just "hit it off." "It wasn't like we had so much in common," Troy tried to explain. Then he told Eddie that Izy texted him that morning and said she needed to talk to him right away and that he promised he would call her tonight.

"Izy said she needed to talk to you and you said okay? And you're planning on calling her tonight?" Eddie summarized.

"That's about it! Now you know the whole story," Troy responded.

"So…you're telling me this now because you want to know what I think you should do, is that it?" Eddie asked.

"Yes, exactly!" Troy said, somewhat relieved. "Sounds to me like you already decided on whatever it is you thought you needed me for!" Eddie said, trying to be straight with his friend. "I get the feeling you're looking more for support, like you're not doing something bad or wrong, right?" Eddie hit it on the head. Troy's smile diminished a little. "Yea, I am feeling a little guilty about it," Troy admitted. "I don't know what to do…I want to be her friend. It's fun, and I enjoy our talks, but I feel like what I'm doing is wrong," he said with his head hanging down some.

"Okay, here is my worldly ten-cent response to your potentially life-altering decision!" Eddie said, trying to lift things up.

Troy laughed. "Great! Let's hear it."

"You have done nothing wrong. It was a circumstance that absolutely could not be avoided. And...as a result of said circumstances"—Eddie tried his best to act like a defense lawyer—"you and Izy became friends, right?"

"True," Troy responded.

"So now, you and Izy want to continue your friendship. However, because she is a woman, a *hot* woman by the way, who also happens to be a filthy rich rock star, you're convinced that should have nothing to do with it!" Eddie told him.

Troy laughed. "Yup."

Eddie continued his defense. "You feel you can't tell anyone because no one—no one but me—that is, would understand, that is if anyone actually believed you." Troy was smiling as Eddie was trying to bring it home. "It is, therefore, my opinion that you maintain your said friendship for the foreseeable future, and you should keep it to yourself, no one will get hurt, and you will be happy," he said, feeling pretty proud of himself. "Wait, except for me, of course, you need to tell me everything!" They both laughed.

"That was pretty good, Eddie! I'm impressed!" Truth is, as silly as it may have seemed, it helped Troy a lot. Just being able to tell someone the whole story felt great. Eddie was so great about it, and Troy felt he could trust him. Although he still felt a little guilty about the whole thing, Troy felt like Eddie understood and told him what he wanted to hear. So he decided he was going to call Izy as promised.

It was a quarter after five, Troy stopped at a convenience store on his way home from work where he picked up a bottle of water. He stops at this store often for gas and sometimes in the morning on the way to work because he loves their coffee. He got back in his car, rolled down the driver's side window, and turned on his radio. *Man, if this doesn't make me look guilty, I don't know what would?* Troy was thinking as he sat in the parking lot of the convenience store, trying to decide if he was absolutely sure he was going to make the call. He checked his watch, it was now five twenty-five. *Would it be weird if I called exactly at five thirty?* he was asking himself. Troy was thinking of being maybe a few minutes late in an attempt to not look too excited or anxious would be better. *Man! I feel like I'm in high school!* he thought as he was starting to get a little upset at himself. Troy was literally staring at his watch, counting down the minutes. "Maybe five thirty-five?" he thought. Troy paused for a few more seconds, then he decided he wasn't going to fight with himself anymore. "This is stupid!" He reached over and turned off the radio and called Izy.

"Troy!" the voice on the other end of the phone shouted excitedly. "I'm so happy you called! I've been thinking about you so much, wondering how you are. I've missed my best friend!" she said, barely taking a breath. "I started to call you so many times, but I wasn't sure if I'd be bugging you, and I was scared I might get you in trouble! So I just gave up and decided to text you! I hope that's okay?"

Troy hadn't said a word yet; he was enjoying hearing Izy's voice and feeling her energy, even through the phone. "It's great to talk to you too!" Troy started. "I thought about calling you many times, but I know how busy you are so—" He was interrupted.

"Are you kidding me!" Izy scolded Troy. "No matter when, no matter where I am, I will always take your call! We *are* best friends, aren't we?" Izy stated firmly. "Isn't that what best friends do?" she asked.

"Yes, I guess they do," he replied. "It's so great to talk to you. I can't believe how long it's been. So ... Izy, is everything okay? You said you *needed* to talk to me?" he asked, getting straight to the point.

"I haven't talked to you in almost a month," she started. "I want to know how you're doing—how is the family, how's the job?" she asked.

"Oh. Well, the family is good. After that long trip, it was so great to get home and be with my kids. I've been spending as much time with them as possible. I'm doing good—really well actually. I got some good news from work when I got back," he started.

"That's cool, what happened?" Izy asked.

"They changed my territories. Areas of responsibilities they call it. I'm no longer handling Asia and the Middle East, which is great for me. Now I am responsible for the entire West Coast and some other major accounts in the US," he told her. "Which means I'll be able to be home so much more."

"Really!" Izy said excitedly. "What does that mean exactly?" she probed for more details.

"I'll be spending most of my time with accounts in the West—like in Seattle, San Francisco, Las Vegas, Denver, and Los Angeles," Troy explained. He felt a little uncomfortable telling her that he would be spending time in Los Angeles. He wasn't sure why but was quickly distracted by Izy's excitement.

"Oh my God! This is great news for you!" she said excitedly. "And…we'll be able to hang out, go out once in a while, this is awesome!" But before Troy could respond, Izy added, "Oops, I'm doing it again! I'm such an idiot!" she said about herself. "I'm sorry, Troy." She took a long pause. "Man, I just jumped right in there, didn't I? I think I may have gotten a little too carried away. Maybe you won't have the time to get together or maybe you don't want to, I don't know?" she asked gently. "I'm sorry if I overstepped…really, I am just so excited at the thought of being able to see you again and maybe see each other and be like real friends"

Troy was a little taken back by Izy's response and then her own reaction to her response. Troy was actually excited that she was so excited. Truth is, he couldn't contain his excitement either, especially now that his friendship with Izy was more real to him than at anytime before. He took a fairly long pause before he responded. He knew he was going to cross some kind of a line. As conflicted as he was inside, he wasn't sure being friends with Izy was wrong. *My wife has plenty of male friends, what's the difference?* he asked himself. However, he knew he would never tell April about Izy—that just wasn't going to happen. "We *are* friends," he started to say. "Why would I come to Los Angeles and not get together with you?" You could hear Izy smiling over the phone. "I think it would be great!" he said with more confidence. "I usually know my schedule weeks ahead so I can let you know, and if it works out, it works out!" he told her.

"I'm thinking that's a little better than perfect!" she said, trying to hold in her excitement.

"So, Izy, tell me about you and what's going on in your life? Every once in a while I hear your name or see a picture of you doing something or another. It's actually kind of strange for me to see you like that," he confided. "Stupid, I know, but I don't know you like that—that Izy doesn't seem real to me," he explained further.

"The truth is, Troy, that's me playing a role, the role of the rock star, it's my job. You know the real me, when you see me like that, I understand how weird it must be, but you and I are real, our friendship is real." Troy was very pleased to hear Izy's explanation.

Izy spent a serious amount of time telling Troy about things that have been going on since she last saw him. Izy had changed record labels; she's been writing some new songs and working on a new album. She was telling Troy how she has tried to lay low so she could concentrate on just her music, but her manager has had her hoping from one thing to another. "Actually, that's kind of what I wanted to talk to you about," Izy told Troy.

"What's that?" Troy asked. Although Troy could not relate to almost anything Izy has said to him so far, he wanted to try to be as supportive as possible. "I'm actually thinking about retiring," she admitted to him in a very serious and somber tone. "I've told no one else!" she said very quickly.

"Wow! That came out of left field!" he said. "This is what you wanted to talk to me about?" he asked.

"Yes, I need your no holds barred opinion about it," she told him. "This could be one of the most important decisions I ever make in my life!" she added.

"I'm a little blown away, I mean, I completely understand why you might need to talk with someone about it," he said supportively. "But why me? I'm not sure I'm qualified to talk to you about such a huge decision! What about your manager or one of your advisors or something like that?" Troy asked. "Why wouldn't you want to talk to them about it?" he questioned.

"No," Izy said sternly, "it's still too early for that. Besides I already know what my manager would say. You are the right person to talk to about this because I trust you and you wouldn't tell me what you think I want to hear, you'd tell me your honest opinion," she said.

"Okay, I don't really know anything about your business, but aren't you sort of at the peak of your career right now?" Troy asked. "I mean why would you want to stop now?" he asked. Troy knew little to nothing about the life of a rock star, so his input was going to be somewhat naïve. Izy didn't care about any of that; she trusted his judgment. "The truth is…I'm tired," Izy started. "I'm tired of being pushed around, I'm tired of people always telling me how great I am even if I suck, and I'm especially tired of feeling the pressure to do better than the last time," she explained. "The whole reason I got into music in the first place has been long gone," she explained further. "I know it sounds a little selfish, maybe even immature to you, but I feel like I've been on tour my whole life, crossing he globe trying my best to entertain, all the while trying to keep the record label happy. It's become so much more work than fun!"

This Troy could relate to. "I'm sorry, Izy. I can only imagine. I can't really relate to most of what your life must be like, but I think I understand. Maybe, and I'm just saying this as your friend, maybe after the next album instead of "officially retiring," you announce a much-needed break. I mean, you can *always* retire right?" he suggested. "After a nice long break, maybe you'll still decide to retire or maybe you've rested enough and you're not ready to be completely done yet. What do you have to lose? This way, you're not reacting emotionally, and you have more time to make the decision that's right for you!" Troy said, trying to think about what would be in her best interest.

"Wow!" Izy responded. "See! That's what I'm talking about! You are amazing, and I am so lucky to have you as my friend. My manager would never have made a suggestion like that. But you know what, Troy, you are exactly right. You just gave me new motivation. I am going to make this next album the best yet, and I'm going to go on tour and make people cry! I feel like a new woman. I am so happy I decided to get ahold of you!" Troy was of course very happy with himself and his advise but was afraid Izy might take him and his lack of experience too seriously. The last thing he would want is to give Izy bad advice.

Izy and Troy talked that night for hours. They completely lost track of time. They were sharing, laughing, and planning together. Troy was having so much fun; it was obvious Izy was too. Neither one of them was paying any attention to how long they had been talking, the time flew by. Just as Troy was talking about his first trip to Los Angeles, his phone beeped with an incoming call. "Oh crap!" Izy we've been on the phone for over two hours! My wife is on the other line, hold on a sec," he asked Izy.

"Hey honey," Troy answered his phone, knowing his wife was the one beeping in.

"Troy! Where the heck are you? Why aren't you home? You should have been home over an hour ago!" April was pretty hot.

"I'm sorry, April. A friend of mine needed to talk, and I guess I lost track of time. I'll be home shortly," Troy tried to explain.

"A friend?" April questioned. "Since when are you the friend that people go to for help?" she rubbed in.

"Wow, that was a little mean! What am I supposed to tell you, a friend asked to talk to me, so that's what I've been doing! I will be home in like fifteen minutes or so." This could be the very first time Troy has ever really stood up for himself with his wife. He wasn't sure if he liked it.

"Okay, fine, get home soon, I have to go out. Next time, maybe you should check in with me first . . . lame story, by the way!" April said in an accusing voice. Troy went back to Izy.

"Hey, I've got to go, I need to get home," he told her.

"Did I get you in trouble already?" she asked in a light hearted way. "No, it's nothing," Troy told her, "but I do need to get going." "I completely understand, Troy, no problem. It has been so great talking to you! One thing, before I go, when are you coming to LA? Can we get together?" she asked with the excitement back in her voice.

"I should be there in about a week and a half, but I can send you the exact dates tomorrow," he offered.

"That's perfect! I am so looking forward to seeing you! Have a great night, I'll talk to you tomorrow!" Izy said good-bye and they hung up.

THE UNEXPECTED MEETING

Troy and Izy exchanged e-mails every day for a week. They came to the realization that they were not going to be in Los Angeles at the same time on Troy's first trip to the coast. Izy was very disappointed, Troy was even more so. They were both really looking forward to seeing each other again.

"I guess we can meet up on my next trip,"Troy texted to Izy.

"That completely sucks!" Izy texted back.

"How long till your next trip out here?" she added.

"I can't say for sure, but it should be within a month or so," he texted back.

"Agggg!" she replied.

Troy laughed. Even after Troy headed out of town, he and Izy continued to text every day and they talked about once a week or so. "Sometimes a text is not enough," Izy remarked. It was like they never lost any time since last being together; they seem to pick things up right where they left off when they separated in New York. They acted like they had been friends for years even though they came from two completely different worlds. They both used each other regularly for a sounding board, an objective ear, sometimes looking for advice, sometimes just to get something off their mind. They seemed to rely on each other more and more when it came to making important decisions, especially Izy. Izy always felt she could trust Troy, but now she felt she could trust him enough to share even some of her most important business decisions. It fact, it actually got to the point where Izy's manager. Mike, would ask Izy why she made a certain decision about something or he would flat out ask, "Where did that come from?" Izy's response was always the same, "I'm trying to take my time and think things all the way through. Your good with that, aren't you, Mike?" she would throw it back at him. "Yes, yes," he would reply, but it was obvious he was beginning to get a little frustrated with her. He knew Izy was a client you could talk to, even reason with, but if she made up her mind about something, you let it go.

First, Troy was in Seattle for several days, then San Francisco for several more. When he arrived in Los Angeles, he went to check into his hotel. At the front desk, the woman checking him in was giggling uncontrollably as she did so. Then between giggles, she said, "Yes, Mr. Anderson, we have your reservation right here. How many keys would you like?" she asked, continuing to giggle.

"Just one should be fine," Troy responded as she handed him his room key. *Weird!* Troy was thinking to himself. *She was definitely acting a little weird.* Maybe it was just an LA thing he was thinking; he's heard all the stories. As he walked toward the elevator, he looked at the sleeve the room key came in and saw that his room was on the tenth floor. He got in the elevator, the floor numbers went to ten, but to get to the tenth floor, you had to insert the key into the elevator keypad. Troy thought this was a little strange but put the key in anyway and pushed the button for the tenth floor. As soon as he got off the elevator, he knew something was up…or wrong. An older gentleman in a tuxedo greeted him at the elevator door. "Good evening, Mr. Anderson, welcome to the Prince Royal Hotel. I've already put your bags in your room. Please allow me to show you your suite," he told Troy as he reached out and took Troy's briefcase from him. *Whaaaaat!* Troy was thinking but didn't say out loud. "Izy!" he did say out loud as he realized she must be involved.

"Excuse me, sir?" the butler asked. "Oh, nothing, sorry. Please continue," Troy told him.

"Yes, sir."

Together they walked to the executive suite where the butler opened the massive door. When Troy walked in, he was a little blown away—actually, an understatement; he was seriously blown away. Troy had been in suites before but nothing like this. The butler showed Troy around the suite. It had a living room with a giant flat screen television, a parlor with a baby grand piano, and a huge chandelier; the suite had a very large master bedroom with the biggest bathtub in the attached bathroom that Troy has ever seen. Every room had a large vase with flowers pouring out of it. There was a large furnished balcony that went around the entire suite. In the living room, Troy noticed a basket sitting on the center table with some cheese, crackers, and a bottle of red wine in it. "A California specialty," said the butler. "Would you like me to open it for you?" the butler asked.

"No, not now, but thank you."

"Can I get you anything else, Mr. Anderson?" the butler asked.

"No, no, I think I'm good for now!" Troy said, trying to act as if he belonged there. "Yes, sir, I am one call away if you need anything," he said as he quietly walked out of the room.

Troy sat down on the lavish couch in front of the table that had the basket on it. He opened the attached card: "Troy it completely sucks that you're in LA when I'm not! Yours@Izy," she wrote. *Yours@Izy? That's the second time she's written that, I wonder what it means?* he thought. He fluffed it off and just smiled as he opened the basket to get to the cheese and crackers. He barely got the basket open when his phone rang; it was Izy.

"Hey, stranger! How do you like the basket?" she asked very excitedly.

"The basket!?" Troy asked. "What about this amazing room. You didn't have to do this, Izy, this is way over the top!" he said to her.

Izy laughed. "Yea, I'm very sorry, they were supposed to give you the presidential suite, but it was already taken!" She laughed harder.

"I'm pretty sure this will work just fine for me. My butler must think I'm nuts or something, coming in here with jeans on and one piece of luggage!" he said to her.

"Naw, you're well-dressed compared to most of the people that rent that room, trust me!" she explained. They laughed together.

Before they knew it, it was midnight; they had been on the phone for hours. Troy hadn't even eaten yet. "Damn it!" he said as he looked at his watch for the first time since they started talking. "What's wrong?" Izy asked, concerned.

"I totally forgot to call my kids! I can't believe it, what an idiot!" He was punishing himself. "Troy, I'm so sorry, it's all my fault. We lost track of time."

"No, it's not your fault. It's my fault, I never or almost never not call my kids when I'm out of town. I'll send them an e-mail, and they'll get in when they get up tomorrow." Troy was trying to make himself, and Izy feel better about his screw up. "Listen, I need to go anyway. I haven't eaten anything except these fabulously fancy crackers and some cheese, and I have a pretty early meeting tomorrow," Troy suggested.

"You're right, it's getting late. Listen, I'm really sorry about you missing calling your kids," Izy said, still feeling bad about it.

"It's okay, we're all good, I'll make it up to them. Have a good night, thanks again for everything! You're nuts, you know that, right?" Troy laughed.

"Yes, I'm afraid it's true, but then, that's why you like me and we are such good friends!" she offered.

"Good night, Troy. I'll text you after I'm out of the studio tomorrow, okay? Good luck with your meeting!"

"Thank you. Good luck in the studio, good night." They both hung up. One phone call, minutes later, the butler showed up with a four-course meal and a couple of ice-cold bottles of Troy's favorite beer. *This is something I could get used to!*

After several very successful meetings in Los Angeles, Troy was on a plane for the last leg of this trip; he was headed to Las Vegas. A nice, short flight. His company has one client there; Troy wondered why they chose Las Vegas to set up shop. He figured they must have received some pretty strong tax advantages or something like that. This was actually Troy's very first trip to Las Vegas. He never had a big desire to go, not being a gambler and not really into the shows and the "Vegas life." But he was quickly taken back as the plane approached the city. *Wow! Look at all the lights!* he thought. *Very cool!* He could start to see some of the better known hotels as the plane got closer to the airport. From his window seat, he could see the hotel New York New York Caesars Palace and the one that looks like a castle. He was starting to get excited about being there. After checking into the hotel, he headed for his room. As he walked through the casino to get to his room, he was completely mesmerized, much like a kid who sees Disneyland for the first time. He walked slowly, trying to take in everything—the lights, the sounds, and the people all buzzing with excitement. *Very intoxicating!* he thought. *Maybe I'll try my hand at something later. After all I am in Vegas!* He was surprised at himself how quickly he was being taken in. April would absolutely not be happy about Troy doing any gambling, and if he tried it, win or lose, he might be better off not telling her. He continued on to his room. Troy was amazed at how massive the hotel was and how far he had to walk to get to his room.

Once in his room, before he did anything else, he called home. He was excited because Maggie answered the phone. "Daddy!" she shouted over the phone.

"Hi, Maggie! How are you?" he asked his daughter.

"Daddy, I miss you! When are you coming home? Will you be here for my game this weekend?" she asked excitedly. "It's the finals you know!"

"Oh, I know, I didn't forget, I wouldn't miss it!" he told her. "Listen, you're not going to believe where I am. When we get off the phone, I'm going to send you a picture from my room," he said.

"Really? Why, where are you?" she asked.

"I'm in Las Vegas! You would not believe all the lights, it's very cool." They continued to talk for a bit, then the phone was passed to Justin. "Justin, how are you, big guy? How's school going?" Troy asked his son.

"Good, Dad, really good," Justin told him. "You're in Las Vegas?" he asked.

"Yes, I just got in a little over an hour ago. You would not believe how big this place is!" he said excitedly to him.

"Dad," Justin suddenly got very serious. "You know, people lose a lot of money in Las Vegas. If you gamble, you have less than a 7 percent chance of winning!" he explained to his dad with confidence and concern.

"Really? How do you know that?" Troy asked.

"I looked it up real quick when I heard you were there," he explained.

"Justin, you are an amazing kid! Thank you for your advice." Troy told his son. They continued to talk for a while more. Justin was telling his dad about a science project he was working on, and how he was anxious to show it to his dad. "That sounds great!" Troy said supportively, "I can't wait to see it!" After a few more minutes, Troy asked to speak to April.

"Sorry, Dad, Mom's not home yet," Justin explained.

"Not home yet? Why, where is she?" he asked.

"I'm not sure." Justin was interrupted by Maggie in the background, "She's at one of her charity functions!" Maggie yelled out. "Oh, I guess she—" Justin started.

"Yes, I heard," Troy replied. They soon said good-bye. Troy was bothered that the kids were home and April was not there. *She should have told me*, he thought. Troy got up and walked to the window. *Really beautiful!* he thought, looking out at all the lights. He took a picture of the view from his room with his phone and texted it to the kids. *They're going to like that!*

Troy wanted to take a shower before he went downstairs to get something to eat. He unpacked his clothes and headed for the bathroom. After several attempts, he finally figured out how to change the water coming out of the bathtub spout to the showerhead. *Do they really need to make it this difficult?* He laughed at himself. After a nice, hot shower, Troy was getting dressed when he noticed the red message button flashing on his phone. *Oh, I bet that's April,* he was thinking. He threw on his shirt and sat in the chair next to the phone. He checked the message, which had just come in.

"Hey, best friend!" It was Izy!

How does she know what hotel I'm in, I don't remember telling her? At least I don't think I did! He was arguing with himself. The message continued. "Have you eaten yet? I hope not. I made you a reservation at one of my favorite restaurants in Las Vegas. It's right in your hotel!" she was saying. "I hope you don't mind, but I made the reservation for nine tonight." It was eight forty-five. *That works out pretty nice!* Troy was thinking. Once again, Troy found himself baffled by Izy. "It's my way of making up for not being in Los Angeles!" she continued. "Go have a great dinner, and if you have time, call me after you're done. I hope you enjoy it!" She ended the message.

Troy was both surprised and happy. *I can't believe she did that! Well... actually I can!* he was thinking as he went down the elevator to the lobby level. Once the elevator doors opened, it was like someone flipped on a switch. It became very loud with many different sounds, the sounds of slot machines, people screaming and cheering, and music coming from several different areas around the casino. *This is nuts!* he thought. As he got deeper into the casino, he stopped every now and then to watch people playing the different games. It was all very exciting to Troy; he's seen people gambling before at some local Indian casinos at home but never so many people with such an excitement in the air. But Troy was starving, and he needed to eat. He kept looking at the signs around the casino but was having difficulty finding the restaurant that Izy made the reservation for. He finally stopped a security guard to ask for directions. The guard pointed Troy to the opposite side of the casino floor. "Of course!"

As he walked up to a roped-off podium, there was one very tall young woman and a younger-looking man, both very well dressed, standing behind the podium with the restaurant name on the wall behind them. Troy didn't see a door to go into the restaurant, *Strange*, he thought.

"Can I help you, sir? he was asked by the young woman as he got closer to the podium.

"I have a reservation for nine," Troy responded. "I think it's under Troy Anderson," he told the woman.

"Mr. Anderson! Yes," she said rather loudly as she looked sternly at the young man who was also there. "Mr. Anderson," the young man said as he stepped up to Troy. "It is a pleasure to have you dine with us tonight. If you would please follow me, sir." The young man turned back toward the wall and lifted his right hand. It looked to Troy like he had a key fob of some kind in his hand; one of those devices you would use to unlock your car. Suddenly right where the name of the restaurant on the wall was, the wall separated exposing a beautiful small inner lobby with a second woman and man standing behind another podium. As Troy was escorted to the podium, the wall behind him closed. The small lobby was so beautiful and lavish; it had a huge crystal chandelier hanging low in the center. The walls were a dark color with drapes flowing everywhere. It was beautiful. Beyond the small lobby area and through a combination of curtains and sheers, you could see into the restaurant. It was dark, but you could still tell how nice it was. *I think I might be a little underdressed for this place!* he was thinking as he was now being escorted by the second young woman. As they were walking to his table, she asked, "Is this your first time dining with us?"

"Yes, actually this is my first visit to Las Vegas!" he admitted.

"Oh, I think you'll enjoy it here. There is so much to do. I know you'll enjoy dinner!" she told him with confidence.

"I'm looking forward to it," he replied. They walked past many booths, all full of people, all very well dressed, everyone eating and drinking and having a good time. Troy was surprised he wasn't turned away at the door because of his lack of dress. They walked so deep into the restaurant they were running out of restaurant, Troy began to think, *She must be taking me to the back of the restaurant so no one can see the way I'm dressed!* he joked to himself.

They really did go to the back of the restaurant . . . and into the kitchen. Troy didn't know what to think. *Maybe she forgot I was following her!* Just as he was going to say something, the young woman stopped. "Give me a second, please Mr. Anderson?" she asked.

"Sure," Troy responded. *Okay this is a little unusual, right!* he thought to himself. While he was standing there feeling totally out of place, he watched the hurried pace of the staff in this very large kitchen, and he was completely enjoying the smells that went by him as food was going out into the restaurant. After a few minutes, the hostess was back with a large man dressed all in white with a big chef's hat on his head. "Mr. Anderson, please let me introduce you to our esteemed head chef, Marco."

"Good evening, Mr. Anderson, welcome to my kitchen," the chef said in a heavy European accent.

German or Swiss, Troy thought as they shook hands. "It's a pleasure to be here." Troy smiled.

"I have something very special prepared for you tonight, I hope you don't mind that I took the liberty?" the chef asked.

"No, not at all, sounds great!" Troy was excited about meeting the chef and having a "meal made especially for him." *This is pretty cool*, he was thinking to himself. *Leave it to Izy!*

The hostess thanked the chef; the chef nodded at Troy then he walked back into his kitchen.

"Shall we?" the hostess asked, motioning Troy to follow her. Instead of walking back out into the restaurant, she took him a little further into the kitchen where there was a small private room right in the kitchen. They went in; inside there was a small table that looked like it could sit four to six people. The room had a large window on one side of it where you could see directly into the kitchen. It was a very beautifully decorated room, impossible to imagine that it was in the middle of a kitchen. The hostess asked Troy where he would like to sit. "You can sit anywhere you like, but the best view of the kitchen is from this chair," she offered as she pulled out the chair.

"Sure, this would be great."

Troy sat down in the chair that was recommended. As he did, the hostess placed his napkin on his lap. Troy turned to her. "Thank you," he said.

"Its my pleasure," she stated. "Your waiter will be with you very shortly. He will be happy to take your drink order. Is there anything else I can offer you, Mr. Anderson?" she asked very professionally.

"No, thank you, everything is perfect," Troy told her.

Suddenly, he heard a very loud "Perfect! How could it be perfect?" Izy was standing in the doorway! She was wearing an oversized leather jacket covered in something that made it sparkle. It had a hood covering her head and part of her face. She had on oversized sunglasses, and she was wearing boots that went past her knees and she had on gloves with the fingers cut off. This time she looked like "*Izy.*"

"So this fantastic dinner that you were about to have by yourself is *perfect*?" Izy said to Troy loudly with a big smile on her face. The hostess practically ran out of the room. Izy laughed a big laugh, closed the door, and then threw open her arms. "Troy!"

she said. "It is so great to finally see you again!" as she walked toward him.

Troy, a little in shock, jumped up from his chair to meet her halfway. "Wow! It's Izy!" he said. "What an amazing surprise!" They hugged like they hadn't seen each other in years, then Izy gave Troy a little kiss on his cheek.

"Man! It's so great to see you!" she said as she started to take off the sunglasses and the jacket.

"Holy cow!" was Troy's reaction. "That's a dress!" Troy exclaimed. "It is a dress, isn't it?" he asked, kind of joking, kind of not.

"You like it?" she asked teasingly. "I was going to tone it down, but then I thought, why? After all, I'm meeting my best friend Troy…it's important!"

"I'm honored!" he said. They sat down at the table next to each other as a waiter walked in.

They were ordering drinks as a second waiter came in and presented them with three or four different appetizers. Troy could tell Izy had already been drinking, but he didn't care. She was being the Izy he knew, even though she was dressed like the Izy he had yet to know. He was the first one to speak up. "You really look great, Izy, how are you doing?"

"I'm definitely doing better now that I'm here with you!" she said while grabbing his arm.

"Yea, me too, I still can't believe your here! I didn't know you knew where I was staying?" Troy stated. He wasn't upset that she knew just surprised.

"I knew you were going to be here in Vegas, and I hated the thought that I missed you in Los Angeles, so I decided I would divert my flight home and stop to have dinner with you. Finding out where you were staying was no big deal. I think one of my people called your office asking to send you some important papers, your office gave him the hotel information," she explained.

"Wow! *That was easy*! Well, I'm glad you did, and I'm glad you're here," he told her with a big smile.

"Me too! But unfortunately, I don't have much time, I have to be back on the plane in about three hours. I have to be in LA for ... something, I forget." She laughed.

They sat there for the whole three hours, eating, drinking, laughing, talking. It was awesome; they were having a great time. The chef would pop in once in a while to see that everything was okay. Izy would say, "Perfect, Chef!" Troy wondered if she might be mocking him a bit because she would giggle each time she said it. The time went by too fast for both of them.

"I've got to go!" Izy said.

"Oh, okay!" said Troy. "I'll walk you out."

"*No!*" she said abruptly, startling Troy. "Aggg, I'm sorry, Troy, that is who you are and you are sweet, but you can't go out with me. I should have explained before. Once I leave the restaurant, no matter how many back doors I use, someone will see me and take a picture. I don't think it's a good idea that we might be seen in pictures together, do you?" she suggested.

"I guess I never thought about that. Of course you're right," he replied. Someone knocked on the door.

"Yes?" Izy asked. A very large man with a black suit on walked in. "We've got to go, Izy!" Troy assumed he must be security. "It's out!" he told her.

"What's out?" Troy asked a little dazed and confused.

"Aw, shit!" Izy exclaimed. "That didn't last long! Someone must have told the press I'm here, so now they're going to be all over the place!" she explained. Troy was sitting there with a blank look on his face. It was a little on the surreal side for him. He knew he was having dinner with a famous rock star in Las Vegas in the back of a private restaurant, but to him, Izy was just his friend. It was hard for him to put the two worlds together. "Is there anything I can do?" he asked as Izy was getting up. Troy stood as well.

"Yes!" she said to him. "Please stay here and have some dessert and let me get well away. I am so sorry for this, but it kind of goes with the territory, you know?" she asked and explained.

"I understand," he answered. They hugged and Izy gave him a short sweet little kiss on the lips. Troy was a little caught off guard by the kiss, but no surprise, he liked it.

"Be safe," Troy said softly just inches from Izy's face. They looked into each other's eyes for a few long seconds. "Thanks for going out of your way to meet with me today, it was fantastic!"

Izy stepped back. "Out of my way?!" Izy laughed. "We are friends . . . best friends, aren't we?"

"Yes, we are," Troy replied. "Best friends go out of their way for each other! Text me tomorrow, will ya?" she asked.

"Absolutely!" and she was out the door.

A GAME CHANGER

Troy did not miss Maggie's soccer game finals. She was amazing, getting two goals in the championship match. It was a great day for Maggie; Troy could not be in a better mood. Troy has always been proud of his kids, but it's times like these when it's hard not to feel a total rush take over your body with happiness for your children's successes. After the final game, they all decided to go out for an early dinner at Maggie's favorite restaurant to celebrate her big win. Maggie's fourteenth birthday was only days away; they could start the celebration early, Troy was thinking. Maggie loved it when the restaurant staff would bring her a special dessert and sing her "Happy Birthday." Justin always thought it was stupid. Troy and April were in two separate cars because April was coming directly from one of her social events, and she needed to stop on the way over to pick up Maggie's team some drinks for the game. Both the kids started to get into the car with their dad. "Why don't one of you go with Mom?" he suggested. Neither one volunteered.

"That's okay," April said. "I can just meet you guys there." Troy thought about going home first and then all of them could go in one car, but that was in the opposite direction. Leaving one car at the soccer fields and then having to come back for it was worse. "It's okay, Dad, I'll go with Mom," Maggie spoke up.

"No, that's okay, Maggie, I don't want you doing me any favors!" April snapped at Maggie. Troy thought that was unnecessarily harsh, especially to Maggie who is always very supportive to her mom, even when her mom was in one her famous "moods." It was an unfair remark; both kids don't see their dad that much and always want to spend as much time with him as possible.

Maggie got into the car with her mom anyway. "That was unbelievably cool of your sister," Troy said to Justin.

"You're right, Dad." Justin had nothing else to say on the matter. Troy and Justin got to the restaurant first; April was definitely a slower driver. He and Justin checked into the restaurant and got a good table right in the middle. Maggie will love the attention when the birthday song comes around. Justin and his dad where talking intensely. Troy loves the fact that he can actually have a real conversations with his kids. Troy was telling Justin about some of the things he saw and did while he was in Las Vegas and was showing him several photos he took with his phone. When Troy was on the last picture, his phone rang.

"It's Mom," he said to Justin.

"Where are you, guys?" he said as he answered the phone in a upbeat tone. "Mr. Anderson?" a male voice on the line asked. "Who is this?" Troy asked, confused and startled. "This is Captain Martinez of the Chicago Fire Department," he explained. Troy's heart sank to his stomach; he suddenly couldn't breath. He was almost immediately overcome with emotion. In seconds, he was thinking all the worst possible things this man's next words might be. "Your wife was in an accident."

Troy gasped for air. "Is she okay? What about my daughter?" he asked in total fear.

"They are both in route to St. Mary's, your daughter is stable with a few cuts and a mild concussion. I'm not sure, but she might have a broken wrist," the captain was explaining.

"Oh, thank God…and my wife? How is she?" he asked desperately.

"Your wife will need surgery. She appears to have some internal bleeding. She has several bad cuts, and she fractured her right leg. She'll be going straight into surgery when they get to the hospital," he told Troy. Troy can't remember, but he's pretty sure he never said "thank you," even "bye" to the fire captain. Troy looked at his son with a face that expressed nothing short of terror. Even young Justin knew something really bad happened. Troy and Justin got up immediately and started running for the car.

"Dad, what's the matter? Is Mom and Maggie all right?" he asked.

"Quick, get in the car," he demanded of Justin. Troy drove like a madman trying to get to the hospital as fast as possible.

"Dad, you're scaring me, what's going on?" Justin asked again.

"I'm sorry, Justin. The phone call I got back in the restaurant was from the fire department. Your mom and Maggie were in a car accident. They are both at the hospital right now," he said as calmly as he could.

"Are they okay, Dad?" Justin asked.

"I think there going to be okay," he told his son, trying not to alarm him more. "I just want to get there as fast as possible!"

Once at the hospital, they quickly parked the car and ran into the emergency waiting area. There were a number of people in the room, some injured, some appeared to be waiting. Troy walked up to the window. "My wife and daughter just came in!" he said rather desperately to the nurse at the window.

"What is your name?" she politely and calmly asked.

"I'm Troy Anderson, and my wife is—" he was interrupted by the nurse.

"Yes, they were checked in together. Your wife is in surgery and your daughter is with the doctor. You can go in and see your daughter, but I'm afraid your son will have to wait here," she explained.

Troy turned to Justin.

"I'm okay, Dad, go see Maggie!" he told his dad. Troy could see a tear coming down his son's cheek. He could see that Justin was scared, and he was trying to hold back more tears. Troy knelt down to be face-to-face with his son; he hugged him very hard. "Everything will be all right, I promise," he whispered in his ear. "I'll be back to get you as soon as can!"

Troy was buzzed into the emergency room; he walked up to the nurses' station. He only managed to say, "Maggie Anderson?" when one of the nurses got up from the desk and said, "Right over here." She walked him past several occupied beds and stopped in the middle of the large emergency room area. The nurse pulled back the blue curtain that was around the bed. Troy saw what he assumed was a doctor with his back to Troy and a nurse on the other side of the bed. Then he heard Maggie's voice. "Is my Daddy here yet?" she asked. Troy was immediately relieved. "I'm here baby!" he said as he stepped forward.

The doctor stepped to the side so Troy could get to Maggie. It was hard for Troy not to cry when he saw Maggie's face covered in bandages and tubes coming out of her arms. "Maggie! I'm so sorry this happened to you... are you okay?" He leaned over the bed to hug her and kiss her forehead. "I'm fine, Dad, a little sore though," she admitted. The doctor spoke up. "Mr. Anderson, I'm Dr. Deny. I'm attending to Maggie. Can I speak to you out front for a minute?"

"Sure, of course." Troy leaned into Maggie and kissed her on her forehead again. "Don't worry baby, you'll be fine," he said to her softly as he stroked her forehead.

"I know, Daddy, I love you!" she told him.

"Don't worry, honey, I'll be right back," he said, smiling at her.

Troy and the doctor walked to the nurses' station. "Is she going to be all right?" Troy asked in a very concerned voice. "She seems fine," he added, trying to physic himself up.

"Yes, she will be fine, she is fine," the doctor said. "She did brake her left wrist, everything else is pretty minor. She does have a concussion. It appears to be mild, so we'll want to keep her overnight for observation, it's strictly as a precaution. She should be able to go home tomorrow, just make sure she gets a few days of rest then she should be back to herself," the doctor explained.

"That's great news!" Troy said to the doctor with a sigh of relief.

The doctor continued, "Maggie's not the reason I wanted to talk to you in private, Mr. Anderson. It's about your wife."

"Yes ... my wife, is she still in surgery? Will she be all right? What exactly happened to her?" Troy asked the doctor. He felt guilty for not asking about her before.

"Mrs. Anderson is still in surgery, she should be out within the hour. She has some serious injuries. I'll be honest, it was touch-and-go when she first came in," the doctor was explaining.

"Oh my God!" Troy exclaimed as he leaned against the counter of the nurses' station.

The doctor went on, "She had internal bleeding that took the doctors quite a while to find, but they've been able to successfully stop the bleeding, that was our main concern and her biggest threat."

"Thank God!" Troy said.

"Yes," the doctor replied. "She had a collapsed lung, but it looks like it will be fine. It's capable of fully functioning on it's own, but right now, we are supporting it so it doesn't have to work too hard and put additional stress on your wife. Mrs. Anderson has a broken ankle and kneecap, both on the same leg, thankfully. We won't be able to work on those until she is out of surgery," he finished.

"So ... she's going to be all right?" Troy asked as he started to calm down and breath again.

"We will be monitoring her very closely for a while, but yes, I believe she will be fine. When the attending surgeon is out, I'll make sure he comes and talks with you. That may still be awhile, so why don't you wait in the surgery waiting room. He'll meet you there," the doctor suggested to Troy.

"Yes, I will. Thank you so much, Doctor. Can I see my daughter before I go?" he asked.

"Of course," the doctor made a hand gesture toward Maggie.

"Thank you again, Doctor."

After Troy visited with Maggie for a few minutes, the nurse told them they were going to be moving Maggie to the pediatrics floor of the hospital. The nurse told Maggie and her dad her brother would be able to visit her there. Troy hugged and kissed Maggie and told her he would see her soon. Troy went back to the lobby area to find Justin deeply engrossed in a large book.

"Justin," he called out in a low voice.

"Oh, hi, Dad! How's Maggie and Mom?" he asked in a very normal tone.

Troy sat down in the chair next to him. "Maggie's doing great. We should be able to both visit her soon. First they need to move her to a different room." He paused for a few seconds, trying to think of the right words. "Mom ... she's not doing quite as well, but the doctors say she will be fine." Troy was conflicted on how much information he should tell Justin.

"So they'll both be okay then?" he asked his dad.

"Yes," he said with reassurance. "Right now, though, we need to move to a different waiting room to talk to the doctor that is helping Mom." Justin got up and walked to the nurse's window. He handed the book he was reading to one of the nurses through the window.

"Thank you for letting me read this," he said to the nurse.

"Sure, honey, anytime. Did you like it?" she asked him coyly.

"It was pretty good," he remarked. "There were a couple of things I didn't agree with, but other than that, I liked it." All the staff behind the glass started to laugh and giggle.

Troy turned to his son. "What were you reading?" he asked.

"Modern medicine," his son said.

"Justin, I'm telling you, you are an amazing kid!" he said as he put his hand on his son's shoulder. "Just amazing!"

Together, Troy and Justin sat alone in the surgery waiting room. They had been sitting there quietly for some time when Justin spoke up. "Dad, why isn't Grandpa here?" he asked.

"Oh *no*!" he said very loudly. *I can't believe I forgot to call him!* he said to himself. He took a deep breath. "You know…I left Grandpa a message, maybe he didn't get it? Let me go try again, I'll be right back!" Troy got up and went out to the main lobby area. He called Frank; he was relived when it went to voicemail. *Whew! That was a lucky break*, he thought as he waited for the beep. "Frank, this is Troy. Listen, I don't want to upset you, but April and Maggie where in a car accident. They're going to be okay. We are all at St. Mary's Hospital. Please come over as soon as you can. April will be coming out of surgery very soon." He didn't know what else to say.

Troy walked back into the surgery waiting room and saw Justin talking to a doctor. "There's my dad," he told the doctor as he pointed at Troy. The doctor was dressed in one of those surgery suits you see so often on television and in the movies.

"Mr. Anderson," the doctor greeted Troy and reached out his hand to shake. "I am Dr. Rose, I performed the surgery on your wife." Justin stood up to be able to hear better. Both the doctor and Troy looked at Justin.

"Justin, why don't you walk back to the front and wait for Grandpa. He's not going to know where to go when he gets here. You can help him," he suggested.

"Okay, Dad, I can do that!" And he left the room.

"First, let me say," the doctor started again, "your wife is going to be fine."

"Oh, thank goodness!" Troy said.

The doctor continued with his diagnoses, "She had some serious internal bleeding, which we were able to get control of, thankfully no major organs were adversely affected. One of her lungs collapsed, apparently as a result of the airbag in her car, which saved her life by the way. It looks good now, but I'm going to keep her on a respirator for a while to make sure everything is functioning as it should." Troy was pretty much just standing there, listening to the doctor holding his breath the whole time. "You may have heard she also broke her right ankle and kneecap. Another doctor is taking care of that right now. She'll need to be in a cast for about eight weeks, maybe less. Beside some bruises and some minor cuts...that's about it." the doctor said as he clasped his hands together. "Overall, very good news, she is very lucky. Any questions for me?" the doctor asked.

"No, sir, I think I got it all. Actually, yes...when will I be able to see her?" he asked.

"I would say a couple of hours, you'll need to wait until we have her in a room. She will be out, though, for quite awhile," he explained. "A nurse will come and get you when we have her assigned to a room."

"Great, thank you so much...for everything!" Troy told the doctor.

"By the way, I heard your daughter is doing great!" the doctor mentioned.

"Yes, she is. I guess all things considered. It's been a very lucky day for me!" Troy said, trying to be upbeat. The doctor smiled, shook Troy's hand, and walked out of the room.

Troy walked to the front of the hospital to find Justin. He felt strange, like he has been in a vacuum for the last several hours and nothing seemed completely real. At the same time, he felt this overwhelming sense of relief, like a huge weight was lifted off his chest. Justin was sitting right by the front door watching for his grandpa. Troy sat down next to him.

"Good news," he told Justin. "Mom and Maggie are going to be all right."

"I already knew that," Justin told his dad.

"Really? What do you mean?" he asked.

"I'm not sure, Dad, but I knew."

"Okay, well, thank goodness you were right!" he told him.

"Grandpa!" Justin shouted out as he ran out the door. Frank was quickly walking toward them. He picked up Justin and gave him a big hug. Troy met Frank at the door.

"How are they?" Frank asked with a very frightened look on his face.

"They're going to be okay," Troy told him. "Let's go see Maggie and I will fill you in on April."

Together they walked through the hospital to the elevators and got off on the pediatric floor. Frank was holding Justin's hand. Troy went to the nurses' station.

"Yes, right down the hall, room 407." They started for the room when Justin stopped and pulled on his dad's shirt. "Dad, we can't go in without a present or something! It's important!" he demanded. Troy turned and bent over to talk to his very upset son. The trauma was starting to sink in, Troy was thinking. "It's okay, Justin, Maggie and your mom would rather see us right now than wait so we can get them something. I'll tell you what, tonight when we get home, can you make them a card? I know they would love that. Then we will bring it to them tomorrow. Is that okay?" he softly suggested.

"Yes, that's a good idea," Justin told his dad. Frank nodded at Troy as if to say "good job." Justin let go of his grandfather's hand and took his dad's hand.

When they went into Maggie's room, she was sitting up, watching television and talking on her cell phone. *Yup, Maggie's okay!* Troy was thinking, feeling even more relieved.

"Maggie!" Justin called out as he ran to his sister's side and hugged her. "I promise, I'll make you a card and bring it tomorrow!" he told her right away. Maggie quickly got off the phone.

"That would be great!" she told her brother. "Hi, Grandpa!" she said as she reached out her arms, looking for a hug.

"Maggie Bear," he said softly. (This is the name he has called her since she was a newborn. Maggie hates it, except in extreme cases like this one.) He hugged her and stood at her side. Justin had already crawled into bed with his sister, so Troy walked around to the other side bed.

"How are you feeling, baby?" he asked after kissing her forehead.

"I'm okay, Dad, but I'm worried about Mom. They won't tell me anything!" she said. Troy decided this was probably going to be the right time to explain everything all at once to all of them. So he told Frank, Maggie, and Justin everything the doctors told him and what he knew about the accident. They all sat in silence until Troy was completely done with his explanation.

Frank sat in a chair next to Maggie's bed, holding his head in one hand. Troy had never ever seen Frank like this—so vulnerable. Frank St. John, except for a few, he is always referred to as "Mr. St. John." Frank is a focused, determined, quiet man that stops all conversation when he speaks. He married young; he never went to college, but he was very smart, common-sense smart. He never really knew what he wanted to do but knew he wanted to make a lot of money. Frank has been divorced from April's mother since April was five years old. No one knows exactly where she is, but the divorce was on the grounds of mental illness and being incapable of raising April—their only child. No one ever talks about it, even Troy's children have been taught to never ask about their grandmother. Troy always assumed she was placed in a home somewhere, and once in a while, he would comment that it might have been Frank that put her there. Frank started his parts distribution business when he was eighteen years old out of his parents' garage. He started by trying to find parts for older cars that were hard to find, cleaning them up and then selling them to mechanics that worked on those kinds of cars. One day, after Frank had been doing this awhile and had already spread his business to new cars, someone Frank knew who worked at a large factory was complaining to Frank about how much trouble the company he worked for was having finding a part for several of their main pieces of equipment. They were always having trouble keeping them running because of this one part. The company they bought the part from was the only supplier and they were always out of stock. Frank was intrigued. He went to the plant and spoke with the plant manager. He asked many questions and then asked if he could borrow one of these parts. Even thought the part was pretty expensive and not something easy to replace, the manager trusted Frank and gave him one. This is where Frank's genius comes in. Frank took the part home and took it apart. It consisted of three main parts. Frank didn't know any one company that could make this, at least make it for the same price or less, but he did know three different companies that might be able to make the individual parts, and then Frank would have to have the three parts assembled. He put the three pieces out to bid, and he received the quotes and some samples back. He quickly figured out not only could he have it made better, but he could have it made cheaper! And most importantly to the customer, keep it in stock. He took the sample to the plant and presented it to the manager. They wrote an order on the spot for one hundred units. It didn't take long and his new company went national, and within three years, global. After a few more years, it went public. Frank has been very rich ever since. He has never remarried, and as far as April knows, he has never really gone out with anyone seriously.

They all sat at Maggie's side, quietly talking. A nurse came in to check on Maggie. "Hello, everyone," the nurse said gleefully. "Maggie, how are you feeling?" she asked.

"Not too bad, a little sore and a little tired," she told the nurse. "I'm sure, it's been a long day for you," the nurse said. The nurse announced to the group that Maggie was going to be checked by the doctor soon, and she was going to need to go to bed, everyone had to leave.

"I have to leave?" Troy asked in an upset voice.

"You can come back after the doctor is done, but I'm sorry the young man can't stay. He can come back tomorrow," she told them.

"That's fine, but can I stay?" he asked again. "Of course, as long as you like." So the three of them walked out to the waiting room. Frank and Troy worked it out so that Frank would take Justin home while Troy waited to see April. After he had a chance to see April he would come home and trade places with Frank.

THE GOOD AND THE BAD

Troy sat in the waiting room for some time. He kept checking his watch. *I can't believe how long things are taking.* After a few more minutes, Troy was approached by the same nurse that was in Maggie's room. "Mr. Anderson. I wanted to let you know the doctor checked on Maggie. She's doing great," she said with a big smile. "The doctor said if she has a peaceful night, there is no reason why she can't go home tomorrow."

"Oh, that is great news, thank you so much!" Troy told her. "Can I see her?" he asked.

"Yes, but we gave her a pretty strong sedative, she'll be out the rest of the night," she explained.

"That's fine! Thank you again." Troy went to Maggie's room, which was now dark. There was only a little night light on one side of her bed. Troy could see the profile of Maggie's face. She was asleep, but that didn't stop Troy from giving Maggie a kiss on her head, then he softly spoke to her. "You are my life, thank you for staying with me!" A tiny tear fell from Troy's eye onto Maggie's pillow. "Maggie, please get better soon." He kissed her again and left the room. He walked to the nurses' station to see if they had an update on April.

"Yes, we just got a call from ICU, your wife is all settled in. Just go to the nurses' station in the ICU on the second floor, and they will take you to your wife," one of the nurses told Troy.

"Thank goodness! Thank you."

Troy made his way to the ICU. It was late; most of the rooms were dark. The nurses' station sat right in the middle with all of the patient rooms circling around it. There were two nurses at the nurses' station as he approached. "Mr. Anderson?" one of the nurses asked. "Yes. Can I see my wife?" he asked her. "Of course. Your wife has had a very difficult day, but she is doing well. Have you spoken with her doctor yet?" she asked.

"Yes, earlier, after she was out of surgery," he told her.

"Okay, good. Then your up to speed on what we were dealing with. We have her under observation because she had a great deal of internal bleeding today, and we also want to monitor her lungs and how they are functioning," she explained. "Your wife is on heavy medication, so she will be out for sometime, but you are more than welcome to see her and you can stay as long as you like," she added. "Right over here," she walked Troy to April's room.

As he entered the small room, he could see his wife was lying on her back facing the door. Her eyes were closed. There were many machines all around her, all on and doing something. He walked up to the side of the bed. April's hair was pulled back; she had several bandages on her face. It appeared like she had a black eye, and she had a tube going down her throat. She didn't look too good to Troy. She was breathing very heavily.

That must be the sedatives? Troy was wondering to himself. He leaned in and kissed her on the forehead. He pulled up a chair to be right next to her. Troy picked up April's hand; it was warm and soft. She moaned a little, which startled Troy. He could see her chest moving up and down with each breath. He could see her right ankle; it was in some kind of cast. The cast looked like it went up past her knee. *What a strange feeling*, he thought to himself. The fog of the day's events was starting to clear. Troy was suddenly overcome with emotion and started to cry. He hung his head low, holding April's hand up to his face. A flash of light startled Troy. It was coming from his pocket; it was his cell phone. He gently put April's hand down on the bed and pulled his phone out of his pocket. Expecting it to be Frank, he was completely caught off guard; it was Izy. "Hey, Troy!" the text started. "Where have you been? I've been trying to get a hold of you all afternoon. I've got a bunch of stuff to tell you. Is everything all right? Get back to me as soon as you can. Yours@Izy!"

Perfect! Troy was thinking sarcastically. He was so down. He looked at April's face; suddenly he felt this overwhelming sense of guilt. He looked at the text again and then turned off his phone. He took a deep breath and picked up April's hand again. He stayed with her for several hours, nearly falling asleep several times. *I better get home so Frank can come over*, he thought. Before leaving the ICU, he checked with the nurses' station to make sure they had all of his contact information and asked them to contact him immediately if there were any changes. Then he drove home.

At home, Frank was sitting in the front room as Troy came in. "I tried to call you a couple of times!" he said rather abruptly.

"Yea, I'm sorry, I had to turn off my phone, and then I forgot I had it off," Troy told him. "How is Justin?" he asked.

"He's good, we barely got home and he feel right to sleep."

"Oh, that's good," Troy said, exhausted himself. "April is in ICU, you can go see her now," he told Frank.

"Good, I'm going to get going then!" he stated as he stood up. Troy could tell he was angry, but what was Troy supposed to do? So he just fluffed it off as Frank being Frank.

"Justin and I will be there as soon as we can in the morning, but please call me if anything changes, okay?" he asked his father-in-law.

"Sure." And out the door went Frank.

Troy went into Justin's room to check on him. He was deep asleep. *Poor guy!* Troy thought. "He's had a pretty rough day too!" Troy pulled the covers up over his shoulders and closed his bedroom door. Troy went into the kitchen to get something to drink before he headed to bed. He was thinking he'd just have a cold glass of water, but a cold beer sitting on the top shelf looked a lot better. He opened the beer, went into the family room, and collapsed down on the couch. He was completely exhausted and overwhelmed. As he was trying to unwind and assess the day, he pulled his phone out of his pocket to make sure it was on and to make sure it was off vibrate, just in case the hospital or Frank called. He sat there a while enjoying the cold beer; even after everything that happened today he couldn't stop thinking about Izy. He really wanted to respond back to her text. *What's wrong with me… this isn't right, is it?* he questioned himself. *Who else am I supposed to talk to about this? Maybe I should call or text Eddie?* he was thinking. *He'd kill me if I called him now!* he thought. *No…I'll call Eddie tomorrow.* He picked up his phone and was scrolling through his contacts; he came to "BFF." He looked at it for a minute then decided to return her text. It was late, but he knew there was a good chance Izy was still up. Even if she didn't respond, at least he got back to her and then tomorrow she would get his message.

He started his text several times. *How do I explain what's happened in a text?* He kept trying to find the right words. *It's just too much.* So instead of trying to explain, he simply texted, "Are you up?"

Within a minute, Izy texted him back, "Yes, I am…but why are you?"

"Can I call you?" Troy texted in response.

"Yes, of course!" She answered the phone in a low soft voice, "Hello?"

"I woke you up! Why didn't you tell me? I would have called tomorrow," he told her in a low voice so he wouldn't wake Justin.

"I was actually worried about you today. It's not like you not to text me back and then when you asked to call…I knew something was wrong," she said. "Is everything okay?" she asked, still sounding like she was half asleep.

"It's been one of the hardest days of my life!" Troy told her.

"Why? What happened?" she asked, very concerned.

"April and Maggie were in a bad car accident today," Troy started to explain.

"Oh my God!" Izy was waking up. "Are they okay, what happened?" she asked nervously.

Troy went on to tell Izy the whole story from the time they left Maggie's championship game to the minute he got home.

"Troy, I don't know what to say, thank God it sounds like they're going to be all right. But what about you? How are you doing?" she asked him.

"I'm better now. I'll be better when they are both home safe," he explained in a very emotional voice.

"Of course!" Izy said. "Is there anything you need…is there anything I can do to help?" she asked.

"No, I really, really appreciate it, though. The truth is, you're helping me now. I needed to call someone, and you were the only person that came to mind!" he confessed.

"Troy, you need to get some sleep. Go to bed and don't worry, everything will be fine. Text me or call me in the morning after you get to the hospital. I want to know how they are doing, okay?" she asked.

"Yes, I will. Thank you, Izy, I'll talk to you tomorrow then." They hung up. Troy never made it off the couch; he fell asleep right where he was.

The next morning, which was only a few hours later, Troy was woken up by Justin. "Dad, I'm hungry!" he said as he pushed on his dad's shoulder. Troy sat straight up.

"What time is it?" he yelled out.

"It's eight thirty, Dad, why?" he asked.

"Oh, that's okay, I thought it was later." He got up from the couch and went into the kitchen with Justin. "Can we just do cereal this morning, Justin? We need to get to the hospital," he asked his son.

"Sure, Dad, that's fine," he answered. "Are we picking up Maggie and Mom today?" he asked. But before Troy could answer, Justin belted out of the kitchen saying, "I almost forgot! I'll be right back!" In seconds, Justin returned to the kitchen and handed his dad two handmade cards, one for his mom and one for Maggie. "I worked on them last night," he said proudly. Troy read the cards to himself. They each had drawings on them; on April's, it was a drawing of Justin and his mom holding hands walking in a park. Maggie's was a drawing of the two of them kicking a soccer ball.

"Justin, these are perfect. I promise. They will love them!" he told his son.

Justin smiled. "Thanks, Dad!"

Troy and Justin were on their way to the hospital. Before they left, Troy picked out some clothes for Maggie with Justin's help. She won't be happy with two guys picking out her clothes, but she will be happy to get home and get in her own bed. Troy was surprised but in a way relieved that he never got a call from Frank or the hospital. *Good news*, he thought. They parked the car and went straight to Maggie's room. Maggie was wide awake and texting on her phone when they walked in. She was beaming with color and life. *Oh, thank God*, Troy was thinking.

"Maggie!" Justin ran to her and handed her the card he made. She carefully read the card quietly then put it down.

"Justin, this is the best card ever!" she told him with a big smile. "I love you!" she said as she leaned over to give Justin a hug.

Troy went to his daughter and gave her a big hug and kiss. "How are you this morning?" he asked.

Maggie was all smiles. "Except for this stupid wrist thing, I'm great!" she told him, but then a second later, she got a little somber. "Dad, Grandpa took me to see Mom this morning. She didn't look too good. I'm worried about her," Maggie said as her face changed. "I talked to her for a minute, but then she fell asleep," she said in a concerned voice.

"Maggie ... and Justin, your mom is going to be okay. She got badly hurt, and like I told you, she had to have surgery. She will be kind of out of it for a while, and it will take her some time to get better. But ... with us helping, she'll be fine in no time!" he told them with confidence.

A nurse walked into Maggie's room. "Good morning, everyone!" she said. "And Ms. Maggie, how are you?"

"I'm good, ready to go home!" she told the nurse.

"I bet you are! So are these two handsome men your escorts?" she asked.

"Yes, this is my dad and my brother, Justin," she explained.

"I see. Well, boys, I'm going to get Maggie ready to go home. It should take about an hour."

"Should we go?" Troy asked her.

"You don't have to. That's up to Maggie!" she said.

"Justin, why don't you and I let Maggie get ready so you and I can go visit your mom?" he suggested.

"No, Dad, I'd rather just stay here with Maggie. Is that okay?" he asked.

Troy was a little stunned, but he understood, maybe Justin was not ready to see his mom after hearing about how she was. "Uh, that's okay with me. I guess it's more up to your sister," he told him.

"It's okay with me! You can help me with my stuff, okay?" she asked her brother.

"Good. I'll be back in less than an hour, okay, guys? If you need me before I'm back, Maggie, just text me, okay?" he explained.

"Sure, Dad, we'll be fine," Maggie told her dad. The nurse nodded her head in support.

When Troy got to the ICU, there were nurses and doctors running everywhere, yelling out things that Troy didn't understand. There was some kind of an alarm going off, but Troy couldn't tell where it was coming from. He started to panic until he saw they were all going to a room next to April's room. *That was scary!*

I hope whoever it is they're going to be okay, he was thinking as he walked into April's room. Frank was sitting in a chair right next to April's bed. They were talking when Troy came in. April looked up and smiled at Troy; he immediately noticed that the tube had been removed from her throat. Frank simply stood and said "good morning." Troy walked to April. "I'm glad to see you're awake. You really gave us a fright around here!"

In a rather raspy voice, she said, "I'm sorry."

"Sorry? You have nothing to be sorry about, that's for sure. You were really put through it yesterday. I'm just glad you're going to be okay," he told her, trying keep things positive. April looked beat up—really beat up. Both her eyes were black and blue, she had no color in her face at all, and she had bruises all over her arms; she looked pretty bad. Troy was upset that Maggie had to see her this way, but he was really glad Justin didn't come with him. Frank told April and Troy he was going to step out for a bit and go get a cup of coffee. He asked Troy if he wanted anything before he left.

"No, thank you, I'm fine," he told Frank. After Frank left the room, Troy pulled up a chair to be next to April. "So how are you really feeling?" he asked her.

She answered in a low, raspy voice, "Right now, I feel okay, but I guess they have me on some pretty strong pain killers. I can barely keep my eyes open, all I do is sleep."

"Sure, that makes sense," Troy remarked. He reached up to hold her hand. "Have you seen the doctors today?" he asked.

"Yes, my surgeon came in sometime early this morning. He gave me all of the gory details. I guess I'm lucky to be alive!" she said as a tear rolled down the side of her face.

Troy got up from his chair, leaned over, and hugged her. He wiped the tear from her face, then he kissed her on the forehead. "Don't worry, April, you're going to be fine," he said supportively. "I heard you saw Maggie?" he asked, deciding to change the subject. "She's doing great! Looks like I'll be able to take her home here shortly!" he added.

"Yes, thank God! Dad brought her in a little while ago. I would not have been able to live with myself if anything worse had happened to her," she told Troy passionately. "Is Justin here?" she asked with some aching in here voice.

"Yes," Troy answered.

"Oh, I'd love to see him! Can you go get him? I need to see him, especially before I fall asleep again," she asked in a pleading way.

"Of course, I'll go get him now."

Troy went back to Maggie's room to talk to Justin. Maggie was sitting in a chair in the room dressed and ready to go. Justin was sitting on the bed playing with his phone. "Hey, guys!" he said as he walked in. "Looks like you are all ready to go, Maggie!" he added.

"Yes, I am!" she said with a big smile. "The nurse said we just need to check in with her before we can leave."

"Great! I'll go check in with the nurse and get you out of here!" Troy told them. Unfortunately Maggie couldn't just walk out of the hospital; she had to be wheel chaired out—hospital policy. So together they walked, while Maggie rode to the front door of the hospital. Maggie got up from the wheelchair; the nurse handed Troy a bunch of papers and then went back inside.

"Where's the car, Dad?" Justin asked.

"Listen guys, your mom's awake and she really wants to see both of you before I take you home," Troy told them. "I think we should all go … we need to go, it will make your mom so happy!" he explained.

Judging by Justin's face, he wasn't too happy about it. He didn't want to go; Troy knew he was scared. But Justin knew he had to go. "Okay, Dad. I really miss Mom," he said, trying to build up his confidence. So they walked back into the hospital and went to the ICU to see April.

Justin's was squeezing Troy's hand tighter and tighter as they walked into the ICU. It was obvious that the sights and sounds were bothering him. As they walked past the nurses' station, Troy stopped both Maggie and Justin. "Hey you, guys, come close," he said as he knelt down. "I want to talk to you before we go into Mom's room," he started to explain. "Mom is doing really well, but she may not look like it when you see her. She has a lot of bandages on her face and quite a few bruises. Just remember, it's still Mom under all that and that those things will go away very soon. She sleeps most of the time so her body can heal faster, so we won't be able to stay long. Let's make sure she knows we love her and that she will be home soon, okay?" They both nodded their heads in agreement.

April was awake talking to Frank when they first walked into the room. Maggie immediately walked up to her mom and hugged her; Justin stood behind Maggie trying to be as close as possible without looking.

"Justin?" April asked. "Come over here so I can see you," she asked quietly. Maggie stepped to the side, and Justin walked to his Mom. First he was looking down at the floor; April reached out and touched his head. She stroked his hair several times before Justin raised his face to look at her. April touched his face gently. "I know I look terrible," she told him.

"That's okay, Mom, you don't look so bad!" he said with a little smile.

"Oh . . . well, that's good," she said, trying not to laugh. Justin stepped up closer, right next to the bed.

"Mom, I'm sorry this happened to you and Maggie," he told her softly. "I really want you to get better soon so you can come home."

"I will, I promise," she said to him assuredly.

"I will." April was dosing off.

"Oh, here, Mom, I made a card for you!" Justin handed her the card.

She read it and smiled at Justin. "Thank you," she whispered. Troy stepped up to her and told her he was going to take the kids home and that he'd be back later in the day. Troy wasn't sure how much she heard, she was out. The kids hugged their grandfather, and they all said good-bye.

BACK TO NORMAL?

April spent three days in the ICU and six more in a regular hospital room. She was recovering very quickly, regaining her strength, although she was often in pain because the doctors were weaning her off the stronger pain medications. Most of the bandages had been removed from her face, and the bruising had all but gone away; at least they could be covered up pretty well by makeup. April was able to receive visitors, and she did. Every day there were people streaming in and out of her room, including Eddie and his wife Barb on one day. When Eddie got to April's room, he asked Troy if he needed to take a number; it seemed so busy! Other than her broken ankle and knee, April was close to being back to normal. Even though Troy was there every day, April had so many visitors he was only able to make small talk with his wife once in a while. She was receiving so many flowers the hospital was distributing them to other patients in the hospital that didn't have any, per Troy's instructions. Throughout this whole time, Troy was still texting Izy nearly every day, and they would talk every once in a while. To Troy, Izy was his voice of calm; she helped Troy by offering support and reminding him that he was a good dad and husband. Izy had threatened several times to send flowers to April or to send food to the house, but Troy talked her out of it each time. She really wanted to help.

As the day that April was getting out of the hospital approached, Frank told Troy that he should be able to get right back to work because he had hired a live-in nurse for April. The nurse would also be taking care of the kids, making meals and running errands. "This way, April can relax and just focus on getting better," he told Troy. Troy was not too happy to say the least. He tried to put his foot down and suggested "*he*" should be the one taking care of April and the kids, and the kids certainly didn't need a nanny. Even before Troy had the chance to discuss it with April, April was already telling Troy how excited she was that her dad got her a nurse, and that Troy could go back to work. *Brilliant!* Troy thought to himself. *Good thing I don't have to make any serious decisions around here!* he said to himself, a little pissed off about the whole thing. "*Am I supposed to be the man of our house, or maybe I'm just the friend who visits once in a while.*" Troy was not happy.

The truth is, once April got home, Troy couldn't wait to get out of the house. She was mean and demanding all the time—worse than ever before. Not so much to the kids and definitely not to her father Frank of course. It was like she had broken every bone in her body and could do nothing for herself. "Please bring me a magazine and some iced tea," she would ask the nurse in a condescending way. "And then after you clean the bathrooms, be a dear and run to the ice cream store…for the kids of course!" The nurse knew full well the kids were both at sleepovers at their friend's houses. Troy could handle it, but he felt terrible for the nurse. April could not have been more demanding. *Frank must be paying her really well*, he thought. *Really well!*

Back in the office where Troy could concentrate, he jumped deep into his work. He would go to lunch with Eddie nearly every day. He loved it; it was a great stress release for him. Eddie always made him laugh. One day at lunch, Eddie asked, "When do you hit the road again? You must be going stir crazy!"

"Yea, Frank wants me out the first of next week. I'll be gone for about ten days or so." He paused. "You know, it's sad I think, but I'm really looking forward to getting out of town!" he told Eddie.

"Why sad?" Eddie asked. "It's what you do, besides I can see being at home while April is on her throne is making you nuts!" Eddie laughed.

"Pretty much spot on," Troy admitted.

"It will be good for you! So listen," Eddie started without a pause. "You and me need to go out for some man time. How about a hockey game?" he asked, knowing Troy was the one with the tickets.

Troy laughed. "Absolutely! I've got tickets for tomorrow night if you're up for it?" he offered.

"Up for it! I think we are both 'up for it'!" He laughed as he hit Troy on the back. "This will be great!" Eddie went on. "I'll buy the beer ... at least the first round!" They both laughed.

Troy was completely dedicated to his wife and kids, even more so while April was recovering. He tried to be home every night to help in any way he could. Although he never felt like there was much he could do; really, he felt like he was more in the way than anything. It was still important to him to show his support and to be there for the kids. There were so many people in and out of the house, at almost all hours, day and night; now he was thinking he's the one that should take a number! He could not work; he could not even relax and watch a movie with the kids at home. To escape, every now and then he would get the opportunity to take the kids out for dinner or something, but even then, April would completely take control and sometimes stop them from going out because she wanted the kids home to do homework or some other kind of project she had for them. It was a little bit crazy and, yes, very, very stressful.

"I am so excited!" Izy said to Troy. "We finally get to get together! What days are you going to be here ... exactly?" she asked. Troy had told Izy he was headed out to the west and planned to be in Los Angeles for three days.

"I should be there on Monday and plan to leave Wednesday night or Thursday morning. This time, Los Angeles is my last stop," he told her.

"That's perfect!" Izy said so excited. "I have nothing formal on my schedule, and I have so much to talk to you about. When can we get together?" she asked.

"I've got a pretty tight schedule, but—" he started to say before Izy cut him off.

"I know you'll be busy, so maybe dinner on Monday or Tuesday night?" she asked. "Or lunch? I can pretty much work around your schedule," she offered.

"I can do dinner on Monday, for sure. Right now I have a lunch and dinner meetings on Tuesday, so Monday would work best," he told her. "How about if I just have Max pick you up from the airport and you can come over here and get cleaned up, do what you have to do, and we can go to dinner from here?" she had it all planned out for him. Max has been Izy's personal bodyguard for almost ten years. He travels with her everywhere and is rarely ever seen not at her side. Max is, unfortunately for him, often an innocent bystander to some of Izy's crazier moments.

Troy laughed. "Okay, that can work…I guess. Are you sure I can't just grab a cab to the hotel and meet you later?" he offered.

"No way!" Izy said. Troy already knew that was going to be her answer. "Nope! I won't have it! When you can, text me your flight information, okay?" she asked.

"Sure, no problem," Troy answered. "I'm really looking forward to seeing you, I have some things I'd like to talk to you about as well," Troy admitted.

"This is going to be great!" Izy exclaimed. "I'll text you later. I want send you some ideas about my album cover!" she said.

"Cool," Troy answered. "I look forward to it, and I'll forward my flight info as soon as I can."

Troy landed in Los Angeles; while the plane was taxiing to the gate, Troy turned his phone back on. He immediately had several texts and a couple of voicemails. Maggie texted him to tell him she really missed him already and loved him "tons!" Troy smiled as his heart warmed. He had two texts from Izy; one was asking if he landed yet and the other letting Troy know that Max would be meeting him in baggage claim when he got in. Troy text Maggie back first: "Love you and miss you too! I hope you have a great week. I will try to call you tomorrow night before you go to bed. I should be home in a few days."

Then he texted Izy: "Just landed! I decided that it might be best if I go straight to the hotel. I hope that's okay?" He was just kidding and tried to send off a follow-up text, but Izy was on him in seconds. "What? I thought we had it all arranged? Why would you want to do that?" Izy received the follow-up text that simply said, "Kidding! I'll see you soon!" Izy did not think it was funny. "Okay ... now I see where we are! You're going to pay for that, you know that!" she threatened.

As promised, Max was waiting for Troy in baggage claim. He walked right up to Troy and greeted him. "Good evening, Mr. Anderson, good to see you again, sir."

"Sir?" Troy laughed. "That will never work ... look, this whole thing is already awkward enough for me, please ... call me Troy!" he asked of Max.

"Yes, sir ... I mean, Troy, except when the boss is around!" he explained.

"Sure, I understand," Troy told him, smiling. "Let's get going!" Troy was sitting in the back of a black SUV that had all of the windows blacked out. The inside was all custom black leather with a small bar, a couple of TVs, a telephone, and a stereo that looked bigger than the one he had at home! The car had a solid partition between the driver and the back of the car. Troy found a call button on the intercom. "Max?" Troy called out over the intercom. "How long does it take to get to Izy's house?" he asked.

"About an hour this time of day," he said. "Welcome to LA!" he joked.

"Yea, I see!" Troy responded, as he looked out his window at all the surrounding traffic. Normally he would have opened the partition, but he wanted to make some calls first. Izy was the first call.

"Troy! Are you here?" Izy asked.

"Yes, I'm sitting in the back of your car on my way as we speak," he told her.

"Great! I'm just wrapping up a call, see you in a few, okay?" she asked politely, not wanting to seem as if talking to Troy wasn't more important.

"Yes, of course, see you soon." Then Troy called his house.

The nurse answered. "Anderson residence."

"Hi, Brenda, this is Troy, is April available?" he asked.

"No, I'm sorry, Troy, she's not here. Someone picked her up some time ago to go to a dinner or something like that," she answered. "She must be feeling better," he suggested.

"Yes, she seems to be much stronger. I don't think you'll be needing me once her cast is off," the nurse suggested.

"How about my kids, are they home?" he tried again.

"Yes, Justin is here. Maggie is over at a friend's," she replied.

"Great, can you put Justin on the phone, please?"

"Hey, Dad!" Justin answered, sounding a bit rushed.

"Hey, buddy, how are you doing?" Troy asked.

"I'm good," he answered. "How are you doing, Dad?" he asked his dad, trying to be polite. "I'm good too."

They talked for a minute or two when Troy asked, "So how are things going around there? Is everything going okay with you, Maggie, and Mom?" he inquired.

"Same ol', same ol', Dad. Mom is a lot better, she's out all the time," Justin told him.

"Really? That surprises me," Troy said. "What is she doing when she goes out?" Troy asked, trying not to sound like he's checking up on his wife.

"I don't know, Dad, she's always doing something. You know how Mom is!" he explained. "Hey, Dad, it's great to talk to you, but my friend Kyle just got here. I gotta go, okay?" he asked his dad.

"Of course. I love you and miss you. I'll see you in a couple of days, okay?" he told him.

"I love you too, Dad, I'll talk to you later!" That was it. Troy smiled.

HOME AWAY FROM HOME

Troy rolled down the partition. "Max, how are you doing up there?" Troy inquired.

"I'm fine, how are you? Is there anything I can get for you?" he asked.

"No, no. I'm good, just getting a little car sick back here!" he explained.

"I understand!" he answered as he chuckled a little. "It happens all the time! You might want to move up here with me for the last part," he started to explain. "The rest of the way we drive up some pretty windy roads! Wouldn't want you to get sick before getting to the house!" he chuckled again.

"Right, good idea! Can you pull over?" Troy asked. He jumped into the front of the SUV. "Oh yes, this is much better," Troy said as he rolled down his window a bit for some fresh air. "Much better!" he said as he took in a deep breath.

"Sorry about that," Max was saying. "No matter how slow I go on these roads, people in the back get sick," he explained. "Except for Izy, she doesn't feel a thing!" he explained further.

Troy looked out the front of the car. "Wow, this is getting pretty steep, how far are we going?" he asked.

"All the way to the top!" Max told him.

"All the way?" Troy stretched out his neck, trying to see the top of the hill through the windshield.

"Yes, sir, all the way," he chuckled some more. Every once in a while, the car would make a really sharp turn, and when it did, Troy could see down the hill into the city.

"Wow! That's a view!" he exclaimed. "Now I know why Izy puts up with this drive!" Troy said.

"That's part of it," Max answered. "It's also great for privacy and security."

"Ahh, well, that makes sense too," Troy said. Sometimes Troy forgets the fact that Izy is an international superstar. He only really knows her as Isabelle, and even though they often talk about her work and what she is doing and who she is with, it doesn't really sink in for Troy. The fact that his friend is Izy, *The Izy* hasn't locked in as real for him. To him, Izy is still just his friend, a great friend.

The SUV comes to a stop in front of a giant wrought-iron gate with a guardhouse on the left side of it. The gate had no markings or names on it. Max waves to the guard, and the guard waves back. Troy leaned over and waved too, not sure why he did. The huge iron gate opened, and they drove through. The driveway was long; it took almost a minute before Troy could even see the house. And what a house!

"Wow!" Troy said. "Did I just say that out loud?" he asked Max.

"That's okay, that happens a lot too!" he told him, trying not to laugh. The entire property was lined with some kind of very tall trees with a ton of leaves. *This must be for security too,* he thought. In front of the house, in the middle of the circle drive was a very tall, beautiful fountain with several cherubs peeing from the three different levels into the base. *This isn't something you'd expect to see at a rocker's house!* he thought to himself.

The house was beautiful, unbelievably large but beautiful. It had an old Spanish-style look with a red tile roof. It had several balconies, and there were vines growing up the sides of the house in several places. It looked as though it was as wide as the property. As they pulled into the circle drive, Izy was coming out of the front door. She was actually jumping up and down, clapping her hands as they pulled up to her. Troy was laughing out loud. "I guess she's excited to see me?" he told Max. Max smiled with approval. Troy was happy to see her too. She was wearing what looked like sweats or something. *The real Isabelle*, he thought.

Troy got out of the car, and before he could take one step, Izy was on him. "You're here!" she shouted out. She gave him a big hug and immediately grabbed his hand and started dragging him to the house.

"Come on!" she said very excitedly as she pulled on his arm. Troy looked back at Max and waived; Max just smiled.

"Come on, come on, come on!" Izy was telling Troy as she pulled him through the front door. Troy was trying to take it all in. As they entered the house, Troy stopped dead. Izy stopped too. "What's wrong?" she asked.

"Oh my God, Izy . . . this place is amazing!" he said as he stood in the foyer, stunned. The entry was, simply put, magnificent. White marble floor with gold and red blended in, large, ornate tables lining the walls. Tapestries and paintings, a chandelier that was so big it had what looked like a ship's anchor chain holding it up. And the ceiling . . . so high, with a mural of a woman laying by a lake in a sheer dress, surrounded by horses and ducks.

Troy was in shock—gawking, to say the least. "Hello?" Izy said, laughing as she passed her hand in front of Troy eyes. "Snap out of it! You can check out the house later. Come on, I been waiting to show you something," she demanded. She grabbed his hand again and starting pulling him deeper into the house. As Troy was being dragged along, he saw the dining room.

"Holy crap! That must be able to sit, what twelve?" he blurted out.

"Sixteen!" was the answer that he got back. They passed what looked like a library and an office of some kind. Then they came to a second foyer that had three hallways, each going off in different directions and two sweeping staircases that curved up the walls with another foyer on the second floor where the two staircases met. Just as Izy was starting down the center hall, a door next to the right staircase swung open, and a woman in a red pantsuit came out. Troy thought it was strange that this woman was in a closet, but as the door opened more, he could see inside; there appeared to be two staircases behind the door, one going up and one going down. *Okay, that's kind of cool!* he thought.

"Good day, Ms. Izy," the woman said with a Mexican accent.

"Hi, Maria! I'm so glad I ran into you. This is my friend Troy. He'll be hanging out every now and then." Maria nodded to Troy; Troy nodded back. "Can we get something to drink and maybe some light snacks?" Izy asked.

"Of course, Ms. Izy. What would you like?" Izy looked at Troy.

"I'm good with whatever you get," he told her, trying to be cool, but it wasn't coming off as cool as he had hoped.

Izy smiled. "Okay, Maria, can you just get use some iced tea and some fresh fruit for now? Can you have it brought to my office please?" Izy asked.

"Of course, Ms. Izy, I will call it in right away." And she disappeared back into the closet.

"Did she just say she would 'call it in'?" Troy asked.

"Yup! Now come on!"

Further down the hall, they passed many doors and many, many windows; some of the windows were made of beautiful stained glass with different scenes in them. To Troy, they looked like they came straight out of a castle; he wanted to ask but he didn't. One large window looked out toward the rear of the property, or maybe *estate* is a better word for it. From the seconds he had in front of the window, he could see the city off in the distance and the corner of a pool. "That looks bigger than my father-in-law's country club," he said to Izy as they finally came to a stop in front of a door at the end of the hall. The door looked like the other twelve they just passed, except this door had a small sign next to it: "Izy's Office, Do Not Disturb!"

Izy opened the door, and they walked in. *This is not an office* was Troy's first impression. The room was large, and it was almost circular in shape. The entire back wall, which faced the back of the house, was almost all floor to ceiling glass with oversized sliding doors that could be opened to make you feel like you were outside. The windows and doors had big, heavy-looking drapes that puddled onto the floor, which was a dark, rich-looking wood. The room had a large stone fireplace with a five-foot high mantle. Over the mantle was a painting of Izy in an all-black leather outfit, with a guitar in her hand and only smoke and fire behind her.

"A little much, I know," Izy said when she saw Troy looking at it. In the dead center of the room was a grand piano, jet black with a black piano bench that had a red cushion. On the other side of the room there were two walls; both were covered with many framed photos as well as a number of posters that Troy assumed were Izy's album covers. Behind him, next to the door they came in, was a spiral staircase that went down below the floor. Before Troy could ask anything, there was a knock at the door.

"Come in!" Izy yelled out. A woman appeared wearing the same all-red pantsuit carrying a tray with a pitcher of iced tea and a large bowl with cut fruit in it. "Ms. Izy," she said. This woman was a younger-looking white woman who was petite and had red hair—a total contrast to her uniform. "Thank you, Melissa, can you just set it over there?" she pointed to an oversized coffee table that was in front of two oversized black leather couches that faced each other. The woman did not respond; instead, she took the tray over to the table and set it down. Then she poured the iced tea into two large smoked glasses and headed back toward the door. "Will there be anything else, Ms. Izy?" she asked.

"No, thank you," Izy replied. "We're good," she said, looking at Troy.

"Good!" he added. And Melissa left the room closing the door behind her.

"So…welcome to my office! Or at least half of it!" she said with a big smile. "What do you think?" Izy inquired.

"Uhhh…I think it's awesome, not like any office I've ever been in!" he told her.

"I know, right! This is where I do all of my best work. In here, I can just relax. This is where I do almost all of my writing," she explained.

"I can see why. This is a great space. I feel relaxed already!" he said jokingly.

"Come on, sit down. I want to show you something," Izy said, pointing in the direction of the couches. Troy had to move a few red pillows before he could sit down. He picked a spot that had a great view; he picked up one of the iced teas and sat down. Izy went to a big wood-dresser–looking thing on the opposite wall and took out a large black leather case, like one an architect might use. Then she picked up a computer tablet device and with it turned on some music. Troy was surprised, the music was not rock and roll; it was jazz or blues—Troy wasn't sure.

Izy could she the puzzled look on his face. "This is my roots," she was explaining. "Everything I learned about music came from jazz and soul," she explained.

"Really! That's not something I would have expected!" Troy told her. Izy sat down on the couch next to Troy and set the big black leather case on the table. "I'm so excited to show you these, but I want you to be honest, I need your honest opinion!" she asked him.

"Absolutely…of course!" he said. Izy unzipped the case and opened it up. There was a small stack of eleven-by-fourteen photographs inside. Izy explained that she was hoping one of these was going to be her next album cover, and she had it narrowed down to the ten in the case. "Oh, that's cool!" Troy replied. "I'm excited to see them," he said as he put down his iced tea. Izy handed him the first photograph. Troy was immediately a little shocked, but he tried his hardest not to show it. "What do you think?" Izy asked excitedly. "Do you like it?" "I ... I do, yes," he told her.

"Ahhh, I can tell you don't. I thought you said you were going to be honest!" she accused.

"I am being honest! I really do like it, maybe just not as an album cover?" he tried to recover.

"Oh, that's fair," Izy said as she handed him the next photograph.

Troy eyes almost came out of his head! "Izy, do you have any clothes on in this one?" he asked a little more shocked.

"No ... But you can see all the important parts are covered! You don't like this one either, do you?" she asked. Izy was getting a little upset and frustrated. "My manager loved them all, I thought you could help me pick the one, you know?" she asked in a kind of desperate way. Troy went through the rest of the photographs with her, taking his time with each one. They all seemed to have the same basic theme; Izy totally naked, covered only in certain areas by strategically placed soap bubbles or a small piece of leather or in one shot a small puppy!

Troy put all the photos back down in the case. Izy was looking at him with her hands clasped together; she had both excitement and concern on her face. "Izy," Troy started, "these are all fantastic, really—I mean, wow!"

Izy smiled.

"But I don't think this is a decision that I can help you with," he explained.

Izy looked puzzled. "I don't understand, you don't have to make this decision. I just wanted to know your opinion," she explained to him. "What's wrong with them?" she asked.

"Do you really want my opinion?" he asked in a sharp tone.

"Yes, of course, you're my friend, and I trust you. Besides, you're a man, right? I think men will like it!" she suggested as she smiled coyly.

"There's no doubt about that!" Troy laughed. "Here's the thing. I am your friend, I care about you, but I know nothing about your business and what might work or not work. Sometimes—actually, most of the time—I forget you're this huge international rock star, obviously something I cannot relate to. I really think this decision should be made by those who know the industry better, people who know you better. But . . . if you want my opinion, well . . . I wouldn't use any of these!" he blurted out.

"What?!" Izy asked loudly. "Why?" she asked.

"Well, again, just my opinion . . . you are so much more than this. I think you are better than this. You don't have to sell your unbelievable talent with sex, do you?!" He was sticking it out there. "I mean there's no question any one of these will get a lot of attention," he told her. Troy was worried that he might have just ended his friendship. Izy said nothing; she just kept looking at Troy. He started to wonder if he'd have to get a cab back to his hotel.

The only thing Izy said was "Huh!" as she sat back on the couch with her iced tea in her hand. "You know what?" she asked, getting excited again. "Let's go to dinner and talk about it, okay?" she suggested to Troy.

"That's a great idea!" Troy said as he was thinking he might have just tested the levels of his friendship more than he wanted.

Izy took Troy to a bedroom where he could change and freshen up. As Troy walked into the room, he turned back to Izy. "I feel like I blew it, and I may have upset you, did I?"

Izy could see he was very concerned. "No, not at all. Actually, I think you gave me something to think about and something for us to talk about! By the way, don't put on a suit or anything like that. This is going to be totally caz," she said, smiling at him.

"Casual? Okay," he replied. Troy opened his suitcase and took his toiletry bag into the bathroom. He couldn't help but think about what he told Izy and how bad he would feel if he upset her or, worse, affected a business decision that was wrong. *She was so excited to show me!* he thought. "What an idiot! Why couldn't I just say yes to a couple of them!" He tried to think of what he could say to make it up, but he really felt like he told Izy the truth, and that was conflicting for him. *I mean, I'm supposed to be her friend, and I answered as her friend*, he tried to convince himself. *Man, those photos were serious, though! Wow! Not the Izy I know, that's for sure!* he said to himself, laughing as he thought about it.

Troy walked out of the room where he was changing and was immediately lost. He looked down the two halls that were in front of him, but he did not recognize either one. So he started down the first hall. When he got to the last door at the end of the hall, it took him to the outside. Then he walked back and went down the other hall; eventually, it led him to two more halls. *Man, this place is huge!* Every door he opened was a bedroom, bathroom, or closet.

"Excuse me, Mr. Troy." It was Maria. "Can I help you?" she asked, smiling at him.

He laughed. "Yes! Maria, I cannot figure out which way to go to get to the front of the house!" he said as he laughed at himself.

"I understand, Mr. Troy, sometimes I even get a little lost," she offered in support. "There are two things you need to know when you're in the main house," she started to explain.

"Main house!" Troy laughed some more.

"Yes, Mr. Troy. First of all, you see these little screens in the wall? These are everywhere in the house, every room. If you just touch it, it will come on. It will tell you where you are and you can click on the map to figure out where you want to go, or you can just push the security button, someone in security is always available to help you," she explained.

"Oh, very cool!" Troy said.

"But Ms. Izy, she is very smart, she knows sometimes it's hard for people to find their way around, so in every hallway if you look up where the wall meets the ceiling, she has the smoke detectors. If you keep the smoke detectors on your right, you'll end up at the front of the house!" she explained further.

"Really? That is smart!" Troy answered. "Thank you, Maria." And he walked on, keeping the smoke detectors on his right. Within minutes, he was standing in the front foyer. "That really worked!" he laughed.

DINNER AND A SMILE

Several women, they appeared to be staff, walked by Troy as he was waiting for Izy at the front of the house. "Good evening, Mr. Troy," each of them would say as they walked by. They all wore the same red pantsuits. *What a strange uniform?* Troy was thinking. He didn't have to wait long when a woman who appeared to be Izy approached him.

"Izy?" he asked smiling.

"Yes it's me!" she said as she threw her arms up over her head. "How do you like it?" she asked him as she posed. Izy had on a blond wig and oversized sunglasses. She looked like she had on almost no makeup. She was wearing a black baseball cap with a crystal number 1 on it. She was wearing plain jeans and an oversized red top. If Troy didn't know it was her, he didn't think he would have recognized her at all.

"I like it!" he laughed. "I thought I was going to dinner with a woman who has very long dark hair, instead I'm going out with a blond!"

Izy laughed. "I hope you don't mind. If I don't wear some kind of disguise, we will never get a chance to sit and talk, let alone eat!" she explained.

This made sense to Troy. "Wow, such a different world, the steps you have to go through just to try to have a little normalcy," he said to her.

They walked out front where Max was already waiting for them with the car door open. "Good evening, Izy," he said so professionally.

"Hey, Max!" she replied back as they got into the back of the SUV. They started down the long, windy road. "Woo, boy!" Troy let out after the first turn.

"What's the matter?" Izy asked.

"Oh ... well, it's this road. It almost got the better of me on the way up to your house!" he explained.

Izy laughed. "Here ... this will help," she told him as she reached for an already open bottle of champagne and a glass.

"Champagne?" Troy asked inquisitively.

"Sure! The bubbles help, and it tastes great!" she said as she offered the glass to Troy. "I'll give it a try, I guess." He was actually concerned it might make him feel worse! Izy was pouring herself a glass when the car went around a particularly tight turn; she slid across the seat right up against Troy, somehow managing not to spill a drop. She laughed as she raised her glass. "A toast!" she started to say. "A toast to being with my real friend and being able to spend some time together. I am really glad you're here," she said with a very sincere look on her face and in her voice.

"To friends!" Troy responded. They clinked their glasses together and took a sip. "Ummm, this is good!" Troy exclaimed.

"I told you!" Izy responded. Before he knew it, they were out of the hills, and Troy's stomach was fine.

They drove for about thirty minutes, talking and laughing and enjoying the champagne. Troy thought he could smell the ocean. "Are we getting close to the beach?" he asked Izy.

"Yes, we are! Good nose!" she laughed. "One of my favorite restaurants is right on the beach," she explained. "I think you'll like it," she added.

"I'm sure of it!" he said.

"There it is!" Izy pointed to a restaurant that looked over the beach. It was a big place, with tiki torches all around it. As they got closer, Troy could see it had cars lined up out of the driveway and going down the street. Max slowed way down and then pulled into a small parking lot for a building several buildings away from the restaurant. There was a chain blocking the way, but suddenly, a man in a valet uniform showed up and took down the chain. *That was impressive!* Troy thought. They pulled all the way into the parking area and got out of the car. It was a brisk night but not cold. Troy could hear the waves crashing on the beach. It was very dark where they were, Troy thought.

"Do you want me to go with you?" Max asked Izy.

"No, thank you, though. You know if you go, I'm busted!" she reminded him. "It's cool. I've got Troy," she added. Max nodded his head in agreement and got back into the car. The valet walked up to Troy and said, "This way please." Together with the valet, they walked down a narrow path between the buildings until they were standing on the beach. They walked a little way down the beach when they came up on the restaurant. It was all beautifully lit up, with more tiki torches everywhere. You could hear people talking and eating on the deck above. A guitar was playing in the background. It sounded like it might be live. The valet walked them to a door on the side of the restaurant; there were no lights on this side of the building.

"This is either really cool or really creepy!" he told Izy.

Izy laughed. "Creepy, I think!"

The valet opened the door, and they walked in. They appeared to be standing in a storage area. An older well-dressed man approached them with a big smile on his face. "Welcome, welcome!" he said to both of them in a heavy Italian accent. "It is so great to have you back!" he said to Izy.

"Thank you!" Izy replied and then hugged the man. "It's great to be back! Let me introduce you to me dearest friend, this is Troy," she said, turning to Troy. "Troy, this is Manny, he owns this place," she said, smiling. Manny reached out to shake Troy's hand. "It's a pleasure to have you here," Manny said.

"I'm honored," Troy replied.

"Your table is all ready for you," Manny pointed toward a door. Izy took Troy's hand, and they walked through the door up some stairs into the kitchen. Manny guided them through the kitchen, stopping only long enough for Izy to say hi to the chef. They continued to a door that was off to the side of the main kitchen doors. They entered into a small private room with a table that would only sit four. The room had its own small but private deck looking out over the beach to the ocean. Manny walked over and opened the big glass doors to the deck. "Should I keep these open for you?" he asked.

"Yes, that would be great!" Izy replied.

Izy and Troy walked out onto the deck. "Wow! This is fantastic!" Troy exclaimed.

"It is," Izy said in a quiet and peaceful voice. A waiter approached them out on the deck.

"May I get you some drinks?" he asked.

"Yes, I believe so," Troy spoke up for the first time ever since knowing Izy. Izy looked at him and smiled.

"What would you like?" Troy asked her. They ordered drinks and some appetizers. They stood out on the deck for sometime, enjoying the view and the sound of the waves. You could hear the people in the main part of the restaurant, but you couldn't see them. The waiter returned with their drinks, another server came in and put the appetizers on the table.

"Shall we?" Troy asked with a big smile.

"We shall," Izy said, giggling at him. They sat down to start what turned out to be a fabulous feast. They drank, ate, laughed, and shared many stories for hours. Other than when the waiter came in to bring them food or drinks, they were never disturbed. Troy had to force the dessert down, but he could not pass on it; it looked and tasted too amazing. "I think I could explode!" he admitted to Izy.

"Do you think we should walk some of this off?" Izy asked him. "Sure, that would be great!" They got up from the table and walked back through the kitchen. Manny was there and waved at them. They walked over to Manny; Izy thanked him and gave him the formal kiss on both cheeks thing and a big hug. Troy reached out to shake his hand. "That was fantastic!" Troy told him. "I'm so glad you enjoyed it, please come see me again soon," he was looking at Izy when he said it.

"We will!" she answered. Together they walked down the stairs, through the storage area and out the side door. They walked out onto the beach and down close to the waves. The air had gotten considerably cooler, and there was a heavy moisture in the air. "Boy, it's been a long time since I've walked on a beach!" Izy told Troy.

"Me too!" he said. "I actually can't remember the last time I did!" There were many people out doing the same thing. Troy was a little worried for Izy at first, but no one even looked at them, let alone recognized her in the dark. Izy was having a blast, skipping and running back and forth chasing the waves.

"Izy. I've got a stupid question for you?" he said.

"Okay," she replied.

"What is the deal with the red uniforms?!" he laughed.

Izy laughed so hard she didn't see a wave coming that caught her from behind and soaked her to her knees, which made her laugh even harder! "Has that been wearing on you all night?" she asked, still laughing.

"Well, kinda!" he said, smiling.

"That's funny! It's no big deal really. You already probably figured out my favorite color is red, right?"

"Right, that I got!"

"Okay, so the real reason is, I have so many people coming in and out of my house my security wanted them to all look the same and stand out, so that's what I came up with!" she explained.

"Huh! In a strange way that totally makes sense! Troy said.

"Yea, so no matter what's going on or how many people are in the house, I know who is staff and who isn't. Plus, then my security always knows who's where and if it's okay for them to be there," she explained further.

"Brilliant!" was the only thing Troy could come up with. He was only asking as a joke, but now he really liked the idea.

They walked for about an hour. It was starting to get pretty cold. "We should head back, don't you think?" Troy asked.

"Head back? Oh, yes, we should get going, after all one of us has to work tomorrow!" she said teasingly. Izy started to walk toward the road and not back in the direction of the restaurant. "Shouldn't we be going back that way?" he asked as he pointed in the opposite direction. "No, we're good," she answered. They walked past some houses and out onto the main road. Right in front of them was Max with the car!

"How'd you do that?" he asked Izy, knowing she never made any calls.

"Well, I guess you should know," she told him.

"Know what?" he asked.

"Max knows where I am at all times, as does the head of my security," she said.

"Really?" Troy was surprised but kind of got it. He seemed to be learning how things are in her world, and he was understanding things much faster now. "I know it might seem kind of creepy, but I had a small tracking device inserted in me, so no matter what's going on, or if I come up missing, certain people can find me. That's how they caught up with me in New York, remember?" she explained.

"Ahhh," he said. "That *is* kind of creepy! I definitely don't want to know where they inserted it!" he laughed.

She laughed and hit Troy on the back as she started to get into the car. "You're bad for a good boy!"

"Max!" Izy yelled out once they started down the road.

"Yes, Izy," he responded calmly.

"Can we stop at IHOP for some pancakes before we head home?" she asked.

"IHOP?" Troy was stunned.

"Yes, oh my God, I am having a craving for their pancakes so bad right now!" she exclaimed loudly.

"Come on?" she begged. "I never get to go anymore! Isn't there one like right down the street?" she asked Max.

Troy didn't know what to say; he was stumped and still so full from dinner.

"Yes, Izy, I believe there is," Max told her. Izy looked at Troy with her big eyes and a pouty face.

"Come on, Troy, it'll be fun!" she said. "Sure, I guess ... I'm cool, I'm not hungry, but that works for me," he said in a supporting way.

"Yea! To IHOP Max!" she said excitedly. It was pretty late, around 11:00 PM, but IHOP was surprisingly busy. "Max, you want to come in?" Izy offered with a big smile.

"No ... I'm good. I'll just stay with the car," he said.

"Okay, we won't be long," she told him and she and Troy walked in. A hostess greeted them at the front; the restaurant was very busy, but they had several open tables, so they were immediately seated. Almost right away, Troy felt strangely uncomfortable, like people were staring at them; at first he thought he was just imagining it. The waitress came to the table and asked to take their order as she flipped open her order book. Izy started to order her pancakes when she looked up at the waitress; the waitress suddenly gasped very loud, "Oh my God!" She said loud enough for half of the restaurant to hear. "You're Izy!" she yelled out of control. Literally within seconds, their table was surrounded by nearly every other patron in the restaurant. They were pushing and shoving, trying to get close to the table. Many had their phones out, taking photos; several were asking her to sign something, but most just wanted to touch her. Troy was freaking out; he didn't know what to do. Izy was handling it pretty well at first, but then

Troy could see she was getting scared. Troy tried to stand up, but there were just too many people pushing against him. Both he and Izy tried to reason with the crowd to move back, but they would not listen. They pushed into the table harder and harder. Now even Troy was a little scared. One woman actually fell onto his lap! Just as he was about to jump up onto the table and start pushing people back, all of a sudden, Max was standing right in front of the table, shoving people back far enough for Izy and Troy to get up. As Izy got up, Max wrapped her under his arm; Izy grabbed Troy's arm, and they rushed out the door. Camera flashes were going off, people were screaming Izy's name—it was total chaos. Once they were in the car and headed down the road, Izy spoke up first. "I'm sorry, Max!" she told him.

"No worries, all's good," he said.

"I'm sorry to you too, Troy, I didn't think anyone would recognize me in this outfit, and especially this late. I feel really bad," she told Troy. "And . . . I didn't get my pancakes!" she said laughingly but upset nonetheless.

"Oh yes, you did!" a voice from the front announced.

"What?" Izy asked, all excited. "I got you some pancakes, just in case!" Max told her as he handed back a to-go box with pancakes and syrup in it. "Max, you rock!" Izy yelled at him. Izy got her pancakes; she was happy. She and Troy ate them on the way to Troy's hotel.

Max pulled the SUV right to the front of the hotel and got out. The valets started to approach the car, but Max waved them off.

"Izy, I had a great time!" Troy started to say. "I am so glad we got to spend this time together. I think I learned more about you and your life in one night than I would have ever expected," he told her.

"Is that a bad thing or a good thing?" Izy asked rather sheepishly. "Good . . . yea, good. Different, but definitely good," he told her.

"Me too, Troy," Izy responded. "I am so lucky to have someone like you in my life. I had a great day!" she said to him. Awkward moment for both, both having mixed emotions about how they felt at that moment and where they were in their "friendship." Izy started to lean in. Troy wanted to lean into her so badly, but he didn't, and he reached up and grabbed her shoulders, stopping her. Izy looked up.

"We *are* friends, aren't we?" Troy asked.

Izy sat back a little. "Yes, we are!" she understood. Troy pulled Izy's shoulders toward him and kissed Izy on the cheek.

"Good night," he said,

"Good night, Troy!" Izy returned. Troy got out of the car and nodded at Max.

"Good night," he said.

"Good night, Troy," Max replied.

TAKE TWO

Troy woke up early; he had several meetings during the day and a dinner meeting that night. He had a busy day ahead. Just as soon as he got out of the shower, his phone was buzzing. It was Izy: "I had a great time last night, the best!" she said. "Will you have time tomorrow for lunch before you head back?" she asked.

Troy texted back, "Yes, I should, that would be great. I'll call you later today," he replied. "Great!" Izy texted back. Troy finished his first meeting, which went very well. Throughout the meeting, Troy had a tough time concentrating but still managed to pull it off. On his way to his lunch meeting, he received a call from the account he was supposed to be meeting for dinner that night. They requested to reschedule for the next morning and apologized for having to cancel dinner on such short notice. Troy was surprised but not disappointed.

He text Izy right away. "Sorry, I can't do lunch tomorrow . . . so how about dinner tonight?" He laughed as he typed. It was as if Izy was expecting the text. "Dinner is all set, my place seven thirty?" she text back. "I have a special surprise for you!" she told him.

"That sounds great!" Troy replied. *Unexpected, but good, I think*, Troy thought. He pulled in front of the restaurant where he was having his lunch meeting.

"See you then," she replied.

Around seven, as Troy was finishing getting cleaned up to meet Izy for dinner, he got a call on his cell phone.

"Daddy! You haven't called in two days!" Maggie said to Troy, very upset. "Are you okay?" she asked.

"Maggie, I am sooo sorry! I have no excuses. I've just been so busy. I promise I will make it up to you. How are you? Is everything okay?" he asked his daughter. They talked for a while, when Troy received a text from Max. "Downstairs, ready when you are."

Troy made sure not to cut his call with Maggie short; it was more important to him than anything else at that moment. They caught up on everything Maggie, including the exciting news that Maggie was expected to be able to get her cast off in about a week. "That's great news!" Troy told her. When Troy asked his daughter about her brother and her mom, Maggie told him Justin was the same, and that Mom was "not around much." Troy was upset to hear about April and didn't understand what was going on, but he was even more upset for Maggie; sadly Maggie was used to it. "I love you, Daddy, see you soon," Maggie told him.

"I love you too, baby. I should be home in two days. We'll do something special, all of us!" he told her.

"Good night, Daddy!" Troy hung up and threw on his jacket. He was feeling strangely guilty but excited to see Izy again. Actually the more excited he got about seeing Izy, the more guilty he felt, but the excitement and anticipation outweighed the guilt. As he walked out the front door of the hotel, there was Max, waiting with the car door open.

This time, Max was prepared. When Troy got in the car there was an open bottle of champagne waiting for him! Troy laughed, but he did not hesitate to pour himself a drink. The drive up to Izy's house went by quickly, and Troy's stomach didn't bother him at all. "Wow, that really works!" he said to Max. Max just nodded. When they arrived at Izy's, she was not out front waiting for him like the first time. Max stopped the car and got out to open the door for Troy.

"Go on inside, they're expecting you!" he told Troy.

He looked at Max. "Expecting me?" Troy shrugged it off, thanked Max, and walked through the front door. Inside, Maria was waiting for him just inside the foyer. "Good evening, Mr. Troy," she said.

"Good evening, Maria, how are you?" Troy asked politely.

"Just this way, Mr. Troy," she said as she began to walk him down the main hallway. They passed the main dining room, living room, and many other rooms before they arrived at a small kitchen toward the back of the house. Inside, there were all the normal things that a kitchen would have in almost any house including a small eating area. It looked very cozy, and it was very nicely decorated, kind of an old world look, very different from the formal look of the rest of the house. Maria went behind the stove, which was on an island. It smelled like heaven!

"Wow! Maria, what is that fantastic smell?" he asked. "This must be what it smells like in an Italian family's kitchen!" he kidded with her.

"Dinner is almost ready, Mr. Troy," she said. "Why don't you sit down and have some wine, Ms. Izy will be here in a moment," she suggested. Troy went over to the table to sit down; the table was set for two. There was a bottle of wine on the table, so Troy poured the wine into the two glasses that were there. There was a lot of food already on the table—bread, salads, and shrimp—but Troy was a gentleman and was not going to eat or drink until Izy got there.

A few minutes later, Izy walked into the kitchen. "Troy is in the house!" she sang as she danced around the kitchen. Izy walked over to Maria, put her arm around her, and looked into the big pot on the stove. She took a big long sniff. "Smells perfect!" Izy told her. Then she walked over to Troy. He stood up and they hugged. "I'm so glad you're here, this is great!" Izy said excitedly as she sat down. They raised their glasses, toasted, and each took a sip of their wine. "Is it bad of me to say I'm so glad it worked out for us to get together tonight?" she asked with a big smile.

"No, it's fine, it just worked out," Troy told her. "After all, it wasn't yours or my fault. I guess you could say it was meant to be!" Troy suggested.

"Well, anyway, I'm glad your here, I wanted to make up for last night," she told him.

"Make up? Make up for what?" Troy was surprised at the comment; he thought they both had a great night, at least until the IHOP incident.

"I'm sorry you had to go through that craziness at IHOP last night. It was all my fault, I should have known better!" she told him. "Really, Izy, it was no big deal. It all worked out," he said to her. "Well, anyway, that's why I decided it might be better for us to stay in, I hope that's okay with you?" she offered.

"Are you kidding? This is perfect! And whatever Maria has going on is making me drool!" Troy admitted.

"Right!" Izy said loud enough for Maria to hear. Maria smiled. "Maria is my go-to girl for everything, but when I need a special meal, she is the best!" She looked over at Maria when she said it; Maria shrugged it off by waving her hand at them in jest.

They sat eating Maria's especially prepared meal, enjoying every bite. They both commented throughout the dinner how amazing it was. They laughed and talked and ate and drank; they were having a great time. Maria went to leave the kitchen after she served the last portion. "Thank you, Maria! You outdid yourself!" Izy told her. "Truly amazing, Maria, thank you!" Troy said to her. Troy and Izy stayed at the table for a bit longer, finishing their wine and winding down their conversation. They never seemed to not be able to talk to each other and truly enjoyed each other's company—each for their own reasons. After the last drop of wine was gone, Izy leaned in close to Troy like she was going to tell a secret. Troy leaned in too.

"Now it's time for your surprise!" she said, giggling like a schoolgirl.

"You're kidding?" Troy replied. "I thought this was the surprise!" he asked with a puzzled look on his face.

"No! No! Come on!" Izy said. They got up from the table. Troy immediately felt a little woozy, and they walked out into the hall. Izy grabbed his hand and guided him through the maze of her house. After a number of different halls and many turns, things started to look a little familiar to Troy. *I've been here!* he thought to himself. There they were standing in front of the door marked "Izy's Office!" They walked in, the lights were low, music was playing. The curtains to the main windows were open, the city was glittering like a cluster of stars off in the distance.

"Amazing!" Troy told Izy. "What a view!" he gasped as he walked closer to the windows. It looked completely different at night; it almost gave you the feeling you were seeing the city from a plane.

"Come, come!" Izy said all smiles to Troy from one of the couches. "Come sit down," she demanded gently as she patted the couch. Troy walked over and sat down next to her. "Are you ready for your surprise?" she asked with a big smile on her face.

"You're scaring me a bit, but…yes, I think I am!" Troy was both very intrigued and a little nervous about where this was going. Izy reached under the table and pulled out an unusual shaped bottle with a clear liquid inside. "Ta-da!" she sang.

"Is that what I think it is?" Troy asked, smiling with the palm of one hand on his forehead. They both started to laugh. Izy had gotten them a bottle of the drink they had when they were in Basil's restaurant back in the little village of Dekemhare.

"This is a reminder of the first time we met and when we became friends!" she told him.

"Holy smoke, how did you get this?" Troy asked, completely astonished. He knew this drink was local and was only made in that village. Izy explained that she was able to get the drink from a friend who was traveling through Yemen. "I asked him if he would make a detour and pick this up for me, and he did," she said. "That was some kind of a detour!" Troy said. "That had to be at least five hundred miles out of his way!" he guessed.

"Maybe so," Izy said as she handed the bottle to Troy. "This is really a fantastic surprise! Thank you for this, Izy, this is great!" Troy told her as he pulled the cork from the bottle. Troy took a sniff from the top of the bottle. "Oh, boy, I remember this stuff!" he laughed. He poured them each a glass of the drink. "How did you even know what to call it?" he asked. "I didn't, but when my friend got to the restaurant, I told him to ask for Basil. Once he mentioned us to Basil, Basil knew exactly what I wanted! How great is that! Oh, Basil also said to say hi to both of us and wished us much health, happiness, and lots of babies!"

Troy choked and laughed at the same time! "Well, that's just funny!" he said, not knowing what to say. Izy laughed hard at Troy's reaction, admitting she almost peed her pants!

"He also wanted to know when we would come back to visit!" she told Troy.

"That is just too cool! What a great guy," he said as he raised his glass. "Here is to my best friend, may this be just the first of many great adventures together!" Troy said proudly. Izy smiled but inside was a little taken back by the toast. She raised her glass, they toasted, and they then both took a drink. The reactions to the drink were nearly the same: "Whoa!"

They sat on the couch for some time, reminiscing, talking, laughing, and drinking. It didn't take long and the bottle was empty. "Oh ... that's too bad," Troy said.

"What do you mean?" Izy asked him.

"We are all out!" he held up the bottle to show her that the bottle was bone dry.

"Are you kidding?" she said jokingly. "You think I went to all that trouble for just one bottle! See that box over there?" She pointed to a large wooden crate on the other side of the room.

The crate was covered in freight and customs tags. He turned back to Izy and smiled. He got up from the couch, more than a little wobbly; he walked over to the crate and took off the lid. He looked in the crate; it was full of the same liquor bottles, all covered in straw. He picked one up and looked at it. "Look! Our favorite year!" he joked.

Izy laughed. "What are you waiting for, let's open it up!" she yelled at him. Troy carefully made his way back to his spot on the couch and plopped down next to Izy. Izy laughed at him; Troy is not a big drinker, and it was starting to show. He pulled the cork out of the bottle and poured them a new glass.

By halfway through the third bottle, they were both feeling no pain. They were leaning back on the couch, resting theirs heads on a couple of pillows. The conversation died down to a couple of chuckles. They both had their eyes closed, relaxed, feeling great, and enjoying the music. Troy was amazed at how comfortable and relaxed he was. He was trying to remember the last time he felt this way, if ever. A song he recognized from when he was a kid came on. His mind was a little cloudy, but he remembered it was always one of his favorites; he used to sing it in the shower all the time, at least until one day when his mom walked in on him! Izy immediately started to hum to the song. Her voice was amazing, so beautiful. Troy opened his eyes and turned to look at Izy. Her eyes were closed; she was humming like the song was in her. She looked so beautiful. The sound of her voice was mesmerizing. The song was a blues gospel song, often sung in church when Troy was younger. He knew Izy could sing, but this was the first time he'd ever heard her voice in person. Troy has heard everything she has ever recorded, at least since he met her. Troy had a new appreciation for rock and roll even Izy's style of heavy rock and roll. Izy and her music are his kids' absolute favorite, her music was always on—around the house, in the car, and in their headphones. Even his wife April was a big fan, likely because the kids were. Until Troy met Izy, he never really listened to hear music, not his thing; he put up with it when he was home because the kids loved it so much. Maggie had it on around the house all the time so she could sing and dance to it.

Troy became enveloped in the music and Izy's humming. Without thinking about it, he suddenly started to sing! Quietly at first, then louder. Izy sat up quickly when she heard him, but she did not stop humming. She was afraid he would stop. She was in shock as she looked at Troy in absolute disbelief that he was singing. She gradually changed from humming to singing along with Troy but in a lower voice. Within seconds, they were both singing, harmonizing seamlessly. Izy was stunned at how beautiful Troy's voice was. She was blown away with his range. He followed her throughout the song hitting all the different notes and pitches. Izy couldn't believe what she was hearing! She stopped singing so she could hear just Troy. The song was coming to an end when Troy realized Izy had stopped; he opened his eyes and sat up.

"What happened?" he asked her. "Why did you stop, was I that bad?" he asked surprised.

Izy gasped, "Troy…that was amazing! You…were amazing!" she said so excitedly as she grabbed his hand. "You never told me you could sing!" she exclaimed. "I'm a little bit in shock right now! Do you see the chills on my arms? I have chills!" she lifted her arm to show him.

Troy laughed. "Wow, I think it's time to cut you off!" he said. "I was just going along with it, it was kind of fun," he admitted to her. "But…I cannot sing, maybe to myself in the shower!" he laughed.

"I'm not kidding around!" she told him. "Where did you learn that song, where did you learn to sing like that?" she asked. Troy wasn't sure if she was being serious or if it was the alcohol that was doing the asking; they both had a lot to drink. Her face said she was serious, but it was hard for Troy to think she really meant it. "That song is one of my absolute favorites!" she admitted.

"Me too!" Troy told her. "But really I never sang before in my life, except once in awhile when I was a kid, and then only in the shower!" he admitted to her.

"Troy, come with me, I want to show you something!" she demanded.

"Again?" he joked. She stood up and took Troy's hand in a very commanding way. They walked toward the door to the room but instead went to the top of the spiral staircase just to the right of the door. Troy knew it was there but never felt right asking about it. He looked over the rail and started to get dizzy.

"Where does this go?" he asked.

"Down!" Izy responded. "This is a very special place to me, only a few people have ever been down there!" she said very seriously. Troy thought of a few jokes but decided to keep them to himself. *Must be the booze*, he thought. She held his hand and they started down the very steep steps. It was a good thing she did because Troy slipped more than once on the way down. Once on the bottom step, Izy let go of his hand. Troy took the last step and then tried to stabilize himself, still holding on to the rail. He looked up and saw a room with all kinds of instruments around, including a small beautiful black piano in the middle of the room. There was a bunch of electronics on a table with chairs in front of it facing what looked like a small sound booth. The only reason he guessed it was a sound booth was because it had several microphones in it, and it was surrounded by big glass windows. There were no windows to the outside in the room at all; Troy thought the room might be below ground level. This room was not like any other part of the house; it was not fancy, nor was there any red furniture.

The walls were lined with gold and platinum albums. There were easily a hundred photos on the walls with Izy and some well-known somebody in every one of them. Every album cover Troy knew of was framed and hanging on the wall. One of the walls had a wood-and-steel case that was full of awards and more photos. It looked like there was even an Emmy inside! Izy walked over to what turned out to be a sound board, flipped a switch, and it lit up like a Christmas tree.

"What are you doing?" he asked. "You'll see ... look around or get yourself something to eat or drink from the fridge," she said, pointing toward a wall.

"Fridge?" he asked quietly as he looked around the room. "There is no fridge down here!" He barely got the words out of his mouth when he saw what looked like a brass handle coming out of the wall Izy had pointed at. *Strange*, he thought. He grabbed the handle and pulled it. Sure enough, a refrigerator! "Wow! That's cool!" he shouted to Izy. She turned to see Troy playing with the refrigerator door, opening and closing it, watching as it appeared and disappeared into the wall.

"I think there's beer in there, will you grab me one?" she asked him.

"Sure!" he replied and took out a beer for each of them. Troy walked over to Izy and handed her the open beer.

"Thanks! Almost ready," she told him.

"Ready for what?" he asked.

"Just a couple more minutes, and I'll show you!" she smiled at him. Troy walked around the room taking in all of the very cool instruments and looking at the photos. The only piece of furniture in the room beside the chairs in front of the sound and mixing boards (Izy's words) was a hugely overstuffed couch chair thing. *I wonder how you get out of that thing?* he thought quietly.

"Okay, all ready!" Izy stated with confidence.

"Oh, that's good!" Troy responded sarcastically. "What are we ready for ... exactly?" he asked again. Troy figured Izy was going to play some of her new music for him or maybe even sing a song. Either way, he thought, *How unbelievably cool would that be!* Izy walked over to him and took his hand. She escorted him around the table and inside of the small sound booth. Troy got very excited, not only was she going to sing for him but right in front of him! She sat him down on a stool in front of one of the microphones. "Here you go!" she said as she handed him some headphones.

"What do I need these for?" he asked her.

"We are going to sing together!" she told him.

"Whaaaat?" he laughed. "Who's going to sing?" he asked.

"We are!" she told him.

"Nooo ... I don't think so!" he said as he started to get up from the stool.

"I would love to hear *you* sing, but there's no way I'm singing! Especially *with* you!" he added.

"Troy, listen ... relax, it's no big deal. We're just going to do what we did upstairs, even the same song," she explained. "A great song that we both love," she added. "Just put on your headphones and I'll start the song, close your eyes, and listen to me. I've already taken out the other voice. If you feel it, like you did upstairs, then just sing. I promise, you're going to love it!" Troy was a little confused but intrigued. He thought even if he sucks, how many people get to sing with Izy! He laughed to himself.

"This is totally nuts, you know that right?" he suggested.

"It's no big deal, this will be fun!" she tried to sound convincing.

"You're not like, recording this or anything, are you?" he asked like he might be thinking about doing it.

"No, no. This is just for fun! I promise, unless you want me to record it?" she teased him. He smiled a coy grin with total disapproval.

Troy and Izy put on their headphones. Izy leaned into her microphone. "Hello, Troy!" she said in a deep voice. Troy could hear her perfectly through his headphones. She asked him to say something into his microphone so she could do a "sound check."

Troy said, "Uhh, hello, my name is Troy!" he sputtered out.

"Perfect!" she told him.

"I'm glad you think so!" they laughed. Troy took a big swig of his beer; Izy started the music. He was nervous but not as much as he thought he might be. He sat quietly as Izy looked Troy right in the eyes as she started to sing. "Oh my God!" he thought very loudly to himself. He was not prepared for the pure sound and the power of Izy's voice. It was like her voice filled his whole body. Izy's voice was so perfect Troy was overwhelmed. By the time Izy got to the second line of this great song, a tear uncontrollably came down Troy's cheek. He heard this song a thousand times but never like this, never so powerful and emotional. Troy didn't know why he was so overcome with emotions. Izy stopped singing and turned off the music.

"Troy, are you okay?" she asked him.

"Yes, I'm sorry. That was, well, that was…perfect!" he told her. Izy got up from her stool, walked over, and hugged Troy. She grabbed his face with both of her hands and pulled his face in close to hers.

"That wasn't me," she told him softly.

"What do you mean?" he asked.

"That was you motivating me." Izy pulled her stool right next to Troy's, then she moved her microphone into position. She sat down and picked up Troy's hand. "Close your eyes," she told him. "Just listen and let the music inside of you just like you did upstairs, don't think about it, think about all the cool things we've done in our short friendship and what that means to you." She started the music again. Troy took another big swig of his beer, then he took a deep breath and closed his eyes. The part of the song where they were supposed to start singing was coming up; Izy gently squeezed Troy's hand. Troy and Izy began to sing the song together. Troy started out softly; Izy was powerful. She squeezed his hand a little harder. Troy started to sing harder, both in volume and emotion. By the third line of the first verse, Troy was all in. They were singing in perfect harmony, too beautiful to describe. They were both completely lost in the moment. Troy opened his eyes, and Izy was looking at him smiling. It was amazing; no, it was unbelievable! As the end of the first verse approached, Izy squeezed Troy's hand again and nodded at him. Troy knew what that meant. There was a part of the song coming up that Izy wanted him to sing alone. He remembered when he used to sing it in the shower; it was his favorite part of the song. He would always go all out but wondered if he should do that now. He stopped thinking about it, closed his eyes again, and just let go.

It came out so naturally. It was perfect, Izy thought as he was singing. They sang this song as if they had been singing it together for years. Now Izy was the one dumbfounded! She could not believe her ears! She has sung with many, many different people, but it never felt like this before; it always felt in many ways like it needed to be forced. They were in the last verse of the song; it was a long multi-range piece with a big and powerful finish. To Izy's surprise, Troy stood up as he was singing it. Izy had visible chills all over her body. Together they hit every note in a perfect and smooth balance. Troy was fully vested into the piece, voice, mind, and body as he raised his hands over his head at the crest of the song, then he lowered his arms, and he brought his voice back down, Izy filled in softly behind him. As the song came to a soft close, they were now singing with their faces inches away from each other, staring into each other's eyes. The song ended, but they did not move. Izy could feel Troy's breath on her face; she leaned in a little closer, neither blinked. Izy moved slowly closer, Troy did not move, still breathing hard, trying to catch his breath. They kissed—a passionate, hard, long kiss. Troy reached up and grabbed Izy's head to pull her even tighter to him. Izy threw her arms around Troy's neck. Then they slowly pulled their heads back, parting their lips from each other. They both opened their eyes, emotions were high; it was the most amazing feeling Troy has ever felt in his life. Izy sat back, turned off the equipment, and took off her headphones. "Troy..." She took a deep breath. "that was the most beautiful thing I have ever done in my life," she said to him softly.

All at once, Troy had a terrible rush of adrenaline race through his body. He came back into focus; Izy could see something was wrong. "Izy . . . I have no words," he said softly as he pulled off his headphones. "I can't explain to you how I feel, but I screwed up. I should never have let this happen . . . this is all my fault," he told her as his head swirled with emotion and alcohol.

"No, Troy, no! This just happened!" She tried to explain. "We just got caught up in the moment. We just got caught up in each other!" Izy knew what was going through Troy's mind. "Izy, I'm married! I have children!" he blurted out.

"I know! I know!" was her reaction. "Can't we just say we made a mistake and laugh this off, like friends do?" she asked pleading, even though that's not really how she felt. What Izy felt she has never felt before, even before the kiss, she knew she was falling in love with Troy. She knew that for the first time in her life what she felt was real.

"Izy . . . I have to go!" Troy walked out of the booth and started for the spiral staircase. Izy reached out for him. "Okay, I understand, you're right, but can't we just talk for a minute before you do?" she asked him. "Are you going to be all right? Can I call you later?" she asked him. He stopped at the bottom of the stairs. "I'm not sure we can be friends anymore, Izy. I don't think that's possible," he said as he started up the stairs. Izy's heart dropped to her stomach. "What have I done?" she pleaded with herself. "What have I done!"

Troy quickly walked through the house, keeping the smoke detectors on his right. As he walked past the main kitchen, he saw Maria inside, so he stopped. "Oh, hi, Mr. Troy!" she said. "Maria, I wanted to say thank you for such a fantastic dinner, it was really special," he told her. "I have to go," he blurted out.

Maria tried to say something, but Troy was already out of sight. Troy knew if he didn't get out as fast as possible, he might not let himself leave. He made it to the front foyer; as he did, his phone vibrated. He took it out of his pocket; it was Izy calling. He didn't answer. He walked out the front door, and there was Max with the car! Troy did not say anything and got into the back. "How did he know I was leaving?" he asked himself. "Strange." Barely out of the driveway, his phone vibrated again. It was a text from Izy. "Troy, please don't leave. Let's talk about this. I know we made a mistake. It's really all my fault. We can fix this," she said. Troy deleted the text. "Oh man!" is all he said.

The car pulled in front of Troy's hotel. Troy didn't even allow the valet to open the door. He all but ran into the hotel not saying anything to Max. He went straight to the elevators and to his room. When he walked into his room, the first thing he saw was the red light flashing on the hotel phone, telling him he had a message. He very quickly got his things together and went back down stairs and checked out.

"There are messages for you, Mr. Anderson, would you like me to get them?" the man at the front desk asked him.

"No, that's okay, I know who it is," he replied. Troy was a basket case of emotions; he had the best and worst night of his life. Leaving Izy's house was one of the hardest things he's ever had to do. Outside he grabbed a cab; he really wanted to go to the airport so he could go home and hug his kids, but he had to go to an important meeting the next morning so he couldn't leave Los Angeles yet. He had the cab take him to a hotel close to the airport where he checked in for the night and went to his room. He opened a bottle of water that was in the room and practically drank the whole thing in one drink. His head was swirling with confusion and alcohol. He sat on the edge of the bed holding his head in his hands; his phone vibrated. It was Izy again. He turned off his phone. He drank the last of the water, got up, and went to the small desk in the room. He picked up the phone and started to call his house. "Damn it!" he said out loud as he quickly hung up the phone before the first ring. "Am I nuts?" he asked himself with the clock on the desk telling him it was two in the morning.

The next morning, Troy could feel the effects of all of the drinking he had done the night before; it was a doozy of a hangover. He pulled himself together, got dressed, went downstairs, jumped into a cab, and headed for his meeting. All the way there he was tempted to turn his phone back on but didn't. "I wonder if Izy called again?" he was asking himself. Troy didn't know it, but she called his cell phone many times and even called the hotel he was originally in, only to find out Troy had checked out the night before. Izy was devastated. "I ruined the only real friendship I've ever had!" she admitted to Maria. "Except for you, of course!" Izy told her, trying to smile and hold back tears at the same time. Maria put her hand on Izy's shoulder.

"Things always have a way of working out." She smiled and handed her her morning coffee. Izy started to cry. Maria held her tightly. Troy pulled in front of the office building where the meeting was. The meeting went well, not fast enough for Troy, but he was more productive than he thought would be possible. He left the meeting and went straight to the airport. He never turned his phone back on.

GUILTY OR NOT GUILTY

Troy landed in the mid afternoon; his family wasn't expecting him until later that night, so he grabbed a cab home. He walked into the front door to the surprise of his son. "Dad! You're home!" he shouted as he put his book down and went to Troy. Maggie came running in from the next room. "Daddy!" she ran up to him and gave him a hug. "I thought you weren't going to be home until later?" she asked him all smiles.

"You're right, I wasn't, but I was able to catch an earlier flight," he told them. Just then, April appeared from the hallway, dressed to go out, putting her earrings in as she was walking toward him.

"Well, hello!" she said, surprised and with a touch of sarcasm. "What are you doing home so early?" she asked with the tinniest of smiles.

"I finished early and was able to catch an earlier flight," he explained. She walked up to him and gave him a small kiss on the cheek. "And what...you don't call anymore?" she snapped. Troy knew this was going to come up so he was prepared. "Unfortunately I lost my phone yesterday. I think I may have left it in one of the cabs, but no one has fessed up yet," he explained. "I've contacted the phone company, and they have already turned the phone off. They told me they will have a new phone for me tomorrow." He went on with his lie. He knew that Izy would be trying to get ahold of him. Strangely, before this incident, Troy never cared about hiding her number or texts from his wife. "If she sees it, she sees it, then I'll be forced to explain my friendship with her." Otherwise, if April never saw it, Troy didn't feel he would have to explain anymore than he needed to. But now things were different, and this he didn't want to have to explain.

"Well, that's nice," was the only thing April said to him. Not a "welcome home," not a "I missed you," just "That's nice." Justin went to sit back down and picked up his book. Maggie was still hugging Troy. April started to head back down the hall.

"I thought that since I'm home early, we could all go out to dinner together?" he announced to them. The kids got excited and were ready to go.

April stopped and turned back to Troy. "You know I can't. I have the Fox Charity event tonight," she explained.

"Well, can't you *not go*?" Troy asked. "Maybe make an exception so we can all be together tonight?" he asked in a stronger tone that April was not familiar with.

"No, I can't not go, what a ridiculous thing to say to me! And what's with that tone of voice?" she asked abruptly.

"You know . . . that's okay," Troy started. "Me and the kids will go out and have some fun, you enjoy your 'event'!" he snapped back. April turned and continued back down the hall. "Whatever works," she said as she walked away.

That went well, he thought to himself sarcastically. The kids were very excited to go out with their dad; they ran and got themselves together, not even allowing Troy enough time to change his clothes.

Troy was more confused than ever. He was angry, sad and unsure of himself. "What happened to April and me?" he asked himself. "What went wrong? Is it me?" He was very upset about the short and unpleasant encounter with his wife. After all, she was the reason he left Izy's house; she was the reason he came home right away—that and his guilt! "*I don't understand why I feel so guilty? My wife obviously hates me!*" he told himself. Troy thought the whole way home on his flight that he should really try to recommit himself to his marriage and try to reconnect with April. Although it wouldn't be the first time he's tried, he still felt a responsibility to try again. "*I'm not sure if a can or if it's worth it anymore*," he thought, but he wasn't ready to give it up, if for no other reason than for his kids. For them he was willing to do whatever he had to. Troy and April's marriage had never been perfect, "except for how they raised the kids," Troy would often think to himself. His kids were perfect in his eyes. April, on the other hand, has never been as emotionally invested in their relationship as Troy was and had hoped for. When they first met, he and April were inseparable, spending most of their time together. But after the wedding and after Troy started working for April's dad, things began to change.

April began to change. She was a different person than the woman he dated and married. Yes, she was still the major socialite and busy body, but how she interacted with Troy was different; she seemed disconnected from him. She was not warm and giving like she was when they first met. Troy had tried many times to be the strong one and make the suggestions or offers to do things together to help their relationship, but April either never wanted to or was just too busy for him. It's funny how April's personality was so attractive to Troy when they first met; now it was the very reason why they were growing apart.

As he and the kids buckled up to go to dinner, Troy thought, *I can't let this happen, I can't let it get worse. I'm going to try to change things*, he confidently told himself. *It's half my responsibility anyway*, he thought.

"Come on, Daddy! What are you doing? Let's go!" Justin was demanding as Troy was just sitting there staring off into the distance.

"Oh! Sorry, all right! Let's go!" he started the car, and they pulled away.

The next morning, Troy was in his office very early. He ordered flowers online to send to his wife with a note that said, "Just thinking about you. Sorry you weren't able to make it to dinner last night. Love, Troy." *That's a good start*, he thought. It turns out it wasn't. Apparently April took the flowers to one of her charity events and never mentioned them to Troy, not even a hint. As he was going over some of his paperwork from the previous week, Frank walked by his office but didn't come in; he didn't even look at him. *That was strange*," he thought but fluffed it off as normal for Frank. Troy knew he needed to get a new phone right away; it was his top priority of the day. He took his cell phone out of his briefcase; he sat there looking at it for a while wondering how many messages where on it from Izy, if any. Then he put it in his top desk drawer. He pondered the thought that he will never see her again, which made him both angry and sad. "I can't believe I walked out on Izy!" he kept thinking. What he is going through at this very moment is exactly the kind of thing he would call to talk to her about.

I guess I lost my best friend, he thought. Just as the thought was in his head, in walks Eddie. "Well, there you are Mister, what the hell!" he started in on Troy. "I've been trying to get ahold of you for days!" It was a slight exaggeration, but it didn't stop him from going on. "You haven't bought me lunch in weeks! I'm pretty sure it's your turn?" he said loudly with a big smile on his face, a face you had to learn to love. Troy could only smile. Eddie has bought lunch maybe five or six times in the five years they've know each other, but Troy didn't care; it was worth it to him.

"I think you're right!" Troy answered. "How about today?" he asked Eddie. Eddie was surprised that Troy didn't want to argue about who was buying lunch.

"Sure!" he said to Troy. "I just have to stop at the phone store on the way," Troy told Eddie. "That works for me!" Eddie said.

On the way to lunch, Troy and Eddie stopped in a phone store to get Troy a new phone. A Salesman approached the two of them and asked if he could help. Troy told him he needed a new phone. When the salesmen asked if he was going to be upgrading from an older phone, Troy said yes. Troy and Eddie picked out a new phone for him and the salesman was getting the new phone set up when the salesman asked Troy, "You want to use your existing number, right?" he asked. Troy hadn't thought about that. Using his existing number would mean everyone that has his number now would still be able to contact him; no, he had no choice but to ask for a new number. "No, actually I need a new number please," Troy told him. "Oh, okay that's fine, would you like me to turn off the old number?" he asked. Troy didn't think about that either. He knew he had to have a new phone number and he knew the right thing to do was to turn off his old number, but that meant severing any ties to Izy one hundred percent. He stood there thinking.

"Hello!" Eddie barked at him. "We are going to lunch, aren't we? What's do you have to think about, just turn off your old phone!" Troy looked at the salesman. "You know, let's hold off on that for right now, let's keep the old number active," he told him.

"No problem, but technically you'll have two phones and two numbers that you're going to get billed for, at least until you decide to turn your old one off," he explained.

"Yes, that's fine," Troy answered. Eddie looked at him like he was nuts. "Why would you do that?" he asked, dumbfounded. "Uh, I have some information associated with that phone that I need, and until I know that all my contacts have my new phone number, it's important to keep it on," he explained, doing some quick thinking. "Oh, that sort of makes sense," Eddie said as he pondered the complexity of the whole thing. "Man, losing your phone sucks!" Eddie remarked.

"Yes, it does!" Troy responded.

Once at lunch, Troy started to mass text his new phone number to the contacts he knew by heart—like his wife, kids, Frank, Eddie, and a few others. "That was a little weird!" Eddie told him, referring to the new phone and phone number. "Why would you want a new number, what a hassle!" he questioned.

"Yea I know. No explanation really, I just wanted a new number," he told Eddie casually. Eddie leaned forward and grabbed Troy's phone off the table. "Cool phone, though!" he said, completely backing away from the subject. "Speaking of weird," Troy started, "has Frank been acting more unusual than usual to you lately?"

Eddie laughed. "No not really, why?"

Troy went on to tell him about his morning and how Frank didn't come into his office.

"I'd consider that a blessing!" Eddie laughed. "I know, I do, trust me. It's just strange. In the seven years I've worked for him, he has never not come to see me the morning that I first get back from a road trip. It's probably nothing. I was just wondering." They went on to talk through lunch—some about business, some about Eddie's latest crazy stunts.

It was funny to Troy that Eddie has never asked him about Izy since the first time he told Eddie about her and how they met. There is no question that it was a pretty crazy story, but he was sure Eddie knew it wasn't made up. Never once did he bring her up or ask if Troy was talking to her. That didn't seem like Eddie. There was no way Eddie forgot. *Maybe he thinks that was all there was to it, and now he doesn't want to embarrass me by bringing it up!* There were several occasions where Troy thought about bringing her up to Eddie, but then, he thought maybe it was better to just keep it this way; that way, no one gets hurt, and no one accidentally says something they'd regret later. Troy was good with it. Izy would remain his "imaginary" best friend. No one needed to know more.

Coming back from their lunch, Troy and Eddie walked into the front lobby area of their office. Troy started to go left toward his office and Eddie to the right. Frank walked into the lobby area. "Oh, hey, Frank!" Troy called out. Frank turned to him without stopping.

"Troy," he acknowledged and walked to the receptionist and started talking to her. Troy looked back at Eddie who saw the whole thing. Eddie held up his hands as if to say "I don't get it" and walked on toward his office, trying to avoid having to interact with Frank. Troy walked to his office as well, the whole time thinking how weird Frank is acting. "I wonder what's going on?" he was asking himself. He sat at his desk thinking he might call Frank and go to his office but then he thought maybe it would be better to finish his reports and e-mail them to Frank to see if he gets any kind of a response from that. Troy put his new phone down on his desk. He already had a text from Eddie. "Okay, you're right, that was weird! What's up with that?' he texted.

Troy texted him back. "I don't know, not sure if I want to know! Let me know if you hear anything!' Troy asked. Troy was looking at his new phone and his short contact list. He knew he needed to turn on his old phone in order to get some of his key contacts onto his new phone. He took his older phone out of the drawer and set it next to the new one. He turned it on; after a few seconds of powering up, the phone made a couple of different sounds, one indicating he had voicemails and another indicating he had at least one text. He decided he had no choice but to check them just in case it might be a business call or in case it was something important he needed to know.

He checked his text messages first; there was only one. Troy got nervous and kind of excited; his stomach was dancing around. Then he saw it was from Eddie.

"Dude! Where are you? Call me! Let's go to lunch tomorrow so we can catch up!"

Well I guess he was telling me the truth! Troy thought. He was a little surprised that there was no text from Izy, actually he was disappointed. Then he went to his voicemail; he had three messages. The first one was from his wife; it must have come when he was on his flight from Los Angeles to Chicago. Her message was short and to the point: "Troy, I don't know when you are scheduled to come in tonight, but you'll have to take a cab home. I have to be at a charity event tonight. I'll see you tomorrow," she said. *Wow! That was heartfelt!* Troy thought.

The next message was from Eddie. "Dude! Where are you? When are you going to be back in the office? Let me know so we can go to lunch! See ya!" Troy laughed out loud.

The last message was from Izy. For the first several seconds, there was no sound, then she spoke up. "Troy, I know you are very upset, I can't even begin to tell you how sorry I am, the whole thing…it was totally my fault. Our friendship means everything to me," she said with a sad and lonely voice, it almost sounded to Troy like she might be crying. "Please call me so we can talk about it, I know we can make this right and be friends again. Please call me when you can," she ended the call. Troy's stomach was turning and his heart was pounding. He felt terrible…sick that he was hurting her. That was not what he wanted; he wished he could somehow believe he could make it right, but he didn't see how that was possible. To be around Izy, after what they experienced together, is something he didn't think he could handle. He thought about that one moment so much it was hard to concentrate on anything else. That moment was something; even though he knew it was wrong, he would never take back. It was a moment in his life he will never forget or even regret. He got the contacts he needed from his old phone and then turned the phone back off.

THE UNEXPECTED

Several months had gone by and Izy was becoming a memory; sometimes the whole thing seemed more like a dream than a reality, except for the kiss. There wasn't a day that went by that he didn't reflect on that moment. Troy never had his old phone number disconnected, and every once in a while, he would turn it on to see if there were any messages; there weren't. Troy's life basically went back to normal, except for his relationship with his father-in-law Frank. Frank went out of his way not to talk to Troy except when he had to, like a mandatory meeting or at one of Troy's kids' functions. It was very strange. Troy tried to talk to April about it a couple of times, but her only response was "You're just imagining it," she would tell him. *Sure, that helps*, Troy thought. So he just accepted it the way it was. Truthfully he didn't care; the less interaction with Frank, the better. It was just such a radical change that it had him confused or at times, even a little concerned. His life with April didn't change much either. He tried and tried to get her to go out with him, to sit down and just talk with him; he even tried to set up a weekend to go away together, just the two of them, but it wasn't going to happen. About the only time they were together was when they were out with the kids, and even then, they didn't really talk except about who was going to pick up who, when, and things like that. Most evenings, April was out of the house doing her "charity thing." It was depressing to Troy; he used to spend more time with his roommates in college than he does with his wife. The demeaning arguments got worse and became more frequent. It was like April was trying to hurt Troy. "*Why is she so angry at me*?" Almost everything he did or said would set her off. Troy didn't understand why or what happened that his wife would shut him out so completely. Eddie's answer was that April was having an affair with one of her charity friends! "Yea, I don't think so!" Troy would always respond.

"Hey, you never know? I mean…you *are* on the road a lot!" Eddie would explain.

"This is my wife you are talking about!" Troy would snap at him.

"Okay, I'm just saying, that's all!" Eddie would reply back. The only silver lining was that Troy got to spend a lot more time with his kids, that part he loved.

Troy still traveled a great deal, most of the time to the West Coast. Every time he would go to Los Angeles, he couldn't help but think about Izy. He would fantasize about running into her somewhere. One time he even went back to the restaurant where they had dinner at the beach in the off chance of running into her. Still conflicted, still confused, he would get mad at himself. "What am I doing?" he would scold himself. "How stupid am I?" Besides, the last thing he would want is to run into her while she was out on a date or something. "That would suck!" he would say to himself. He never ran into her, but she was always around, no matter where he was, on the West Coast or at home. If his kids weren't blasting her music in the house or in his car, then her music would be on in a restaurant he was eating in, or she would be on a magazine cover or two or three. Izy was always around; she was everywhere. Some days he would pick up his old phone to call her but then talk himself out of it. "Not a good idea, besides she probably wouldn't take my calls anymore." Other days he would see or hear her so much, everywhere he went, he couldn't take it and would just lock himself in his office for hours at a time.

One Saturday afternoon, Troy and his family, including April who would only go now and then, were at Eddie's house for a barbecue. A fairly common occasion that Troy always liked, it was a good diversion from his everyday life. Eddie has been married to his wife Barb for two or three years longer than April and Troy. Barb was one of April's best friends in college, which is where Barb met Eddie. Eddie and Troy became friends through their girlfriends—now wives. It was no accident that they ended up both working for the same company. Eddie and Barb have two children, Missy, fourteen, and Nathan, twelve. All the kids get along great. It was a beautiful day, not too hot with a nice afternoon breeze. Everyone was outside enjoying the beautiful day while Eddie was cooking. The adults were sitting at a table next to the barbecue having drinks; music was on in the background. Three of the kids were running around playing on the grass; Justin was reading a book in the shade. April was in an unusually happy mood, engaging with Eddie and his wife Barb and even Troy now and then. *This is great!* Troy thought. Everyone was having a really nice time. Troy was chugging down the last of his beer when a song he immediately recognized came on the radio.

Troy choked and his beer went flying out of his mouth, nearly missing April! "What's wrong with you!" April shouted. "You almost spit on me!" She was super pissed off even though Troy missed her.

"Are you all right, Troy?" Eddie asked as Barb wiped the table of any beer that landed on it.

"Yes, yes, I'm fine, sorry about that!" the lyrics to the song started. "Holy shit!" Troy belted out, startling everyone.

"What the hell Troy?" April snapped at him. Eddie looked at Troy as if he had two heads. "Dude! What's going on? Are you okay?" he asked, very concerned. "Eddie, can you do me a favor and turn up the music a little?" he requested. Strange request, but Eddie turned it up. The three of them stared at Troy, uncertain of what he was going to do or say next. Troy sat there, listening to the song with his mouth hanging open; he realized he was listening to the song *he* and Izy sang together in the basement of her house . . . on the radio!

Maggie came running up. "Eddie, can you turn it up, this is my absolute favorite song!" she requested.

"Sure!" he replied and turned it up.

"What do you mean your favorite song?" Troy asked his daughter.

"It's the best!" she told him. "How long have you been listening to it?" he asked very confused.

"Oh, I don't know, maybe a week," she replied.

"A week!" he asked, shocked.

"Troy, what is wrong with you?" April snapped at him. He couldn't believe it; he was listening to the song—*the* song he and Izy sang together, once, while drunk and goofing around in her studio. "I thought she said she wasn't recording it?" he said under his breath.

"What?" Eddie asked.

"Oh, nothing, sorry," Troy replied. "Do you know this song?" he asked Eddie.

"Of course, dude, I downloaded it a couple of days ago, isn't it awesome?" he asked.

"Yea, sure, awesome," he answered, barely able to breath. "This isn't rock and roll, I thought rock and roll was her thing?" he asked generally.

"It is, Daddy, but she decided to do this song with this guy and now it's number one!" Maggie told him. Troy put his head in his hands and bent over in his chair. He thought he was going to be sick.

"Number one?" he repeated.

"Dude, where have you been? Everyone is talking about it!" He sat up, his face as white as it could be.

They must not know, right? How could they know? Otherwise someone would have said something, right? he was thinking to himself while panicking at the same time.

Troy truly felt like he was going to be sick and excused himself to go to the bathroom. His head was swirling. *What's going on?* he kept asking himself. He splashed cold water on his face; he'd look at himself in the mirror, then he'd splash himself again. *Okay, it's not a dream! Oh my God, what am I going to do if anyone finds out! How will I ever explain this!* he started to panic again.

Eddie showed up at the door, "Hey, Troy! Are you okay in there?" he asked. "Come on, food's ready!" he shouted through the door. Troy opened the bathroom door and walked out. "You look terrible!" he told Troy. "Did you see a ghost or something?" Eddie joked as they walked back outside together.

"You have no idea!" Troy thought.

"No idea!" When they got back to the table, the food was all ready and sitting on the table. Eddie handed Troy a fresh beer. The food smelled great, but Troy wasn't sure if he would be able to eat. April and Barb had already started.

"Troy, you need to eat something," April commanded. Troy sat down and put a small amount of food on his plate. The two wives continued their conversation. "So who do you think it is?" April asked Barb.

"I have no idea!" she answered. "It's all anyone is talking about!" she added.

"I know! I even heard that one radio station is giving out a reward if you know who he is?" April told her.

"Oh, I heard that too!" Eddie chimed in. "I heard they were giving away ten thousand dollars if you knew and had proof!" he said all excited.

"Have you heard some of the names people are suggesting? It's so funny!" Barb added. Troy was in complete disbelief; he could not believe what he was hearing. "If you know who *who* is?" Troy asked the group, trying to be somewhat naive about it.

"The male singer in the Izy song, you goof!" April answered smartly. "Yeah, Izy released this song but won't say who the male singer is!" Barb told him. "It's all kind of exciting, isn't it!" April added.

"Exciting?" Troy was not in his right mind. "Sounds like a publicity stunt to me!" he said with authority.

"You think?" Eddie asked.

"No, I heard the guy agreed to do the song with her but only on the condition he would not be named!" Barb told everyone.

"That's just silly!" April offered her opinion. Troy tried to eat something. It remained the topic of conversation till the end of the get-together, even Maggie and Justin would offer up their opinions about the song and the mystery male.

"It's got to be someone we know!" Maggie said.

"What do you mean by that!" Troy sort of snapped at her.

"Nothing, Daddy, I'm just saying it has to be some singer we already know but no one has been able to figure out who it is yet, that's all," she explained. "I'm sorry, baby, I'm just tired, we need to get going you, guys," he said, addressing Eddie and Barb. April was giving Troy one of her looks. She turned back to Barb. "Yes, thank you so much, it was great to get together, and Eddie the food was out of this world!" she told him. They all hugged, and the Anderson family headed to their car. April couldn't help but get in a shot once out of hearing range of Eddie, Barb, and their kids. "I don't know what was going on back there, but act like that again and see what happens!" She hit Troy hard on the arm. "Ouch!" he said, but he wasn't referring to the pain.

Now that Troy knew, he was hearing *their* song all of the time. He wasn't sure how he felt about the whole thing but found himself unable to resist downloading it. He would listen to it at his desk, in his car, and on his phone, especially when he was flying. He was so tempted to contact Izy, but every time he would try to pick up the phone and call, he would chicken out. He couldn't help but wonder why she decided to release the song; he really wanted to ask her. He checked his old phone constantly to see if she has reached out to him at all, but there were never any messages or texts. There was no question the song was a huge hit; it had already been number one on both the rock and soul charts for almost four weeks. Troy saw an interview that Izy did by one of the big gossip television shows where she was asked repeatedly about the male singer in the now global hit. She would simply answer, "A friend."

HERE! Troy would smile every time he heard her answer that question, which she was asked constantly in interviews on television, radio, and in print. The other question she was asked was why she chose to make such a wide departure from her normal rock and roll recordings and take what the interviewers referred to as being "so risky" for her. "The truth is, this type of music is who I am, this is where I came from. I just needed to be reminded and I felt it was important to put it out there. Don't get me wrong. I love rock and roll…I breathe rock and roll," she would tell them.

For some reason, this monumental secret made Troy feel special. He was happy all the time, even around his wife and even when Frank was around, who was still acting strange with him. Troy was much more talkative and outgoing, he smiled at everyone that walked past him. He has always been able to talk to people, but usually there had to be a subject to launch the conversation. Now he would start the conversations and talk about nothing, just chatting. Everyone noticed the change, his co-workers, including Eddie, his kids, and April. He couldn't put his finger on it but he liked it; he felt energized. If he was having a particularly stressful day, he would put on the song, and by the end of the first verse, he was already feeling better, ready to move on. It was like he had some secret power that only he knew about and only he could control. It was very liberating. Eddie accused him of doing drugs, jokingly of course, but sometimes he wasn't completely sure he was wrong.

"Troy, you have to share, dude! It's not fair!" he would say to Troy. Troy would just laugh. He thought many times about telling Eddie the truth, but knew if he told anyone even Eddie it would eventually get out, and life as he knew it would be gone. And he couldn't trust that even Eddie could resist the now twenty-thousand–dollar reward!

CHANGE OF FORTUNE

Troy could not believe that ten weeks later that the song he and Izy's sang together was still number one. He couldn't believe that the secret was still intact and his life was not disrupted. However, even with Troy's elevated state of mind, he and April's relationship only seemed to be getting worse. They moved past arguing to fighting, they hardly ever saw each other, and Troy had reached the point of giving up; it was not worth trying anymore. Troy was very upset about it, but he felt it was no longer in his hands. Even Justin asked him one day if he and April were going to get a divorce.

"What!" he asked his son. "Where did that come from!"

"I don't know, Dad, you and Mom never seem to be happy around each other, and when you're home, she's gone, when you're gone she's home. It doesn't look good!" he explained. "Maggie and I already know it's coming," he said as a matter of fact.

"What do you mean?" Troy asked with a great deal of concern in his voice. "Has Mom said something to you or Maggie?" he questioned raising his voice.

"No, she hasn't said anything, it's just an observation," he told Troy.

"Look, Justin, yes, you're right. Sometimes your Mom and I don't get along so well, but we still love each other, and yes, we are both very busy, but we manage," he tried to convince Justin. "We are a family!" he explained.

"I know, Dad, it just seems like you both might be happier without each other," he was telling his dad from his heart.

"Please don't worry about it, things will be fine, I promise!" he told him and gave Justin and big hug. *This sucks!* Troy thought to himself. *What am I supposed to do?* he argued with himself. "If it's affecting the kids, that's bad. I have to talk to April about this," he decided.

Troy was in his office trying to work, thinking mostly about what to do about his home life when the receptionist called him on the intercom. "Mr. Anderson, FedEx is here for you," she said.

He sat there shaking his head. *Okaaay, can you sign for it please?* he asked her.

"I tried that, Mr. Anderson! The FedEx man says only you can sign for it!" she explained.

"What? That's just weird...okay, fine, I'll be right there," he told her. He walked to the front and the FedEx delivery guy approached Troy.

"Mr. Anderson?" he asked.

"Yes, I'm Troy Anderson," he answered.

"May I please see your ID?" he requested.

"My ID?" Troy asked, a little flustered but pulled it out anyway.

"Yea, I'm sorry, we have to ask for identification on our high-priority deliveries," he explained.

"High-priority delivery? I've never heard of that!" Troy told him. The receptionist was shaking her head in agreement with Troy. "They're pretty rare, only certain accounts have that level of service," he explained further. "It's not something we advertise." The delivery guy handed Troy the flat envelope, thanked him, and walked toward the elevator. Troy looked at the label, some company in New York. *Strange*, he thought. He shrugged his shoulders at the receptionist, suggesting he didn't have a clue, then went back to his office.

Huh, I can't imagine what this is, he said to himself as he pulled the tab to open the large envelope. From inside, he pulled out a regular-size white envelope with his name neatly written on the outside. He looked back inside the large envelope; there was nothing else. The white envelope was not sealed. He reached inside, and to his amazement, he pulled out a check! "A check?" he reacted. "Who would be sending me a check?" He looked at the front of the check, and the first thing he noticed was his name clearly spelled out across the check, then his eyes wandered to the amount: "Twenty-two thousand eight hundred thirty-five dollars and no cents."

"Holy crap!" he yelled very loudly as he fell back in his chair holding the check with both hands. He read it again, "Troy Anderson, Twenty-two thousand eight hundred thirty-five dollars."

"This has got to be some kind of a mistake!" he thought. He read it again. "Who would be sending me this kind of money?" he was excited, but he was sure it had to be some kind of an error. He thought maybe it was some scam that you hear about, and it's really just a way to get you to sign up for a loan of some kind. But it looked like a real check, no small print. He looked in the big envelope again, turning it upside down and shaking it to see if he missed something. *Okay,* he tried to rationalize. *If it's for me, why is there no explanation about who it's from or what's it's for?* he thought. *Maybe I have some long-lost uncle that sent me this?* he laughed. He spent quite a while looking at the check, fantasizing about where it came from, if it was really for him, and if it was, what he could do with it. He read the sender's name again from the FedEx envelope; it was from some company in New York. He never heard of them.

He was still imagining what he could do with the newfound money when Eddie appeared at his office door, startling Troy. "Hey, dude, what's with the special delivery?" he asked.

Troy smiled. "Oh, I see it made it around the office already!" Troy responded with a little disgust as he slid the check into the middle drawer of his desk. "It was no big deal, just a client that needed to send me some contracts," he tried to explain.

"Oh, that's it? Everybody was making such a big deal about it!" Eddie told him.

"And that surprises you?" Troy asked him.

Eddie laughed. "No, not really, I guess I should know by now, right? I'll catch you later!" He waved and walked away. Troy turned to his computer and went to his favorite search engine. He typed in the name of the company: "Masters Management, New York." He hit return; only one listing came up, so he clicked on it. They did not appear to have much of a website. The page it took him to only consisted of some contact information, including a New York phone number. Troy picked up his phone and called the number.

"Masters," the woman on the other side of the phone answered.

"Hi, my name is Troy Anderson—" he was cut off.

"Can you hold please, Mr. Anderson?" she asked politely.

"Sure, I guess?" he responded. He was only on hold for a few seconds when a man came on the phone.

"Mr. Anderson?" he was asked in a deep voice.

"Yes," Troy answered.

"My name is David Masters, how can I be of assistance?" he asked.

"Mr. Masters," he started. "I think there has been a mistake. I received a check from your company today and—" he was trying to explain when David cleared his throat, trying to interrupt politely. "Mr. Anderson, I apologize, but there is no mistake. That check is for you, that money is yours," he explained.

"But…I don't understand…why does it belong to me?" Troy questioned. "We were told you might be calling, and again, I apologize for the unusualness of the situation. What I can tell you is that a client of ours has asked us to forward to you your percentage of any royalties from a recent release of hers," he explained.

"Izy?" he asked.

"Unfortunately, I cannot explain any further, we have strict instructions regarding this matter," he told Troy.

Izy! It's got to be her! What is she doing? he wondered.

"Mr. Anderson, if I may, I would advise you that if anyone inquires about the check or any conversations with me, it would be best for all parties involved if you just denied it," he suggested to Troy.

"Really?" Troy asked. "Okay, that's fine," he offered.

"Any other questions for me, Mr. Anderson?" David asked him.

"No, I guess not. I'm good for now," he implied.

"Great, please have an excellent rest of the day!" And he hung up.

Troy sat at his desk, staring at the check completely confused, repeating in his mind what Mr. Masters had told him: "The money is yours."

"Amazing! This must be some kind of a royalty from our song!" He was blown away. "I wonder why she didn't tell me," he said, thinking of Izy. "Maybe this is her way of trying to protect me? Why would she send me this money anyway? I didn't really do anything, and as far as the world is concerned, I don't exist," he told himself. His mind was jumping all over the place not sure what to do or what to think. "This is crazy! It's not like I can really keep this! What would I do with it? How would I ever explain this to anyone, least of which…April! But, boy, it would be nice to be able to keep!" He took his old phone out of the drawer and turned it on. "I'm just going to call her!" he decided. His phone came on, and he pulled up his contact list. His thumb hovered over "BFF." He wondered what he would say to her. He wondered what she would say. *She might hate me by now for all I know*, he was thinking. *But then, why would she send me this money? So what do I say anyway…* "Hey, thanks for the twenty-two thousand!" He closed his phone. *Wow!* he said to himself out loud. He turned off the phone and put it and the check in the desk drawer. "I need some time to think about this," he decided.

For the first couple of days, it was hard to not think about that check just sitting there in his desk drawer. He questioned himself throughout the day about whether or not he should call Izy. He even was tempted to talk to Eddie about it but changed his mind almost as quickly as the thought entered it. Troy went on a quick trip to Seattle and was home by Saturday morning. April wasn't around, but he and the kids enjoyed a nice afternoon hanging out over at Eddie and Barb's house. Troy really enjoys their company; they were truly great friends even when Eddie was being Eddie. Both Eddie and Barb could tell something was wrong; it must have shown on Troy's face.

"Are you okay?" Barb asked him.

"Yea, Troy, you've been a little out of lately!" Eddie added.

If they only knew! he was thinking. "Yea, I'm okay. Things have been a little rough at the house lately," he admitted, somewhat relived that he was either finally comfortable enough or tired enough to tell someone.

"Really?" Barb questioned. "I know you guys have had some difficulties, but it's not that bad, is it?" she inquired. Truth is Barb knew exactly how bad it was, but she didn't want to hurt Troy by saying anything. "To be honest, I don't know. We barely ever see each other and then when we do, if we don't fight, we don't talk! Even the kids think we are done!" He poured out.

"Your kids?" Eddie asked.

"Yea, apparently they have been talking about it with each other. It's very upsetting," he told them.

"That's such a shame!" Barb said. "Have you tried to go to counseling?" she asked.

"When I bring up the subject, I am summarily dismissed. April says her dad says that counseling is just for the weak!" Troy explained.

"Wow!" Eddie responded. "That's nuts!" he added.

"Well, you should keep trying, shouldn't you? I mean for the kids' sake, right?" Barb suggested.

"Yes, I should, and I do. It kills me that we may be hurting them or confusing them," Troy said sadly.

"Oh, they're fine!" Eddie told him. "Look!" He pointed at the kids chasing the family dog, "They are great kids, smart and always happy. I think they're fine," Eddie told Troy with remarkable depth. Troy smiled as they all watched them playing.

On Monday, about midmorning, Troy was planning his next trip; this one was going to be for at least a week. He hung up the phone from confirming one of his appointments in Los Angeles when the receptionist called him on the intercom. "Mr. Anderson?" she asked.

"Yes," Troy responded.

"FedEx is here for you again," she told him.

"Really?" he said to her. *What now?* he thought. "Okay, I'll be right up."

"Mr. Anderson." It was the same FedEx delivery guy greeting Troy as he approached the reception area.

"Oh, hi!" Troy said.

"Please sign here," the guy said, handing him his little computer thing.

"No ID?" Troy asked. "No, we're good. I have it in here from last time, thanks, though!" he handed Troy the envelope and headed for the elevator. Troy looked at the envelope; it was from the same company in New York. Troy turned toward the receptionist. "I guess I've been a little popular lately?" he suggested to her. She smiled and nodded. Back in his office, Troy was going a little crazy with anticipation. *What are they sending me now?* he wondered as he pulled the tab to open the envelope. Inside was a single white envelope with his name hand written on the front, "Naw…it couldn't be!" was his reaction. But it was, it was another check. Troy pulled the check out of the envelope; only this time, his eyes went straight to the amount: “One hundred twenty-seven thousand three hundred eighty-six dollars and ten cents!”

“Oh my God!” Troy burst out, then he started to laugh uncontrollably. Several of his co-workers, including Eddie, came running into Troy’s office. Troy quickly put the check into his desk drawer.

“Are you okay?” Eddie asked him while the others looked on.

“Yes, yes, I’m fine,” he said with this smirky smile on his face. “I’m sorry, that was a little loud, wasn’t it?” he was trying to cover. “I just got word that I was able to get an appointment with a really big potential client, I guess I got a little too carried away,” he told them. The co-workers seemed to accept his excuse as they left his office shaking their heads; Eddie didn’t.

“Dude, what the heck is going on?” he asked with some concern in his voice. ”You are definitely not yourself lately!” he told him. Man, he wanted to tell Eddie so bad, but he just couldn’t. “No . . . really, I’m fine—actually, I’m a little better than fine!” he told Eddie.

“Really?” Eddie asked in a very condescending way.

“I promise. I’m leaving tomorrow for a week or so, so you want to try to do lunch today?” he asked his friend.

“Absolutely!” Eddie responded. “Great!” Troy said, knowing that would change Eddie’s train of thought.

WHAT GOES AROUND ...

Troy was having a successful trip in Los Angeles. He was trying to stay focused on his work but between *their* song always being on wherever he went and Izy's face being everywhere he looked, it was a little hard not to be distracted. He thought about her every day; he wondered how she was, if she was happy. He hated himself for ending their friendship. *What an idiot!* he thought. "Did I really need to do that?" he would ask himself. Inevitably, he would always come up with the same answer: "Yes, I had no choice. I crossed a line, and if we would have tried to stay friends, that line would have moved! I did the right thing for her, for me, and for my family." He pretty much had this same argument with himself at least once a week or so. It was always a little more intense when he was in Los Angeles, because he knew how close he was to Izy. Since receiving the checks, it's only made things that much harder, even more confusing. The checks just sat there in his desk drawer; he had no clue what to do about it. He had no one he could talk to about it.

Troy got home to little fanfare; actually no one was home when he got in. There was a note from April on the refrigerator: "I'll be home late, Maggie is at Courtney's house for the night, and Justin will be home around ten. April."

"Nice!" he said, pretty upset that even his kids weren't home to greet him. There was no way Troy was sitting around by himself, so he took his bags to his bedroom and went into the bathroom to clean up. He walked back to the front door, grabbed his car keys, and headed out the door. He had no idea where he was going; he just wanted to get out of the house. He called Eddie to see if he wanted to meet him for a drink, but Eddie was already on his way to his son's basketball game.

"I can meet up with you after the game," he offered, but Troy explained he needed to be home for Justin before ten. Troy drove around a bit and then spotted one of his and April's favorite watering spots; at least it was when they were first married. *This will be good*, he thought. *I'll just stop in for a quick drink and then head home*. He walked through the door; he forgot how dark it was inside. It was pretty crowded; a hostess approached him and asked him if he wanted a table. "No, thank you though. I see a spot at the bar," he told her. Troy had some trouble maneuvering around the tables and the crowd but made it to one of the only open bars stools. He sat down and a napkin was immediately placed in front of him. "Evening!" a young, attractive barmaid asked him. "What can I get you?" She had to lean in and speak up because it was so noisy.

"Hi! Can I just have a beer please?" he requested.

"Sure thing!"

It was very unusual for Troy to go out on his own, especially to a bar. He was really enjoying it, the music and watching all the people; it was very entertaining to him. He especially enjoyed watching the young men talk and plan on how they were going to approach some young women in the bar. Troy was having fun keeping track of the successes and failures; it was very amusing to him. He didn't recall the bar being such a pickup place. It was always more of a hangout joint where you could meet friends or take a date. Suddenly he was concerned that someone he knew might see him there. He did not want to have to try to explain why he was in a singles bar by himself! He quickly finished his beer; he got up and put enough money on the bar to cover his beer and the tip. He was becoming more anxious, and he wanted to get out quickly. As he worked his way back to the front door, he came upon a table with a man and a woman sitting at it. The woman looked somewhat familiar; now he was really nervous, *Should I walk by or go around?* He was thinking how to best avoid being seen. He slowed down trying to decide the best route to the door. He looked at the woman harder through the dim light when his stomach fell to the floor; he realized he was looking at April!

He stood there for what seemed like a minute without moving. The guy sitting across from April couldn't really see Troy; Troy thought he recognized the man but wasn't sure. But he was sure it was April. They were laughing and drinking, every once in a while, April would put her hand on the man's arm. "What the …" he started to say not loud enough for anyone to really hear when he was bumped from behind, distracting him for a moment. He couldn't believe what he was seeing. At first he tried to think logical and not jump to any conclusions. *This could just be one of her meetings, maybe they are discussing their next charity event!* he tried to convince himself. At least until the man leaned into April and kissed her! He kissed her on the cheek, but he still kissed her. Troy was enraged. He started to approach the table.

No! he said to himself. He turned around, walked to the rear of the bar, and went out a back door.

April's having an affair? he asked himself in total disbelief. *Is that possible?* he questioned. As he headed for his car, he was tempted to go back inside and confront his wife, but he didn't. He wasn't scared—well, maybe a little; he was more confused and frustrated. What he really wanted was to get home in time to be there for Justin. On the drive home, he was nonstop shaking his head, and he would hit his steering wheel with his hand a number of times; he was beyond frustrated. He was confused beyond words. "*All this time I have been working so hard, trying everything to keep my family together*!" he was not hurt, he was mad!

What do I do now? he asked himself. *Is this really an affair, maybe I'm overreacting*, he thought. *Maybe it was just an innocent gesture?* He made himself more confused. He had so many different things going through his head right now he didn't want to think at all. What he really needed was a friend, someone he could tell everything to, someone who would understand. He wanted to call Izy. But he didn't; he couldn't. Instead, he went home, and within a few minutes, Justin was walking in the front door.

"Hey, Dad!" Justin said.

"Hey, big guy! How are you doing, did you have fun?" he asked his son. Troy tried his hardest to hide his emotions from his son.

"Sure, it was great! I'm starving. Do we have anything to eat around here?" he asked as he headed for the kitchen. Troy followed.

"I don't know, let's see what we can put together!" *The perfect distraction*, Troy thought.

Troy didn't really see April too much for the next couple of days and over the weekend. He went to hockey game with Eddie on Saturday but said nothing about his solo trip to the bar. It was a great game, but Troy was only half there. Eddie noticed but didn't say anything; he knew Troy was going through a tough time, and if he wanted to talk, he would be there for him. On Monday, Troy was finishing up a discussion in his office with Eddie about an account when Frank walked in. "Troy, when you have a few minutes, I'd like to see you if my office," he told him. Eddie sat there and didn't move; he didn't even turn to acknowledge that Frank was there.

"Sure, I can come over in a few minutes," he told him. Frank nodded and walked out of his office.

"Tell me that wasn't strange!" Troy said to Eddie.

"Yea, man, that was definitely strange! I wonder what he wants?" he asked.

"No clue, I guess I'll find out soon enough!" he told him.

"Mr. Anderson?" came over the intercom.

"Yes," Troy answered. "FedEx is here for you," she said.

"Okay, I'll be right there," he told her.

"What's up with all these deliveries lately?" Eddie asked.

"Oh, it's one of my new accounts. They are all paranoid about the contracts and signatures so they send everything by FedEx. It's no big deal, they're just kind of strange that way!" Troy explained.

"That's cool!" Eddie said. "I'll leave you to deal with the wolf—good luck! Let me know how it goes!"

"Yea, thanks!" Troy half smiled.

Troy met the FedEx guy at the front; only this time, he had two envelopes in his hand.

"Two?" Troy asked.

"Yes, sir, Mr. Anderson, you weren't here last week," he explained.

"Oh, of course, thank you," Troy went back to his office. He set the two envelopes on his desk, side by side. Strange, he wasn't nervous or anxious at all. He looked at them, picked them up, then he noticed that one envelope was considerably thicker than the other. *Hmm, something different!* he thought. *Okay, I'm saving that one and I'll open this one first*, he joked to himself. He opened the first one and pulled out the same white envelope that has come before. He took out the check like he's done it a hundred times and read it; only this time it took his breath away. "One hundred ninety-two thousand six hundred ninety-nine dollars!"

"Wow!" he said, much more quietly than he had the first two times. He gently set the check down on his desk and picked up the other envelope; now he was nervous! He opened it, and inside was the same white envelope he has been getting but also a second slightly larger envelope that was thick. He took them both out. The one had his name written on it like usual but the second one, the larger one, said, "Yours@Izy." It appeared to be her handwriting. *This was from Izy!* he said to himself. He excitedly opened the sealed envelope. Inside he found eight tickets to an upcoming concert; Izy was going to be in Chicago! Attached to the banded tickets was a sticky note that read, "I hope you can come!" That was it. The concert was for the end of next month; Troy didn't even know Izy was on tour. Troy sat there looking at the tickets for a bit, thinking, *This would be amazing, but*… He interrupted his own thought. *Of course we're going to go, my kids will go bananas! This will be awesome!* Realizing it was very unlikely that he would actually see Izy, but what a great gift! He picked up the other envelope. *Another check?* He laughed. "One of these days they're going to show up and take all of these back!" he joked.

He was right, and he pulled out another check; only this time, it was different. Troy set it down next to the other check; he looked at both of them carefully, then he got up and went over to his office door and closed it. He grabbed a pillow off the small couch that was in his office and sat back down at his desk, putting the pillow on his lap. He looked at the checks again, reading them carefully, then he crushed the pillow into his face and screamed as loud as he could! The second check…was for one million two hundred thirty-five thousand one hundred twelve dollars! Yup, Troy was a millionaire.

THE RECONNECT

Troy must have screamed into the pillow for three or four minutes! He got light-headed from all the screaming but then finally calmed down once he started to lose his breath. He picked up both of the checks along with the tickets and put them in the drawer with his other checks. A bead of sweat appeared on Troy's forehead. Suddenly, Frank's voice came booming over the intercom, scaring the crap out of Troy.

"Troy!" Frank barked.

"Yes," he replied.

"I thought you said you'd be here in a few minutes. I've got things to do!" he barked again. "Oh, sorry, I'm on way right now!" he told Frank. Troy quickly gathered himself; he took a deep breath and headed to Frank's office. Frank's secretary smiled and greeted Troy. "Hi, Troy, you can go right in," she said.

"Thank you." Troy has never gotten nervous when meeting with Frank before, but Frank has been different, distant really, and Troy was not exactly walking on the ground at the moment. So he was probably more anxious than nervous. Maybe now he would find out why Frank has been acting so unusual.

"Good," Frank started as Troy walked in. "Take a seat, Troy." Troy sat down but Frank stood up. "I've been needing to talk to you," he told him. Troy was suddenly starting to get nervous. Frank continued, "I'm concerned about you and April," he said.

Whoa, not what I was expecting! he thought to himself. A new bead of sweat showed up on his forehead. "You do a good job around here, but as you know, my whole life is dedicated to April's happiness, and of course my grandkids!" he stated.

Where the hell is he going with this? Troy was starting to get upset.

"Sure I know that" Troy answered strongly.

"I don't claim to understand or know exactly what's going on, but I want you to do whatever you have to, to make that family work. You need to make my daughter happy, you getting me?" he stated bluntly. Troy was about to burst; he was sure his face was as red as it could be. He wondered what kind of crap his wife was telling him. He sat up and took a deep breath. "No, actually, I'm not sure I'm getting you!" he responded back to him. Frank looked surprised by Troy's response. "Yes, we are having a very tough time right now, but I'm not sure what I can do about it, I've been trying for years to get April and I back to where we were when we met. I would love nothing more than to have a happy and healthy relationship, but I'm not so sure it's me you ought to be talking to!" Troy put it out there. "What's that supposed to mean?" Frank snapped at him.

"You know, it takes two, right? I'm just saying maybe you should be asking your daughter what she is or isn't doing to help the relationship!" Troy was on an unusual role, bubbling with newfound confidence. "And, look, if you really want to stick your nose in it, maybe you should have thought about it years ago when you started sending me out of town for weeks at a time! How much do you think that helped our relationship?" He threw it back at Frank. Frank stood there saying nothing, one of first times Troy can ever remember Frank being speechless. "I'm scheduled to be out of town the rest of this week and part of next," Troy was telling him. "Why don't you spend some time with your daughter and ask her the same questions you're asking me, see what you find out! Oh, and maybe ask her if she might be letting her charity events get a little too personal!" he put it *all* out there now—why not! Troy got up and walked for the door, just as he was about to walk out of the office he turned and looked at Frank, nothing; Frank just stood there looking down at his desk. Troy went back to his office.

He sat down at his desk, leaned forward, put his elbows on his desk, and rested his head in his hands. He took several deep breaths. *I guess I should have seen this coming*, he was thinking. Eddie walked into Troy's office and closed the door behind him.

"Dude, are you okay?" he asked. "People said they could hear yelling!" he added.

"Yea, I'm fine. A little pissed ... but fine," he told him.

"Pissed? Why?" Eddie asked.

"Our meeting? It had nothing to do with business and everything to do with my relationship with his daughter!" he told Eddie.

"Really? Wow! How did it go? How did you take it? What did he ask you?" Eddied drilled Troy.

"He really didn't *ask* me anything. He mostly told me what *he* thinks I need to do or should do, it sucked! I'm not sure, but I think he threatened me with my job!" he explained. "No, he didn't ... did he?" Eddie asked. "Yea, I think he did!" Troy told him. "Your like the most important guy in this company, why would he threaten you?" he asked. "I don't know, really, it's a little nuts. This couldn't have come at a better time!" Troy said sarcastically. "Look, why don't we head out to lunch a little early, we can take a long lunch and let you cool down," Eddie suggested.

"I would love to, Eddie, really I would, but I am going to take off. I need to be alone for a bit, then I'm going to go home and see my kids," he told him.

"Sure, I understand. If you need me or want to just go out for a drink or something give me a call, okay?" he offered.

"Thanks, Eddie, I'm sure I'll be fine, but I appreciate it."

Troy didn't want to go home; he wanted to call Izy. An hour ago, he found out he was a millionaire; thirty minutes ago he was being threatened by his father-in-law who was also his boss. He needed to talk to Izy; she's the only one that could possibly understand. He drove his car around for a bit looking for a good place to make the call from. As he was, he suddenly realized, "What if she doesn't want to talk to me? I'm assuming she'll take my call, and even if she does take my call, the last thing she'll want to do is talk about my problems!" He started to get depressed. He found a park and pulled into the parking lot. There was a tree that he could pull right up to that partially shaded his car. He took his old phone out of his pocket and turned it on. He went to his contacts, and without hesitation, he pressed "BFF." *She's not going to pick up!* he thought as the phone was on the third ring.

"Troy?" she answered. Troy all of a sudden couldn't speak. It was so great to hear her voice; his mind was racing. "Troy, are you there?" she asked.

He spoke up. "Yes, I'm here, sorry," he replied.

"No, that's okay, how are you?" she asked.

"I'm fine," he answered.

"I feel like I probably interrupted you or something. I called at a bad time, didn't I?" he suggested.

"Troy, no matter what you might be thinking, we are friends. We've never stopped being friends. You don't ever have to apologize for calling me. I wanted to call you a hundred times!" she admitted to him. "But I just couldn't," she told him.

"Wow! Me too!" he told her. "I think I screwed up huge, and honestly, I'd understand if you didn't want to talk to me or be friends anymore," he confessed to her.

"Troy!" she snapped at him. "What's wrong with you? Do you honestly think I would have sent you those tickets if I didn't care about you, and I didn't want to be friends with you!" she started becoming Izy again. "Something's wrong, I can feel it, what is it?" she demanded.

So there Troy sat, in his car, in a parking lot of a park, laying out his troubles with his best friend who he hasn't talked to in months! He rambled on for a least an hour, with Izy only interrupting once in a while to ask a question. Troy finally got her all caught up and he took a long pause. "I'm pretty sure you would qualify as a therapist!" he told her. "Just talking with you has already made me feel better!" he said.

"Troy, I have one more question for you, and you don't have to answer if you don't want to," she told him.

"Sure, of course, what is it?" he asked. He could hear Izy take a deep breath.

"Do you love her?" Izy asked him.

Troy sat there for a few seconds, with everything that has gone on, he never stopped long enough to ask himself this question, undoubtedly scared of what the answer might be. He knows he loved his wife, but did he still love her today? He had a hard time dealing with Izy's question, so he quickly changed the subject. "Izy, what's with all these checks you're sending me?" he asked her. "You've sent me almost two million dollars!"

Izy laughed. "Really, is that all?" she said. "Huh . . . you must not have gotten some of the other checks yet!" she told him as she laughed harder.

"You're joking with me, right?" he asked her.

"No, not really!" she responded.

"I don't understand why you're sending me this money?" he asked her. "I can't keep it. I don't feel right about it!" he told her.

"You're kidding right?" she replied. "That's your half of the royalties from our song," she explained. "Well, yes, I kind of figured that, but why? I didn't do anything, I just sang the song with you that one time?" he asked.

"Troy . . . that song, that moment, changed my life. I introduced the song as a single, without your approval by the way, and you could easily sue me," she started.

"Like that's going to happen!" Troy interjected.

She laughed. "I wanted to see if my audience would respond. I wanted to see if they would feel the same way I do about the song, and as you know, they did! So now it's on the album and it's on tour with me!" she explained further.

"You would not believe how often I hear that song!" Troy laughed. "I couldn't get you out of my head even if I wanted to!" he admitted. They both laughed.

"We definitely hit a soft spot with our song, it's been number one on the charts for over twenty weeks, and the album has gone ballistic!" she told him. "By the way, it's almost seems weird to talk about it now because I didn't ask you before, but I hope you understand why I didn't put your name on the song?" she told him.

"Oh no, I totally understand and appreciate it," he told her. "I didn't think about it then, but by doing so, I've made you a mega superstar that no one knows, it's crazy how much I get beat up about who you are!" she said laughingly. "Yea, I've heard some of the interviews, pretty nasty some of them!" Troy suggested.

"Naw, no big deal. Trust me, this is nothing. It just rolls off me," she told him. "It's kind of fun having this mystery man that no one knows!" she admitted. They continued to talk for hours; it was like they never lost touch. Troy felt like he had air in his lungs again; his head began to clear. They agreed to talk again and text when they wanted or needed. "Troy, you understand I would never do anything to hurt you or your family?" Izy told him. "Yes, I know. I'm truly sorry for hurting you, Izy, I feel …"

Izy stopped him. "Troy, we are good, you and me. I hope you work things out at home. Oh! So you did get the tickets, eight of them?" she asked excitedly.

"Yes, I did, that's pretty great!" Troy told her.

"So you're coming then?" she asked.

"Wouldn't miss it!" he said.

"Great! I'll talk to you soon!"

TROY'S BIGGEST SELL

Troy went home feeling better, still pissed off at his father-in-law, and unsure of the state of his marriage, but somehow, after talking with Izy, he felt better. Out of the hours of conversation they had together the one thing that stuck out in his mind was when Izy asked him if he loved April. He was upset at himself that he couldn't answer the question; he felt like he should have been able to and it should not have been something he had to think about. He pondered the question all the way home. "I do love her…or I did love her," he continued to question himself. If Troy was nothing else, he was old-fashioned; he did not take his commitment to his marriage lightly. He felt that no matter what, he was supposed to see it through. He hated the idea of not being a family; he hated the fact that his kids might be forced into a situation that they are not responsible for. Troy knew, but he would not admit it even to himself that his feeling for Izy are strong—very strong. Troy tried his hardest to convince himself that he could be just friends with her, but that was not what he really wanted. After only knowing Izy for one day, he knew he never wanted to be her friend. There's no question; Izy got under his skin and it gave him a new outlook. It put excitement in his life again; she motivated him and she helped him realize that he was a different man, more so than even he thought. As he pulled into the driveway of his house, with his car still running, hands firmly gripping the steering wheel, he finally admitted to himself, "I love her…Oh, man, this is crazy…I love her!" He wasn't thinking about April. It almost came as a relief being able to say that to himself. "Jeez, this is just great, now what?" he asked himself. He didn't know, but this revelation gave him energy; it put a fire in his belly that he hasn't had in a long time, maybe ever.

Troy walked into his house. "Oh my God, what is that smell?" he asked loudly. The house smelled fantastic; something was cooking, and instantly, Troy was hungry. He put down his briefcase and walked into the kitchen. Everyone was there; April was wearing an apron standing behind the stove—a rare site—Maggie was cutting up some vegetables, and Justin was sitting at the kitchen table reading.

"Hi, Daddy!" Maggie was the first to speak.

"Hi, guys, what's going on here?" he asked.

"Hi, honey!" April said with a big smile. "We're making a family dinner," she explained.

"Well, it smells fantastic!" Troy told her as he took a big gulp and cleared his throat. His face had to be nothing less than a look of shock! April walked from behind the stove, grabbed a cold beer out of the refrigerator, and went over to Troy. She handed him the beer and kissed him softly on the cheek. Troy was stunned.

"Who are you and what did you do with my wife!" he joked. April smiled and the kids laughed. "Honey," he started, "I thought you had one of your big events tonight?" he asked.

"I did, but I decided not to go, they'll be fine without me," she told him. Troy needed to sit down, so he went to the kitchen table and sat next to Justin.

"Hi, Dad!" he said, looking up from his book.

"Hi, son!" Troy smiled. Everyone was talking and laughing, including April. *Maybe this is a dream?* he thought. *Maybe I'm going through some kind of guilt-trip vertigo thing*, he was asking himself. He drank down his beer and walked over to the counter where Maggie was just finishing up. “How are you today?” he asked her.

“I’m great, Dad, how are you doing?” she asked back. Troy wasn’t sure how to answer the question. Up until ten minutes ago, it was a bad day, a great day, a day of self-reflection, and now it’s a confusing day. “I’m good, honey, I’m good,” he answered.

They all sat at the dining room table, enjoying the fantastic meal April had prepared. “April, dinner is fantastic!” Troy told her.

“Yea, Mom, it’s really great!” Justin added.

“Well, thank you,” she said graciously. “I wanted to do something special for you, guys, you all deserve it, and I’ve decided I’m going to cut back on my work and spend more time at home so we can have dinners like this all the time,” she proclaimed. Troy just about came out of his seat.

“Yeah!” the kids shouted out.

“Wow, that’s great, honey,” Troy said in support of her decision. “That’s great news, right, guys?” he asked his kids. They nodded their heads in support as they both had food in their mouths. Troy looked at April as she was talking with the kids; something was different. Troy didn’t want to ask, and he wasn’t complaining, but “Why now?” He had to ask himself. “Well...” Troy started. “In light of this sort of celebration, and since we are all here, I have a little surprise for you, guys!” Troy told them.

“Surprise!” Maggie shouted.

“What kind of a surprise, Dad?” Justin asked.

“Well, it just so happens I got us tickets to see the international superstar Izy! Her concert is coming to Chicago next month!” he announced to everyone with a big smile on his face. The kids jumped up from the table and started screaming and dancing around, even April looked a little excited. Maggie ran to her dad and gave him a big hug. “Wow, Daddy, that’s fantastic, I can’t wait to tell all my friends!” she said.

“Troy, this is fantastic, really. We are all big fans, but how did you manage to get tickets? This concert has been sold out for months! Barb told me she has been calling radio stations every day trying to win some tickets. You didn't buy these from some scalper and pay some ridiculous amount of money, did you?" she asked, drifting back to the April he is more used to.

"No, not at all! Actually one of my new accounts sent them to me, apparently they couldn't go for some reason," Troy told her.

"A new account?" she questioned.

"Yea, as a matter of fact, they sent me enough tickets that we can invite Eddie, Barb, and their kids too!" he told them. The kids screamed even louder.

April shifted away from the drill sergeant. "Do they know yet?" she asked excitedly.

"No, I haven't had a chance to call Eddie yet," he told her. April snatched her phone from the table, and started to call Barb. "Is it okay if I tell Barb?" she asked with her finger on the button.

"Sure!" Troy told her. April was like a schoolgirl telling Barb the news; you could actually hear Barb screaming through the phone.

The next day, Troy was back in his office doing some paperwork and planning his next trip. He was going to be in Los Angeles but was disappointed that he wouldn't be able to see Izy because she was on tour. Troy opened his desk drawer that he kept the checks in; he pulled them out of the drawer and lined them up on his desk. He rarely looked at them, but for some reason today, he wanted to. Maybe because the money reminded him of the song and the song reminded him of Izy and the day they sang it together.

"Troy!" Frank was at his door.

"Yes!" Troy responded as he hurriedly slid the checks off his desk and into the drawer. Frank walked in and closed the door.

"Everything okay at home?" he asked. Troy was not happy that they were headed down this path again. "Yes, everything is fine, Frank, thanks for asking!" Troy snapped at him.

"Good, my talk worked then," he said with a smirk of confidence on his face. "I don't know what you're talking about. Our talk didn't help anything," Troy told him.

"No, not *our* talk, my talk with April," he explained.

"You talked with April?" Troy asked, standing up from his desk. "What did you talk about with my wife?" he asked angrily.

"I just told her what she might be doing wrong and told her she needs to fix it. I explained that she needs to understand what a value you are to her, the kids and this company. That's all." Before Troy could ask or say anything else, Frank turned, waved his hand in disgust, and walked out of Troy's office. Troy sat back down. *Oh man... this company? Now I get it! Why can't any part of my life just be a little bit normal?* he questioned himself. *I guess now I know now why April was so different last night!*

Troy called Eddie over the intercom. "Hey, Eddie, you want to go to lunch today?" Troy asked.

"Are you kidding!?" was Eddie's response. "I guess I'm buying today!" he said happily.

At lunch Eddie could not stop talking about the concert and how excited his family was to go, especially Barb. "Dude, I don't know how you pulled this off, but this is huge!" he told Troy. "You know how hard these tickets are to get, heck, my wife was literally listening to the radio all day every day trying to win some tickets. It's the only thing she and my kids will talk about!" Troy was only half listening; he was thinking about what Frank just told him, or more like admitted to him and of course Izy. What was it going to be like seeing her in concert? This would be the first time Troy has ever seen her preform and the first time he's seen her since they had their little mishap. Although Troy knew it wasn't likely he was *really* going to be able to see her, he'd be watching like the other fifty thousand people in the audience. Troy snapped out of it.

"Eddie ... you don't have to pretend. I appreciate what I think you're trying to do, but I'm pretty sure you know where I got the tickets from!" he told Eddie.

Eddie completely ignored the comment. "By the way, not that it matters, but where are our seats?" Eddie asked.

"You know I'm not really sure. I never looked, but I have to imagine they are going to be pretty good!" he told Eddie reassuringly. "I mean this is a pretty big account, wink wink, I don't think they would cheese on something like this!" he joked.

Around the house, things were definitely different; April was different. She was home most nights, hanging out with the kids, making dinner, talking, and engaging them in whatever they were doing, even Troy got some attention. It was nice, it was peaceful, it was the way it was supposed to be, Troy thought. *How long can this last?* he would ask himself. At first he felt as if he was waiting for the "other shoe to drop" but it didn't happen. Slowly, the difficult days seemed to drift away from his mind. April was more attentive to him, more affectionate, and she seemed genuinely interested in Troy's work and whatever it was he wanted to talk about. Troy looked forward to coming home again. He and April even went to dinner a couple of times and actually had a nice time. Troy hated the thought of it, but Frank may have made a difference; but was it real?. Frank still avoided Troy at work, now probably more because Troy's confidence scared him a little. Frank came around the house once in a while; it was good—better. Frank will always be Frank, but at least he didn't make Troy feel like an outsider in his own home anymore.

Although very skeptical Troy accepted the change, he wanted it to be real. With only a few minor exceptions April was like a new person. Troy and Izy stayed in touch the whole time, texting a lot and talking when possible. Izy was very supportive of the new April and the happiness it has brought with it. "I am happy for you and your family Troy. It's the best thing. Maybe April finally realized how lucky she is, at least I hope she has!" Izy told

Troy. Troy could tell something wasn't right in Izy's voice but he respected and appreciated her support. Troy knew he loved Izy but he also knew he needed to keep that to himself if he wanted a chance to succeed with his family and be able to stay friends with Izy.

THE FINAL CURTAIN

The big night was finally here! April and the kids were beyond excited; April wore a glittery rock-and-roll T-shirt with some jeans and high heels, she looked good. The kids were both wearing Izy T-shirts and had their cameras in hand. They were waiting in their living room for Eddie and his family to get there. Eddie went all out and got them a limousine. "It was the least I could do!" he told Troy, although Troy had already found out from April it was at Barb's insistence! The eight of them piled into the limo and started for the concert. The kids sat in the front and along the side, the adults sat in the rear, and Troy sat next to Maggie on the side bench seat. Everyone was buzzing; Izy was playing loud in the background. Everyone was having a great time, even before they got to the concert. Troy was having a great time too, but he had major butterflies in his stomach. He had talked to Izy just that morning. *She is amazing!*" he thought. She offered to send a car for Troy and his family; she even tried to insist that they come backstage before the show so they could all meet, but Troy turned her down.

"I don't think I could handle that!" he told her.

"I understand, just let me know if you change your mind," she offered. Troy was unsure how he was going to feel seeing her on that stage, if he could separate the international superstar from Izy his friend. *Is she my friend?* He continually asked himself. Troy was afraid his feelings for Izy were taking ahold of him. *Maybe it's just because I haven't seen her in such a long time*? he questioned himself. April broke his thoughts. "Troy wake up, why don't you pour us all a drink?" she suggested.

"Oooh, that's a good idea!" Barb added.

They approached the arena, the same arena where Troy goes to watch hockey games. The place was nuts: people walking everywhere, cars and limousines all trying to find a parking spot or maneuver closer to the front. Somehow, their limo managed to get pretty close; they all got out and walked to the main doors. The lines to get in were very long, but no one in their group seemed to mind. The arena was covered in giant posters of Izy, all with different outfits on. There were laser lights blasting everywhere and Izy's music filled the air. They were having a great time just taking it all in. They went through security successfully, and Troy handed their tickets to the woman who was scanning the tickets. They walked deeper into the concourse trying to not be run over by the masses of people. Troy walked up to one of the directories to see which way to go to get to their seats.

"I don't see them on here?" he told Eddie.

"What do you mean?" April snapped at him a little but then smiled.

"Let me take a look," Eddie offered.

"That's a good idea!" Barb laughed. "We'll end up in the basement for sure!"

Everyone laughed. "I don't see them either," he told the group.

"Let's find an usher or security," April suggested.

The kids were losing it. "Come on, Dad, the concert is going to be starting soon!" Maggie was stressing.

"Excuse me, Mr. Anderson?" asked a familiar voice. Troy turned around, it was Max! Troy almost said his name, but in a breath, he answered, "Yes?"

"If you and your party would come with me, sir, I will be happy to escort you to your seats," Max offered. Eddie, Barb, and

April all looked at Troy like "what the heck is this?" Troy looked at Max. "Uh, that would be great, thanks!" Max turned and the group followed. Troy was starting to sweat!

I thought we talked about this! he was thinking about the conversation he just had had with Izy. "This is crazy, I'm not ready! This is not going to be good!" he was saying to himself, trying not to get sick.

April grabbed his hand. "Where are we going, and who is this guy?" she asked in a coy but demanding way. "He's obviously not an usher, although he is big enough to be security. I didn't know they wore such nice suits!" she continued sarcastically.

"Honestly, April, I'm not sure. Let's just see where he takes us, okay?" he countered sharply.

Barb looked back at April. "This is kind of exciting!" she told her. April smiled while gritting her teeth at Troy's last remark. They walked for quite a ways, nearly to the other side of the arena. Then they walked down all of the stairs until they ended up on the floor. "Look!" Eddie shouted to Troy, we are standing right where the Blackhawks play! He said as excited as a kid seeing Disneyland for the first time. "Your right!" Troy told him. They went behind a big curtain where they came to a door with a uniformed security guard standing in front of it. He nodded at Max. Max nodded back and the security guard opened the door. "Here we go!" Barb yelled out.

Troy was thinking about running. They entered what looked like a backstage area. "This way!" Max called out.

"Where are we going, Daddy?" Maggie said excitedly.

"I'm not sure, honey!" he answered nervously. "Let's just follow the man," he suggested. They continued through several more backstage areas; there was equipment and cords everywhere; people shouting and working very feverously. Then Max took them up a small set of stairs and opened a door.

"Oh crap!" Troy said out loud. Everyone turned and looked at him, even Max. Troy looked at Max; Max winked and continued into the room. "Sorry, guys!" Troy said. "For a second I thought I forgot my phone! No worries, it's right here!" he held it up for everyone to see feeling like an idiot.

They all walked into the room. It was a large suite with three high top tables, a bar, and a buffet table going down one side. It looked like the inside of a little palace, with big flowing drapes and small statues mixed in and around the room. It even had a small fountain next to the bar. *This is very Izy!* Troy thought to himself, but it definitely wasn't her dressing room or anything like that. *Maybe this is like a reception room?* he worried.

Max spoke up. "Please relax and have some food and drinks, there are things for the kids here as well," he explained.

"Where do we go to watch the show?" Barb inquired.

"Oh, sorry!" Max said as he walked to the front of the suite. He grabbed the middle of these long, heavy-looking dark curtains; first, he pulled one back then the other.

"Wow!" Justin said, looking out over a rail, as everyone else moved closer to see. They were actually up above the stage, just to the right of it. They could see the entire stage and part of the auditorium.

"This is amazing!" April yelled out. Barb, Eddie, and the kids were in awe.

"Is anyone else coming?" Troy asked Max coyly.

"No, sir, you are the only ones," he answered Troy's question, much to Troy's relief.

"You mean all this food is for us?" Eddie asked, all too excited.

"Yes it is! Enjoy! The first band will be on shortly," he told them and left the room. Troy was able to relax a little and breathe again. *I really thought I was a goner, I should have known better!* he scolded himself for not trusting Izy. Everyone was getting into the food with a vengeance; Barb was making drinks for everyone.

"Just a beer for me please, Barb!" Troy requested. April came and sat down next to Troy at one of the tables with her drink and a plate of food.

"This is pretty spectacular!" she said, very pleased.

"Yea, it is!" Troy responded.

"Did you know about this?" she asked as Eddie sat down with them.

"No, I had no clue!" he told them both. "I guess you're going to owe your client big time!" Eddie said to him.

"You have no idea," Troy said under his breath.

The first band started; they were good but loud. Troy wasn't really into their music. Everyone else seemed to enjoy them. The kids obviously knew the music; they were singing every word. It was unreal how close they were to the stage; you could practically reach out and touch the band. Every once in a while, the lead singer would come over just below them and sing right up to the kids; they screamed with excitement. The lead guitarist would throw up a guitar pick when he would walk by; everyone scrambled to get one. Troy sat back at the table and watched everyone having a good time, jumping, singing, and dancing. After the first band was done, everyone came back to get more food and drinks. "That was amazing, Dad!" Maggie told him.

"Unbelievable!" Barb was saying. "No one's going to believe us!" She started taking pictures of everything and everyone with her phone; Maggie and Justin got into it too. Just then, a man came through the door.

"How did you like the first band?" he asked with a big smile on his face.

"Loved it!" was the unanimous response.

"Hi, everyone, my name is Rocky. I know, but it is, and I will be your host tonight. Is there anything I can get for you or do for you right now?" he asked. No one had any needs, so he offered to take a group photo that looked out over the concert hall. "That will be special!" he said after taking the photo with almost everyone's camera or phone. He looked at Troy. "If there is anything you need, just pick up this phone, and I will be on my way!" he told Troy. Funny, with all the other goings on, no one noticed the phone before!

"That's perfect, thank you," Troy responded. Everyone was so excited to be there and take it all in.

"I can't wait for Izy!" Barb shouted excitedly. Everyone screamed excitedly and ran back to the balcony as the next band started to play.

The second band was much more well-known; they must have been—even Troy knew a few of their songs! They played for about an hour. The last song they played was their most recent hit; everyone in the building went crazy. The stage was surprisingly small with a couple of different levels; both of the bands so far used the stage very well, moving around so everyone could see the action. After the song was over, the lead singer, Troy found out later his name was "Snake" stood at center stage right at the edge of the stage and thanked everyone in the audience. "Thank you so much, Chicago! You rock!" he screamed. The audience screamed even louder. "And a special thank you to Izy for letting us be here tonight!" he yelled into his microphone, jumping around the front of the stage. "You are so lucky right now!" he told them. "Izy is next! Keep rocking!" then he and the band walked off the stage, waving and flashing the rock symbol with their fingers.

One of the cool things about where they were watching from is you could partially see the stage after the curtain dropped, so you could see stage hands taking down and setting up equipment. It was very exciting to watch; it was a controlled madness in almost no light. Each time a band was about to come on, the lights in the room they were in would dim to almost dark, then as soon as the band was over, the lights would come back on. It was very cool. This time, when the lights came back on, everyone headed back into the room for drinks and potty breaks. Troy went to the bar to get himself another beer.

"Hey, check this out!" Eddie said as he lifted the top to one of the food serving dishes.

"What is it, babe?" Barb asked. Eddie picked up a brownie the size of his hand!

"Wow, let me see!" Connor said as he pushed aside his dad. The kids started taking the lids off all of the pans; each one had an amazing dessert inside—oversized cookies, brownies, pastries, and candy. "They must have changed the food sometime during the last show!" Justin concluded as he stuffed a cupcake in his face. Rocky walked in. "I see you discovered the treats!" he said, smiling. "If you didn't already know it, there is milk in the refrigerator!" he said, smiling at the kids who were all now covered in chocolate. "Is there anything else I can get you before the show starts?" he asked the group.

"I have a question for you Rocky," April spoke up.

"Sure!" he said.

"These aren't tickets that someone can buy, right?" she questioned.

"April!" Troy snapped at her.

"I'm just asking!" she snapped back.

Rocky looked at Troy, not sure how to answer but tried anyway. "No, that's okay. You're right!" he said excitedly. "You must be important or know someone important, not just anyone can get this suite!" he explained. "I don't know anything past that, I'm not allowed to ask who, I'm just told how many to expect," he explained to the group.

"Interesting," April said. April didn't seem completely satisfied with the answer but didn't push it any further. She went and got herself another drink.

I wonder why she felt it necessary to do that? Troy asked himself.

You could hear the stage hands still working on setting up for Izy's show. There was music on in the background in between each band, generally a lighter rock. Eddie came and sat down next to Troy. "Dude, this is exceptional!" he said as he put his hand on the back of Troy's neck and squeezed it—a man hug.

April and Barb came and sat down with them, both with a drink and a plate of desserts.

"Troy, I don't know how you managed this, but this is something Eddie and I and our kids will never forget, thank you!" she told Troy, reaching out to squeeze his hand.

"You guys are welcome, seriously, it's no big deal. I'm just along for the ride with you, guys, and I am very happy that we are all here together to experience this," he said genuinely. He looked at April; he could tell April wanted to say something, but instead she took another bite of a brownie. By this time, April was feeling no pain. She hadn't stopped or even slowed down her drinking since they got there. "It can't be much longer now!" Barb said, totally excited. Most of the kids had already moved back to their seats at the front of the balcony area. Troy was starting to get really, really nervous.

"This is pretty cool, don't you think?" Eddie asked April.

"Yes, I do!" she replied. "Your husband, he's the rock star!" Eddie told her.

Troy nervously looked over at Eddie. "What do you mean by that?" he asked him.

"Dude! Look at where we are! We are about to see the hottest rock star in the world, and we have better than front row seats! That's makes you a rock star in my eyes!" Eddie explained.

"Oh…thanks, Eddie," Troy said, breathing a sigh of relief. April didn't say a word.

The lights throughout the concert hall dimmed to almost black. Everyone started to scream—really scream. It could be one of the loudest things Troy has ever heard. The longer it was dark, the louder the screaming got. The curtain started to come up, the whole place was going nuts. Troy looked on anxiously to see Izy preform, anxious to see Izy. From his position, he could see the entire stage; the band which was only five pieces—drums, two guitars, a base player, and a keyboard—were already on stage. The hall was still almost completely black. Then a loud click and a pinpoint spotlight shown into the audience. The audience went crazy; within seconds, another laser sharp spotlight, then another, then another. There must have been dozens. The spotlights started to race around the hall, moving quickly over the audience in a random pattern. It was working; the audience was at a fever pitch, everyone grabbing for the lights as they pass by. Then came a single thunderous drum strike and all the lights simultaneously snapped into one light pointing at the absolute center of the stage; no one was there. The band broke into one of Izy's latest singles and the fans went crazy, but still, no Izy. Everyone inside the room was pressing up against the balcony bar trying to strain to see Izy. Then right under the spotlight, a perfect circle opened in the floor, unless you were up high, you wouldn't have been able to see it. The band repeated the music to the first chorus. Then from the circle in the floor with the spotlight streaming down on it, a hand appeared as Izy rose up to the stage level. The screaming was so loud it almost hurt. Izy was dressed in a flowing black and red dress, short, very short, with black studded boots that went halfway up her thigh. He hair was blowing back from some fans that must have been in front of her.

Beautiful! Troy said; over all the noise, the only one that heard him was April. She gave him one of her famous death stares. Troy turned back to the stage. Izy was all the way on stage, the band was playing louder and louder, the drums were reverberating throughout the hall, the sound was inside you whether you wanted it to be or not, and then Izy hit her first note.

"Wow! Troy said. Everyone in their group all started to sing, scream, and jump up and down to the music. Izy was rocking it hard right out of the gate. She was running all around the stage, screaming out her lyrics. The guitar players were chasing each other around the stage, jumping and pounding on their guitars.

The first half of the concert was nothing short of incredible. "Amazing!" is what everyone was saying as they took a break from the screaming and dancing to go get something to drink. Even

Troy had a blast. He was completely blown away. He has listened to Izy's music every day since they met, but hearing her live was beyond anything he could have imagined. She put it all out there on stage; her rock lyrics were hard, powerful, and beautiful all at the same time. Just when he thought Izy couldn't affect him anymore, she has figured out without even knowing it how to reach into Troy's soul. "Tell me that wasn't unbelievable!" Eddie said to the group as he got Troy and himself a beer.

"Unbelievable is the word, honey!" Barb said.

"What do you think, Troy?" April asked. Troy felt like the three of them were staring at him, waiting for his response.

Was April asking this because she really wanted to know, or was it something else? he asked himself. "I . . . thought it was fantastic!" he said, comfortably telling the truth. "She was remarkable. I know all of you are fans, but I had no idea what I was missing out on!" he added.

"What about you April?" Troy asked as he drank his beer.

"I have to admit, I'm usually disappointed when I hear people live, but Izy did not fail to deliver," she told them.

"I think she was even better live!" Barb added.

"Hey, Dad!" Maggie came over to the table. "Do you think Izy will do 'Life of One'?" she asked.

"Oh, she has to!" Barb jumped in. "How can she not? It's the biggest song ever!" Barb said.

"Yea, but what about the guy?" Maggie asked. "You know the guy that sings with her?" she explained.

"Oh, I read she does the song on her own when she's in concert" Eddie answered.

"That's cool, I guess," Maggie said and walked away. "Could you imagine if the guy was here?" Barb asked them, getting all excited about the possibility.

"It's actually very disappointing," April added. "I wonder why this guy just doesn't come out of whatever closet he is in and sing with her. The guy must have some kind of a complex or something!" April laughed.

Troy wasn't laughing, neither was Eddie or Barb. April had a little venom she felt she had to put out there; Troy couldn't understand why. "I mean really, it's a little ridiculous at this point, don't you think?" She was on a role. "Personally, I think it's just some kind of a stunt!" she added.

Maybe she had too much to drink? Troy was asking himself. *She loves Izy, why the sudden change? Maybe she is reacting to something else.*

Eddie and Barb walked over to talk with the kids leaving Troy with April.

"You okay?" Troy asked her.

"No, not really!" she snapped back.

"Why? What's the matter?" he asked sincerely.

"Troy . . . I can't pretend any longer, no matter what Daddy says. I don't know how else to say this, so I'm just going to say it, I'm sorry . . . but I just don't love you anymore!" she said bluntly and loud enough for Barb to hear. Troy was stunned but somehow not surprised; he wasn't sure what to say.

"There, I've said it!" she shouted as she finished off the last of her drink.

Why now? "Why here?" Troy asked her, sort of pleading, trying to understand.

"Why not? I can't keep up this lie anymore, it is what it is!" she said as she got up and went to the bar. Barb immediately walked over to Troy; he was pretty sure she was the only one that heard the whole thing.

"Troy, are you all right?" she asked him.

"I guess so . . . I think so?" he replied.

"Did you hear the whole thing?" he asked her as he was shaking his head.

"Did the kids hear any of that?" he panicked.

"No, they all look like they're too busy having fun!" she told him. Maggie did. Troy looked over at the kids; they were playing like they were in the band and Maggie was being Izy.

"Wow! That was a little out of left field!" Troy turned back to Barb.

"It was!" Barb said, trying to be supportive. "It's crazy, I can't imagine how you're feeling but you know what, you're a great guy! You deserve happiness, and maybe you and April just can't give that to each other anymore?" she suggested. "It could have been handled better that's for sure, but then that might be the reason for all of the drinks? Who knows?" She questioned.

Troy looked up at Barb. "Maybe you're right, but how am I supposed to process this? Especially right now?" "Troy, I don't think you're supposed to, and I don't think you should try. Have a beer, take a deep breath and enjoy where we are and enjoy who you *are* with!" she stated confidently speaking right into his ear. Right then, Eddie walked up.

"What's with the serious conversation over here!" he said, joking around. "We are supposed to be having fun, we are supposed to be partying!" he shouted, waving his arms all around. Barb leaned into Troy and gave him a hug. "We'll figure this out later, try to forget about it for now, let's have some fun!" she told him, pulling him up off the stool.

The lights went dark! Everyone but April hustled to the balcony. April stayed at the bar. Barb didn't let go of Troy's hand and walked him to the balcony. Everyone in the place started yelling out Izy's name. "Izy! Izy! Izy!" The music started and Izy appeared from backstage; they went right into full rock mode. In seconds, Troy had his conversation with April zoned out and was rocking with the rest of the group, never taking his eyes off Izy.

This time, Izy was dressed in a red skintight, all-leather jumpsuit that had black sparkling stripes that went across the chest area, like tiger stripes. Every song Troy knew by heart; he would sing along under his breath. Izy ran back and forth across the stage in her giant stilettos, singing and dancing. At one point, she was directly below their balcony, everyone in the group started screaming and trying to take pictures; Izy must have been only fifteen feet away! She sang directly to them for a few seconds, then in between verses looked up and threw a kiss. Troy stepped back; Izy smiled and ran back to center stage. "Did you see that, Dad!" Justin was sure it was meant for him, and it may have been. It was awesome. The concert seemed to get better and better as it went on. Izy must have been on stage for the second half of her show for over an hour with no signs of letting up. Her voice never quivered once, hitting every note. "*Wow, she's a machine*!" Troy thought. Barb tapped Troy on the shoulder. Troy leaned in to hear her.

"Look!" she pointed behind them. Troy turned around. April was gone! "Where did she go?" Troy asked.

"I don't know, I turned around and she was gone!" Troy walked over to the door and went out. There were two security guards in the hall. "Did a blond woman come by here?" he asked one of them.

"Yes, sir, she went by about twenty minutes ago, one of the other security guards escorted her back outside the arena, I believe," he answered.

"Outside? Really! Thanks!" Troy said and went back inside the suite.

Troy was finally done with April's moods and craziness. He had enough.

"Where is she?" Barb walked over to ask.

"I'm not sure," he said. "She may have left!" he told her.

"Left? Really?" she asked.

"Do you think she will come back? Maybe she just wanted to get out for a bit, clear her head," Barb said, not knowing what else to say.

"Naw, I think she's leaving," Troy responded. "I think she's leaving for good!"

"I'm sorry, Troy." Barb was feeling really upset for him.

"No, don't be, like you said, it's been a long time coming. This needed to happen and why not now...look at the distraction we have!" he said, changing his expression to a smile.

"That's awesome! Come on, let's go back and watch!" Barb suggested, trying to do her part to help distract from the strange situation.

"I think I'm just going to sit here for a minute," he told her. Barb looked concerned. "I'm okay, really. Please go back and watch, I'll be over shortly," Troy said. Barb nodded and went back to the group. Even with the music blasting through the room, Troy was able to reflect on what just happened.

So she doesn't love me. he told himself. *I wonder how long this has been going on?* In a way, he was confused, somewhat conflicted, but he also felt clarity. In a strange and uncomfortable way, he was relieved, and then in the next second, he would feel like maybe he failed. He suddenly had so many questions. *What happens now? I wonder if I'll lose my job!* He laughed out loud! *"Like I really care!" What about the kids! Oh man, what about the kids, how are they going to deal with this?* he asked himself. His thoughts were interrupted. "Hey, dude! What are you doing sitting here? Where's April?" Eddie inquired. Troy just looked at him.

"Look, I think the show is almost over, come check it out!" Eddie insisted. So Troy got up and walked to the balcony, unsure of just about everything in his life. He saw what a great time his kids were having and smiled when Maggie turned to look at him. *What do I tell them?* he thought. Izy finished the song she was singing with a bang—literally. She stood at center stage. The audience was screaming and cheering. They started to chant her name again. "Izy! Izy! Izy!" Over and over, louder and louder. Izy opened her arms wide with the microphone in one hand and took a long, deep bow. "Thank you, Chicago! You are my new favorite city!" she screamed to the audience, who only got louder.

Izy stepped back from the edge of the stage; three stage hands ran out onto the stage, each carrying what looked like small black screens. They placed the screens all around Izy, creating a makeshift changing room that completely hid her from everyone. The lights in the hall went black again, with only one spotlight focused on center stage. From inside the curtains, Izy started to speak. "This last song is a very special song," she was saying, the audience was so loud it was hard to hear. "This song is a part of who I am and I want to share it with you!" she said, suddenly a shoe came over the curtain, the audience went bananas. They loved it, then the other shoe, then the jumpsuit. Everyone was going crazy. Eddie and Barb were laughing and clapping their hands. Troy was trying to figure out where this was going. Every once in a while, the keyboardist would play a couple of notes to tease the audience while Izy was apparently changing. He and the drummer even did a little striptease music when Izy first started throwing out her clothes. Izy continued, "My very best friend . . . who I love with all of my heart, performed this song with me"—mad, out-of-control screaming from the audience—"and thanks to him, it has changed my life!" she told everyone. "And thanks to *you*! You have made this the number one song in the world!" she screamed out from behind the curtain. The audience was in a rage with excitement. Four men ran out on stage, three stood, each holding a section of the curtains; the other grabbed her clothes and ran off stage. All at once, the stagehands pulled away the screens and Izy screamed again at the top of her lungs, "Thank you, Chicago! You guys really know how to rock!" It was cool, very cool. Izy was now wearing blue jeans, an 'Izy' T-shirt, and some tennis shoes. "She's getting comfortable!" Troy laughed. Izy walked around the stage talking to the audience. "I am so happy to be here!" she was saying. "And I'm so happy you're here!" she said, pointing to the audience then turning and pointing to the suite. "What do you think? Should I do one more?" she teased.

"Okay, okay…it's time to get a little more serious," she told them. From the other side of the stage, a platform rolled out on stage; on it was a twenty-piece orchestra! The lights in the hall came up only slightly; the one spotlight was still on Izy. A stagehand came running out to center stage where Izy was standing and set down two stools. Everyone was watching in anticipation; Troy didn't know what to think. Izy sat down on one of the stools, a second spotlight lit up the stool next to her. Izy took a drink of water from a water bottle that the stagehand set next to her. Izy turned and looked directly into Troy and his group's suite. "This is for you!" she said as she pointed up to them. The group went absolutely crazy. Troy smiled and took a deep breath. "*And* this is for *you*!" Izy belted out, pointing out to the audience. The orchestra started playing. Izy's head was down, the audience was remarkably quiet, only a few single screams. The music was building. Izy raised her head. She began to sing. It was so powerful, so beautiful only someone who was there could understand. The first verse was beyond words; Izy sang it as if the music was inside of her.

Every single person in the audience was touched, most of the women were crying or tearing up, even Eddie was affected. He looked over to say something to Troy, then he turned to Barb. He said quietly, "Where's Troy?" Barb looked over where Troy was standing, then back inside the room.

"I don't know?" she shrugged her shoulders. "He was right here a minute ago. Maybe he went to look for April?" she suggested. They both turned back to the stage.

The orchestra was moving to the second verse. Izy put one leg down on the stage, getting ready to sing the second verse. She raised her head and lifted the microphone to her mouth. Just as she sang the first chord, a powerful male voice jumped in over her! Izy gasped and stood up immediately. She turned toward the back of the stage. The male continued to sing. Izy started to cry. The audience was completely freaking out. Was this the guy? Izy's eyes were locked on the voice coming from the dark. Even all the members of her band turned to see who was singing. About halfway through the second verse, Izy was able to compose herself to sing. Troy emerged from the dark and walked to Izy. They continued to sing. Izy was holding her chest. Troy just kept his eyes locked on Izy. They stood center stage—singing, staring into each other's eyes. Izy was trying to hold back her emotions; Troy reached out and touched her face. "Who is it? Who is it?" Everyone in the suite was screaming with excitement; they knew they were at the show where the mystery male singer finally came out. It wasn't until the spotlights moved away from the stools and shown on Izy and Troy that Barb said something: "Doesn't that look like Troy!" she screamed.

Maggie screamed, "It's Dad!" Shock and disbelief would be an understatement; Barb started crying. Eddie held his hand over his mouth, trying to take it all in. Maggie was screaming so loud, "You go, Dad!" She was shocked but had this overwhelming sense of pride for him. Justin jumped up and down and kept screaming the whole time.

The third and last verse was coming up as the orchestra opened it up with a long instrumental; Izy dropped her microphone to her side and leaned into Troy. They hugged. Izy put her hand on Troy's face and kissed him on the cheek. "I love you!" she said softly in his ear. Troy turned and looked at his friends and family in the suite. They were all smiling at him. They were all screaming his name. He turned back to Izy. "I know . . . I love you too!" he said to her, then he leaned in closer and they kissed, a small gentle kiss, but this kiss changed their friendship forever. Everyone, I mean everyone, screamed, and cried, and laughed—if you were there, you felt like you were seeing a moment, a special rare experience where you knew many people's lives just changed. They sang the last verse together holding hands and singing with everything they had, never taking their eyes off of each other, except for one quick second when Troy looked over Izy's shoulder across the stage and he saw Max. Troy held up his left hand and gave him the rocker sign; Max nodded and walked back into the dark.

After the song was over, Troy took one quick bow with Izy, hugged her, and quickly left the stage. When he walked in the door of the suite, everyone started screaming and clapping. Everyone was so excited, he could feel the energy in the air. Maggie and Justin ran to their dad and hugged him so hard they nearly knocked him over. Maggie was out of her mind in excitement. Barb was crying while smiling and laughing.

Troy felt great, excited, strange, and sad all at the same time. Everyone, even Rocky was in the moment. Everyone was trying to get to Troy; everyone had a million questions especially about him being the 'mystery' half of Izy's famous hit. "When did you meet Izy? How did it happen? When did you guys decide to sing together?" were just some of the questions being shouted out. "You guys! You guys!" Troy tried to talk over them. "Calm down; it's still just me. I'll answer all of your questions, but you need to let me catch my breath first!"

Eddie spoke up right away. "Everyone get a glass! I want to make a toast!" Eddie looked at Troy, took a long pause and everyone got quiet. "Troy…wow! I mean *wow*!" Eddie stood on his toes with excitement. "That might have been the craziest, most exciting, and most memorable thing I have ever had the pleasure to witness and be a part of in my life! Troy, you rock!" Everyone cheered and toasted their glasses. It was an amazing moment.

"What? No one wants to toast with me?" said a voice entering the suite. "Oh, my God, it's Izy!" shouted Maggie. Instantly Troy was relieved as the center of attention. As everyone converged on Izy, Troy pulled Barb aside. "This is nuts, right? I feel unbelievably excited and guilty as hell; you know what I mean?" he confided. "What kind of a message is this sending to my kids? Did I make a mistake?"

"Troy," Barb responded calmly. "This isn't an accident, it's definitely not something you need to feel guilty about. Here." She handed Troy an envelope from her purse. "What's this?" Troy asked. "I wasn't supposed to give you this until we got home, but I think now is the right time. April gave me this before we even left for the concert. I think she planned to leave the concert alone all along," she explained.

"What is it?" Troy repeated, a little confused.

"They're divorce papers," she told him.

"You're kidding me! Really?" He handed the envelope back to Barb. "Wow! I don't know what to say!"

"This is your life Troy, it's *your* life! Take a deep breath, have a drink, enjoy this craziness, and you'll sort it out later, I know you will. Trust me, your kids will be fine!" Troy leaned in and gave Barb a long hard hug.

Barb looked up and standing right in front of her was Izy! "You must be Barb? It is truly a pleasure to meet you!" she said as she put out her hand. Troy stepped back from Barb, Barb tried to speak, but nothing came out; all at once, she jumped into Izy's arms and gave her a monster hug! Everyone, including Troy and Izy laughed uncontrollably.

"Troy I have to go. Will you call me later?" Izy asked.

"Sure, no problem." he replied, a little confused about how he should act at that moment. Izy stepped toward him and gave him a hug. As she did, she whispered in his ear, "Nice job, best friend! I'm pretty sure you just changed our lives forever!"

"Yes, I guess I did. Are you okay with that?" he asked, already knowing what the answer was.

"Can we talk about that over dinner, maybe my place?" she backed away from Troy and smiled.

She stopped several times on the way out the door for pictures with everyone that wanted one and left the suite. Troy stood there with one kid under each arm, "You guys—"

He was interrupted by Maggie. "Dad, we love you and we couldn't be more proud of you!" she told him with total confidence. Troy started to tear up.

Just then, Eddie walked up to them. "So, does this mean I have to have *my* people contact *your* people if I want to go to lunch with you?" Everyone started laughing. Troy loved his family, and he loved his friends, especially his *best* friend.